THE BUTCHER

NATHAN BURROWS

Rub-a-Dub-Dub,
Three maids in a tub,
And who do you think they be?
*The **Butcher**, the Baker, the Candlestick Maker,*
And all of them out to sea.

English 15th Century Nursery Rhyme

1

Norma dried her hands and looked through cloudy eyes at the joint of pork on the kitchen table in front of her. It was indeed, as the butcher had told her, a fine cut. She clasped her arthritic fingers across her thin chest, as if she was about to say a prayer, and thought about what she needed to do with the joint of meat before putting it in the oven. With a quick glance at the kitchen clock, its hands large enough to make out through her cataracts, Norma inhaled a satisfied breath before blowing it out of her cheeks.

Later that evening, Norma's only granddaughter was coming round for supper. She was bringing her new boyfriend, the young man who might well be 'The One'. Norma patted the pork with a tea towel, enjoying the sensation as she did so, half-listening to a bunch of politicians arguing about import and export something or other on the radio. Whatever they were arguing about, it was getting quite heated and Norma tuned them out, her thoughts drifting to her granddaughter. The poor little thing had been in an awful place for about a year after

travelling halfway round the world with some young
upstart. He was, according to the granddaughter, utterly in
love with her. It turned out he wasn't, and the poor girl had
come back to Norfolk with a broken heart and equally
broken credit rating. Norma had put her up for a little
while, just until the youngster got her feet back on the floor
and found a decent job.

Shuffling her way to the cupboard to get the salt she
needed to rub into the joint, Norma squinted at the photo
on top of the fridge. Although she couldn't see it very
clearly these days, she knew the picture very well. It was
Peter, her husband, standing next to Norma in front of the
Eiffel Tower just over two years ago. The year before The
Lord took him. Norma had disagreed a lot with The Lord
at the time, arguing that it wasn't Peter's time. The Lord
didn't need him yet in her opinion, but Norma hadn't won
that argument.

Peter had popped out to the allotment one sunny
evening, saying to Norma as he left he was just nipping out
to earth up the potatoes, and that he might be a while.
Norma had smiled, knowing full well he would spend some
time at the allotment, and an equal amount of time at the
pub. He'd be back later, smelling of beer and Polo mints.
Except he hadn't come back that night, or any night at all.
Another allotment owner had found Peter face down in his
King Edwards, dead as a dodo. The hospital said he had a
heart attack, and that he wouldn't have suffered. But that
wasn't the point, not to Norma. When The Lord did
decide that it was time to take Peter, she'd wanted to be
there herself, holding his hand and letting him know how
loved he was. But Norma knew it wasn't her sad, smiling
face that Peter had seen just before he died. It was a pile of
King Edward potatoes, which still needed earthing up,
rushing toward his face at a rate of knots.

Norma shook her head just as she always did when she got all maudlin about Peter and peered into her kitchen cupboard to find the salt. Walking back across to the joint of pork, she put the salt down and got her best knife out of the drawer. It was sharp as anything. Peter used to joke he could shave with it. The knife had been sharpened so many times that soon Norma would have to buy a new one, and that would cost money she didn't have. Not since Brexit, anyway. She gripped the knife in her gnarled fingers and drew it across the fatty top of the meat. Norma noted with satisfaction the way the knife cut through the skin just to the right depth for the salt. Norma was sure the crackling would be perfect. Her granddaughter liked the crackling, and Norma hoped that the new boyfriend would as well. She concentrated hard on what she was doing. This joint was a real treat, what with the price of pork going through the roof since all the foreigners stopped buying British. It hadn't helped that the British, in return, had stopped buying foreign.

Putting the knife on the side, Norma sprinkled a generous amount of salt onto the joint of meat and rubbed it in with a satisfied smile on her pinched face. The pork felt just right underneath her fingers. Firm but not too firm, pink but not too pink. The butcher had promised her a special joint for a special occasion, and he hadn't disappointed her. As Norma brushed the excess salt from the skin, she noticed with a frown that there was one of those animal marking tattoos on the joint. It must be the farm's symbol or maybe the animal's number, she thought. Hopefully by the time the skin had turned into crackling, the marking will have disappeared.

Norma didn't follow football. She never had. It wasn't something that either Peter or she were the slightest bit interested in. If she had been keen on the beautiful game, and if her eyesight had been better than it was, Norma might have recognised the tattoo.

It wasn't a farm symbol, or animal number. It was a tattoo. A proper tattoo of an Arsenal Football Club crest. There was another thing that Norma didn't know about the joint of pork on her kitchen table.

It wasn't pork.

2

E mily Underwood sat in the driver's seat of her little red Mini and tapped at her laptop keyboard. With a couple of clicks on the trackpad, she brought up the previous health inspection of the Chinese takeaway that she had come to inspect. With a glance across at the closed takeaway, she pushed her seat back to give herself more room and started reading. What she read wasn't pleasant at all.

Since qualifying as a Food Standards Agency inspector three months ago, Emily had gone on five visits, all to establishments like this one. Eateries with track records of less than ideal conditions behind the public areas. This visit was going to be different though — it was the first one she would be doing on her own. Her five mentored visits had all gone well, and her boss, Mr Clayton, had signed her off as competent. So now, she was on her own. With a carefully trimmed fingernail, she tapped at the trackpad again to read the next page of the report. It didn't pay to have long fingernails in this business.

The Chinese takeaway she was sitting outside was

called 'The Wong Way'. Whether this was an unsuccessful attempt at irony or just a reflection of the fact it was run by an elderly chap called Mr Wong, Emily didn't know and didn't care. One thing she did know was that the takeaway was almost shut down after the last inspection. It was safe to say that Emily wouldn't be eating from the place any time soon.

Emily looked up as she heard a noise from the take-away just in time to see the sign on the door flip from 'Closed' to 'Open'. A young Chinese woman twisted at the lock and pulled the door ajar a couple of inches. *This was it*, Emily thought. *Showtime.*

She got out of the car, closing the laptop screen and shoving the computer under the passenger seat of her car. Norwich wasn't a particularly crime-ridden city, but the takeaway was on the edge of one of the less well-off council estates in the city. Emily grabbed her briefcase from the rear seat, smoothing her short blonde hair back behind her ears, and got out of the car. She took a deep breath, straightening out some of the creases on her trousers. The Food Standards Agency didn't have an offi-cial uniform, so she was wearing the unofficial uniform. A trouser suit, one of three she now owned. Today, Emily was wearing her navy blue one. The advantage was they were practical, especially on farm visits. Emily could tuck the trouser legs into a pair of wellies with no problem at all. The downside, at least according to her flat mate, Catherine, was that they made her look like a lesbian.

As she walked toward the front door of the takeaway, Emily could feel her heart fluttering just a tiny bit in her chest. It wasn't really nerves, more the fact that she was about to do her first solo inspection. Emily pushed the door open and stepped into the waiting area, a tinkling bell above the door announcing her arrival. While she waited for someone to come out from the kitchen area, she looked around the waiting room, taking in the musty smell of old Chinese food. It smelt like her ex-boyfriend's flat on a Sunday morning, but his flat also had the added odours of spilled beer, sweat, and — very occasionally — sex. There were many reasons why he was now an ex-boyfriend, but housekeeping and personal hygiene — or rather, the distinct lack of both — had been the key ones. A budding Health Inspector like Emily had no place being with an absolute slob like that, no matter how good looking he was. At least that was what her friends had told her at the time. If Emily had realised how difficult it was meeting a 'nice young man' in Norfolk, she wouldn't have been as hasty in getting rid of him, but what was done was done.

On the walls of the waiting room was the obligatory dragon wallpaper, adorned with rice paper calendars advertising The Wong Way restaurant. It was, according to the calendars at least, a taste of the Orient in Norfolk. Set into one of the walls was a fish tank filled with murky green water. Emily took a step towards it, peering into the gloom. When a large fish appeared out of nowhere and startled her with unblinking eyes, she jumped. Laughing, she took a step back. As she did so, the door behind the counter opened and a young woman walked through. She was just as slim as Emily, shorter than her by a couple of inches, and had jet black hair cut into a similar bobbed style. The two women stared at each other for a few seconds. Emily smiled, trying to get the girl to relax.

'Hello,' Emily said, broadening her smile. The Chinese girl didn't smile back, but continued to stare at her. After a few more seconds of silence, Emily continued, 'Do you speak English?' The girl finally stirred into life.

'Yes, I speak it pretty well, all things considered,' she

replied, the Norfolk accent obvious even to Emily who tried to hide her surprise.

'Oh, okay,' Emily said, scrabbling in her pocket for her identification card. 'Good stuff. My name's Emily Underwood. I work for the —'

'I know who you work for,' the girl interrupted, raising her eyebrows. 'The Food Standards Agency.' Emily felt her mouth open an inch before closing it again.

'How do you know that?' Emily asked.

'It's obvious. You've got that look. All prim and proper, like butter wouldn't melt when in reality all you do is go round wrecking people's livelihoods.'

'Well, that's not strictly speaking true,' Emily started to defend herself, but when she saw the look on the girl's face and her tightly folded arms, decided against it. She got her notebook out of her briefcase instead. 'What's your name please? I need it for the report.'

'Wang.'

'Thanks, and your last name?'

'Wong.' As Emily wrote 'Wang Wong' down in her notebook, she had to press her lips together to stop any trace of a smile from appearing. She glanced up at the young woman whose lips were equally as compressed. 'My middle name's 'Fang'.' Emily felt the corners of her mouth start to twitch as she said 'Wang Fang Wong' in her head, and to her surprise she saw Wang suppressing a smile as well. 'It's not as bad as my brother,' she continued. 'He's also called 'Wang', but his middle name's 'Wei'. It could only be worse if it was the other way round.' Wang paused. 'Because then he'd be 'Wong Wei'.' Wang's face broke into a broad smile, and Emily grinned back. This wasn't turning out how she thought it would. Wang took a couple of steps towards Emily and lowered her voice. 'Look, I'm sorry for being stroppy. But I know my grandfather's going to be in a right old mood for the rest of the evening what with you visiting.' Hearing Wang use a colloquial Norfolk phrase — right old mood — appealed to Emily's sense of humour, and she started laughing.

'No, that's fine. I get we're not often that popular,' Emily said. 'But after the last inspection…' She let the sentence hang.

'Yeah, I know. I've tried to talk to Granddad, but he's quite stubborn. His shop, his ways. I'm only helping out here because he doesn't speak English, and Gran's not well.' Emily remembered the Grandmother described as a translator from the report.

'Oh dear, I hope she gets better soon,' Emily said, smiling with what she hoped was a sympathetic expression.

'Come on, let's get it done. But I warn you, you're probably not going to like it,' Wang said, her smile fading as she turned away and walked back towards the kitchen door.

An hour later, Emily was sitting back in her Mini with her mobile phone pressed against her ear.

'Mr Clayton, it's desperate in there,' she said. 'If anything, it's worse than the last visit.' Her manager's disembodied voice echoed down the line.

'How'd you mean?' he said.

'Well, the food storage is still all over the place. The top shelf is seafood. All types of it. Prawns, fish, something else that smells like it was in the sea at some point. Next shelf down is what I think might be beef, but it's difficult to tell,' Emily flipped the pages of her notebook. 'And on the bottom shelf is something that I can only really describe as something that's almost pink, but tinged with blue. None of it's refrigerated.'

'Well, that's an offence right there.'

'There's more,' Emily continued. 'Mice droppings everywhere, open bags of dried noodles and rice on the floor. There's a bunch of eggs in a bucket, and something's died in there.'

'Something?' The incredulity in her boss' voice was obvious. 'What sort of something?'

'I think one of them might have hatched.' There was a silence on the other end of the line before her manager went on.

'What's going on with the disabled toilet? In the last report, it was blocked.' Emily could hear paper rustling as he paged through the report.

'Well it's not blocked now, but it's not a disabled toilet anymore,' Emily replied. 'It's been, er, it's been converted.'

'Into what?'

'A bedroom. There's a bunk bed in there now. I mean, it's still a toilet, but it's now one with people living in it.'

'Sweet Jesus,' Emily's boss breathed down the line.

'I spoke to the poor girl working there, and her grand-father won't do anything about it. He says that only Chinese people eat there, so it doesn't matter.'

'Okay,' Emily's boss said. She could hear the resigna-tion in his voice. 'We're going to have to close them down. I'll get a team out to you to give them the good news.'

'No, it's okay Mr Clayton. I can manage it. There's only the young woman helping out and the grandfather here. I get on fine with her, and he's quite elderly,' Emily said. She was desperate to finish this job off and didn't want Mr Clayton to think that she couldn't cope with a simple closure notice. 'I'll say we're just closing it for the evening, and that we'll be back tomorrow to help them get sorted out. They won't know it'll lead to a prosecution.'

Mr Clayton wasn't at all convinced, but Emily managed to talk him round.

'Any problems at all, you just let me know Emily, okay?' he said.

'Sure, no problem. I'll have the report for you in the morning.' After saying goodbye to her boss, Emily got back out of her car just as another car pulled into the car park. A man in his forties and a small child of about nine or ten got out and started walking toward the takeaway.

'Sorry, excuse me,' Emily called out to the man. He turned to face her. 'I'm afraid the Chinese is closed for the evening.'

'No it's not,' the man replied, pointing to the sign on the door. 'Look, it's still open.'

'Well, it won't be in a couple of minutes' time.' Emily showed the man her Food Standards Agency identification card. 'Trust me.' The man's face paled as he shepherded his son back to the car.

'So, I'm afraid we're going to have to ask you to close the takeaway for the evening, Mr Wong.' Emily looked at the elderly Chinese man standing on the other side of the counter and waited for Wang to translate. As Wang finished speaking, Mr Wong shook his head from side to side. He spoke in rapid Mandarin, his anger obvious.

'He says that this will not be possible, not tonight or any night,' Wang said. Emily looked at her, not wanting to come across as pleading.

'Could you tell him that this isn't something we're asking him to do?' Wang started translating, and Emily added. 'It's something we're telling him to do.' When Wang had finished talking, Mr Wong looked at Emily, his eyes almost completely closed. He whispered at Emily what

sounded like the words 'gun dan', turned on his heel and
marched back into the kitchen. 'What did he say?' Emily
asked Wang.

'Never mind. You might want to think about leaving,'
Wang called back over her shoulder as she followed her
grandfather into the kitchen. Emily listened as they argued
behind the closed door, Mr Wong's voice becoming louder
and louder. When she heard pots and pans banging
together, Emily took a step toward the takeaway entrance.
The clashing of metal got even louder, and when Wang
joined in with the shouting, Emily turned and unlocked
her car through the window with the remote. Maybe it was
time to admit to Mr Clayton that this wasn't something she
could deal with after all? Her suspicions were confirmed
when Mr Wong came bursting back through the kitchen
door. Emily took one look at the huge machete in the
elderly man's hand and sprinted toward the door.

'Shit, shit, shit,' she said, heart pounding as she struggled with the door. Push not pull. Fail. She managed to fall
through the door just as Mr Wong rounded the counter,
waving the machete above his head and screaming at her
in rapid Mandarin. Emily couldn't understand a word of
it, but it was obvious he wasn't being friendly. The little old
man was a lot quicker than he looked, and Wang's
desperate attempts to hold him back weren't working. He
was gaining on her fast as they both ran across the car
park. Emily got to the car, threw open the door, and got
the key in the ignition with the second attempt of her
trembling hands.

As she left two streaks of rubber on the Chinese takeaway's car park, Emily started laughing. Partly out of fear,
but mostly out of relief. That was something that she was
going to have to leave out of her final report to Mr Clayton. She slapped her hand on the steering wheel. She was

still full of adrenaline, but as she looked in the rear view mirror at the receding Mr Wong, she started laughing much louder than she normally did.

'Chicken Chow Mein!' she shouted at the top of her voice. 'Pork Balls!'

Tom Pinch was fed up being a pig farmer. Even though his father was a pig farmer and his father before him, that didn't mean Tom had to enjoy what he did for a living. He sat in the seat of the eight-year-old tractor that the bank still owned, at least for another year, and looked out across his small slice of Norfolk.

The farm was small by most standards, and compared to most of the farms in Norfolk it was tiny. Tom and his older brother, Frank, owned just over twenty-five acres of what was some of the most barren land in the county. When his grandfather ran the farm, it was over five times the size it was now. Then the county council decided that Norwich needed to be connected to 'that London' by a bigger road and that the road had to go right through the middle of their farmland. Tom's father, who was by then the farmer, had sold off the more profitable half of the farm on the other side of the brand new A11 dual carriageway a few years later. He'd done this 'to make the family more comfortable' but Tom had known the money would prop up both the farm and his father's fondness for alcohol.

One thing that the money hadn't done was convince Tom's mother to hang around. She'd done a runner as soon as the cash from the sale of the land had come in, taking her half of the windfall with her. Tom's father had been killed a few years later after wandering down the middle of the dual carriageway with a blood alcohol level that would have finished most people off. It wasn't the alcohol that killed Tom's father, but an Eddie Stobart articulated lorry called 'Kayleigh-Louise' — according to the name written on the wing of the cab. Tom Pinch, aged just thirty, had become the reluctant co-owner of a pig farm. His older brother Frank was already a qualified butcher by the time their father died, and had little to no interest in the farm so Tom had been running it ever since.

He shivered, pulling his fake Barbour jacket tighter around him, and started up the tractor. It coughed into life, and Tom cast a worried look at the black smoke that billowed from the exhaust. Once it had declined to a dirty grey colour, he put the tractor into gear and headed over to the pig sheds. Behind the tractor was a large trailer full of food waste from one of the local supermarket chains, Kett's of Norwich. Anything, or pretty much anything, that was out of date, misshapen, or otherwise unsellable was offered to local farmers at a heavy discount. Tom wasn't ashamed to say he'd fed himself on the food on more than one occasion. Until a few years ago, Tom bought food scraps from a local old people's home. He'd once found a set of dentures in the food, scraped off a plate by an overzealous nurse — or so Tom assumed. The food scraps had been a much better arrangement in Tom's opinion. They were much cheaper, and the pigs didn't care. The only people who cared were the busybodies from the Food Standards Agency who had stamped the practice out. It contributed to Foot and Mouth disease, they said. Tom had never worked that one out. Old people didn't get Foot and Mouth disease, so what was the problem?

As Tom drew up outside the pig sheds, he saw a group of emaciated scruffy men get to their feet and shuffle around. The oldest was maybe in his fifties, the youngest much closer to Tom's age. This was the latest group of itinerant workers who he'd recruited from 'Marko', the Albanian gangmaster who provided illegal immigrants to a few select farms in the area. A few years ago, before all the Eastern Europeans had gone home after deciding that England wasn't the best place to be anymore, he'd had much better workers. For a start, most of them spoke English, even if was only a bit. This bunch in front of Tom could barely write, let alone speak another language. Tom knew it wasn't their fault, and he tried to look after them as best he could, but it made things bloody difficult. He'd had to pay more for the Eastern Europeans, but they were much better workers. Whether it was because they were better fed, Tom wasn't sure. Either way, he'd have them back in a heartbeat.

He jumped down from the tractor and made his way over to the group. There were five of them altogether, and Tom had no idea where they were from. They didn't look European, nor did they look African, and they were all dressed in a random assortment of clothes. Some of them fit, but most of them didn't. They looked at him with a mixture of nervousness and excitement.

'Does any of you lot speak English?' Tom asked. In reply, he only got confused stares. Obviously not. With a deep sigh, Tom acted out what he wanted them to do, which was shovel the feed from the trailer into the pig troughs. He had to mime it out three times before one of them twigged and explained it to the others in a language that Tom didn't recognise.

For the next hour, Tom drove across the fields from pen to pen, followed by the workers who filled the troughs in the pens up. To their credit, although they were pretty slow with the shovels, they weren't fazed in the slightest by the pigs jockeying for position at the troughs as they filled them up. What was particularly galling was that most of them weren't even Tom's pigs. They belonged to the farmer next door, a miserable old bastard called Jones whose wife was in the hospital. The only saving grace was that Jones was paying Tom for babysitting his pigs.

A couple of times as they were travelling between pens, Tom saw one of the workers grab something from the back of the trailer and eat it, but he said nothing. Hard as things on the farm were, Tom couldn't begrudge any of them eating the odd misshapen carrot that was too ugly even for the people of Norfolk.

Once all the troughs were full, he pointed to the now empty trailer.

'In you get,' he said, slapping his hand on the trailer floor. There was one worker who Tom had seen struggling with a limp earlier, and Tom hooked his hands to give him a step up. He received a broad yellow-toothed smile by way of a thank you. Once the group looked as comfortable as they could be in the back of a farm trailer, Tom returned to the tractor and started driving back across to the pig sheds for them to have their lunch. As he drove, Tom wondered how bad things would have to be for him to even consider going to work in a foreign country let alone on a pig farm. The poor bastards had probably paid an arm and a leg to get over here, and now they were being hunted down by the authorities and forced to work for peanuts. Tom knew he was adding to the problem by using them, but he didn't have a choice anymore. He hated being a pig farmer, but it wasn't anywhere as bad as the life that those unlucky buggers had.

He unloaded the immigrants in the centre of the complex, next to the fridge shed and a disused building that had been an abattoir. A few years ago, they'd slaughtered all their own livestock on the farm, but the Food Standards Agency had put a stop to that as well. It was only used now when they were slaughtering pigs for their own kitchen. That was the only thing that was still allowed. Frank had said a few times now that they were out of Europe, they'd be able to go back to the good old days and do all their own processing instead of paying through the nose for a commercial abattoir, but there was no sign of that yet.

While the strange group tucked into their sandwiches, Tom went into the largest of the pig sheds in the complex to see his own stock. Most people would have choked at the smell inside, but Tom's nose had long since given up on trying to tell him how awful it was. He looked around at the empty stalls. This time last year, they had all been full of sows, some pregnant and the rest nursing piglets. Now there were only three pigs inside, but at least they were Tom's. He was waiting for them come into heat so that he could unleash Boris the Boar on them. Tom glanced across at the reinforced pen where the massive boar was fast asleep. Boris was a bad-tempered thing at the best of times, and Tom certainly wasn't going to wake him up to say hello. With a wry grin, he looked at the three female pigs in the other pen. They had no idea what they were in for. Boris had mated with one of Jones's sows a couple of weeks ago, and Tom hadn't been able to watch. It was brutal.

Tom left the shed to see how his workers were getting

on with their lunch. To his surprise, they had finished and were sitting on the straw bales outside the sheds playing a card game. Tom clapped his hands together to get their attention and pointed toward the trailer when they all looked up at him.

'Come on you lot,' he said, even though he knew they couldn't understand him. 'Back to work.'

As the first of the workers started climbing back into the trailer, Tom heard one of them shout something. He looked to see the man who had shouted pointing across the field. All the workers' eyes followed his finger, as did Tom's, to look at a white Transit van bouncing its way down the track toward them. There was a rapid exchange of views between the workers in whatever language they were speaking. Tom watched, fascinated, as the rapid-fire conversation intensified. The next thing Tom knew, he was looking at the backs of the workers as they sprinted as one across the field and toward the woods on the edge of his land.

4

'That'll be four pounds ninety please, my love,' Frank Pinch said to his customer as he handed the old lady a bunch of sausages carefully wrapped up in greaseproof paper. He waited while she rummaged in her bag for the money. She was the only customer in his butcher's shop at the moment, so he was in no hurry, and she had been the only customer all day. Frank watched as the little old lady counted out change onto the glass cover of his half-empty display counter. Each coin that was plundered from the depths of her bag was held up to the light, squinted at, examined, and then announced.

'Fifty pence!' the woman exclaimed with delight as Frank took a deep breath. 'Now,' she continued, 'that's only forty pence left. Let me see…' Her gnarled old hand disappeared again in the bag up to her elbow. It was the world's crappiest lucky dip as far as Frank was concerned. He took another breath and waited for her to finish rummaging. When she had finally managed to pay for the sausages, he wished her a good day and kept a painful smile fixed on his face as she shuffled her way out of his shop.

'Good God, that was painful,' he muttered under his breath as he looked at the clock on the wall. Almost lunchtime, and only one customer. Mind you, she had bought the most expensive sausages in the village. Frank wiped the counter down with a piece of kitchen towel and threw it into the bin, covering the sausages' original wrapper. He should really have hidden the packaging before selling the sausages to the woman, but he knew she couldn't see much further than the end of her nose, so he was safe enough there. Every week she came in, regular as clockwork, to get her bloody sausages. Frank had told her that he kept some 'special' sausages for his regular customers under the counter, reserved only for people like her. He wasn't lying. What the old lady didn't know was that the only thing special about them was that Frank had bought them from Lidl. With a theatrical grin, he had winked at the old woman and crouched down behind the counter, unwrapping the sausages and re-wrapping them in some greaseproof paper, also from Lidl. Four sausages for her, two for him. It was the same every Wednesday morning.

Frank looked around his butcher's shop, wondering not for the first time how long he could keep things going. A few years ago, before the whole Brexit debacle, he'd been so busy that he'd had to take on additional help in the shop. He'd hired a young Polish lad, who not only was a very good butcher but also brought a steady stream of attractive young women into the shop. The women were mostly Polish themselves, but a fair few locals had become regulars as well. They might not have left with the sort of meat that they'd hoped to walk out with, but at least they were spending money. These days he could barely afford to pay the rates, and it was only the fact that he owned the shop outright that was keeping his head above water. There had been two butchers in the village until a year ago, a convivial rivalry that had gone back years. Then one morning Frank had driven through the village and seen a sign in the other shop window thanking customers for their support and announcing its closure. The last he'd heard, the other butcher had embarked on a second career as a fuel and retail management technician in the Sainsbury's petrol station just off Pound Lane.

The only customers who used his shop these days were like his most recent one. Elderly people who still realised the value of a proper butcher, a local butcher who served local meat. That was the main reason he was wearing a white coat underneath a red striped apron, with a white hat topping off the outfit. At least he looked like a proper butcher. Frank knew that if his brother Tom didn't pull his finger out and start producing something on the excuse of a farm they both lived on, even the shop wasn't going to carry on for much longer. Frank's customers all had one thing in common. They didn't drive, so couldn't get into Norwich where the price of meat was marginally cheaper, and they didn't order stuff off the internet. Most of them didn't even know what the internet was other than a place where perverts lived.

Frank walked into the back room of the shop, past the industrial size fridges that hadn't been turned on for months and had to be left open at night to stop getting mouldy, and opened the small under-the-counter fridge where he kept his lunch and most of his stock. As he sat on a small stool and munched on his cheese sandwich, he thought about Tom's latest scheme to get back on track.

Fed up with buying pig sperm at top prices, Tom had invested in a male pig, a boar. His idea was to use the boar to get the farm's stock of pork back up to sustainable levels and sell extra sperm on the side to other local farmers. Apparently, the market for unused pig semen in Norfolk was quite buoyant. Frank had queried this with Tom, on the grounds that if pig semen was that much in demand, then every farm would have its own supply of the stuff. Tom was adamant though, and he'd come back from the livestock market a few weeks ago with the world's ugliest male pig. They'd named it Boris after deciding that it had more than a passing resemblance to the Prime Minister.

Frank sighed as he thought about his younger brother. It was fair to say that Tom wasn't a people person and that he was happier around pigs than he was around other human beings. Frank wouldn't mind if Tom could actually run the pig farm at a profit, as opposed to the steady drip of their dwindling savings. Boris had almost cleaned the pair of them out of their savings, and it wasn't as if the butcher's shop brought much money in anymore. They had just had a whole load of meat back from the abattoir that was sitting in a fridge back at the farm, so at least in the next couple of days, he would have some more meat in the counter in the front of the shop. As Frank wondered how long it would take them to get back on terms, or indeed if they ever would, he heard the door of his shop open. He got to his feet, brushed the front of his red striped apron to get rid of any crumbs, and walked back into the main shop to see which old lady it was this time.

To Frank's surprise, it wasn't an old lady in the shop. It was a young one, and a rather attractive young lady at that. She was slim, dressed in a dark blue trouser suit, and was looking into the half-empty display counter with a curious expression on her face. Frank licked the tips of both index fingers and thumbs and ran them over his eyebrows. He didn't get the chance to talk to many women near his age, and he was determined to make the most of it.

'Can I help you?' Frank said, twisting his face into what he hoped was a welcoming smile. It certainly worked on the over-eighties. The woman looked up at him, and after a brief pause smiled back at him.

'Hello,' she said before returning to look back in the display.

'So, you're not from around here, are you? Are you just passing through?' The customer looked at him, her eyebrows raised, and Frank was worried he'd offended her. 'I mean, most of my customers are locals, so I know them all. I don't get much passing trade, you see.' She smiled at him, her face relaxing, and he noticed a slight gap between her front teeth.

'Goodness, you don't have much in your cabinet, do you?' she asked. Frank examined her, not quite sure what to say. She had an almost round face, a button nose dusted with freckles, and as he told Tom later that evening, the most mesmerising green eyes. He ran through a few replies in his head before deciding on what he thought was the best one.

'That's only the display, my love,' he replied, catching the faintest trace of irritation on her face as he said 'my love'. Frank made a mental note not to use that expression again. 'I keep the good stuff in the fridges,' he nodded at the empty fridges behind him, 'and out the back.' He hoped she wouldn't ask what was in the fridges. It wasn't as if he could open them. 'Were you looking for something in particular? If I don't have it in stock, then I can always get it in for you.'

'No, not just now, thank you,' she replied, looking again into the glass display counter. 'I'm not here to buy anything.'

Frank watched her place a small briefcase on the countertop just as his mobile phone buzzed in his pocket. While the woman opened the case, he pulled the phone out and looked at the screen. It was Tom, so he rejected the call. Given the choice of talking to Tom or talking to this young lady, Tom could wait. He could wait quite a long time as far as Frank was concerned. The young woman pulled out some paperwork from her briefcase.

'I'm guessing you're Frank? Frank Pinch?' she asked. Frank started to get a sinking feeling in his stomach as she put an identification card on the counter.

'Yes, that's me,' he replied, leaning forward to read the name on the identification card. A much more serious version of the woman looked back at him from the card. Emily Underwood, Food Standards Agency Officer.

'Your annual inspection's due in the next week, so I thought I'd drop off the self-assessment paperwork.' Frank's phone buzzed again. He ignored it again as his visitor continued. 'I know it normally comes in the post, but I was in the area, so thought I'd pop in and introduce myself.'

'Well that's very kind of you, Miss Underwood,' Frank said, trying to summon up a smile. 'Very kind indeed.'

Frank watched as Emily walked back toward the door, her briefcase tucked underneath her arm. 'I'll see you next week, Mr Pinch,' she said as she opened the door. Frank's phone started buzzing again.

'I can't wait,' he muttered as he stabbed at the phone to answer the call. 'Tom, what the hell is it?' He paused, listening to his brother shouting down the phone. 'Calm down, Tom. What sort of accident?' A few seconds later, Frank flipped the sign on the butcher's shop to 'Closed', locked the door, and jogged toward his battered ten-year-old Land Rover. As he opened the door, he wondered why on earth his little brother had a dead body in one of his pig sheds.

5

T he boardroom of Kett's of Norwich was on the top floor of a tower block called Partridge Towers right in the middle of Norwich. The latest addition to the management team of Kett's of Norwich, Andy Robertson, was setting out a large oval table in preparation for the board meeting later the same day. He wasn't technically a member of the management team, he was an intern, but as far as his mum was concerned, Andy was about to take over the company.

Partridge Towers was a new building next to the bus station. Some of the city's residents loved its brown brick walls, angular construction, and huge windows. Most of them hated it, and the statue of Alan Partridge outside the front door was vandalised almost weekly. The boardroom sat on the top floor in the corner of the building, with two full walls that were floor to ceiling glass. Even if people hated the building, anyone who'd been in the boardroom couldn't help but admire the view.

Andy put glasses by each of the embroidered placemats on the table, turning them upside down as he placed them carefully on the table. If one got chipped, it would come out of his wages, and Kett's of Norwich didn't pay their interns much at all. As he placed a glass at the head of the table, where the Chief Executive Officer would be sitting, Andy entertained a daydream in which he rubbed his testicles around the rim of the CEO's glass before putting it on the table. If the boardroom didn't have a glass wall that looked out onto the main office of the company, it might not have remained a daydream. Andy hated the CEO with a vengeance. Most of the company hated the CEO with a vengeance, so Andy wasn't on his own there. For a second, he wondered if anyone would do anything if he did drop his trousers and taint the glass with some man sweat. It might turn him into a company legend and persuade Karen in Accounts to give him a second look and say something other than 'thanks' when he delivered her post. He looked at her through the glass wall, sitting at her desk only a few feet away from him. Outrageously beautiful, well aware of it, and a head buried up her own arse. She didn't even notice him, as usual, and might as well have been sitting in a different building.

Glasses distributed, a brief fantasy about Karen in Accounts and what they might do on the office photocopier abandoned, Andy turned his attention to the computer in the corner of the room. He wiggled the mouse to get rid of the screen saver — a rotating graphic that spun the Kett's of Norwich logo — and entered his password. His monitor was mirrored on the huge television mounted on the wall of the boardroom. Andy took a seat at what would be his position when the board meeting was on. Sitting in the corner and pressing the mouse button every time someone said 'Slide, please'. He looked at his emails, but that didn't take long as he hadn't received any, and was looking for the main presentation when a small box popped up in the corner of the screen. If he'd been at his own computer, the message would have been accompanied by a 'ding', but in the boardroom the speakers were turned off. It was from Martin, his only friend in the company, and the only other intern.

Fancy a beer tonight, mate? the message with 'Martin the Intern' in the status bar read. All the company messenger accounts had first names and departments across the top. Apparently, the CEO had read somewhere that was what Google did. No last names, only first names and departments. The word in the canteen was that the CEO was 'Charles the Big Cheese', but as no-one Andy mixed with had ever been messaged by the big man himself, it stayed a rumour.

Sure, meet in the Murderers, Andy typed before setting his messenger status to 'Do Not Disturb'. He found the presentation and brought up the first slide just as the door to the boardroom opened and the first of the attendees filed in and took their seats, ignoring Andy as they did so. Twenty minutes later, and ten minutes after the time the meeting was due to begin, the CEO lumbered into the room and took his seat.

'Right then, thanks all for coming,' Charles the Big Cheese said, looking around the room through rheumy eyes once he had settled his oversize frame into the chair. The room had filled up with people in suits. There were only two women amongst them, one painfully thin, the other at the opposite end of the eating spectrum. 'Let's get going, shall we? Rob, over to you,' the CEO barked. A thin man got to his feet, his suit hanging from him. Andy looked at the man who had stood up, noticing not for the first time the thin sheen of sweat on his oversize forehead. Rob from Marketing. Might as well have been Rob from

Belsen, Andy thought. Technically, he was Andy's boss, but this was a tenuous connection at best.

'Thank you, Charles,' Rob said in his trademark high-pitched voice. 'Adam, slide please?' Andy decided to ignore him. 'Adam? Slide please?'

'It's Andy, Rob,' Andy replied, emphasising the word 'Rob' as he pressed the first slide. A graph appeared on both Andy's screen and the main screen in the boardroom, showing a graph with a whole load of lines. 'My name's Andy, you cock,' Andy muttered under his breath as he looked up at the screen on the wall. The only thing that Andy understood about the graph was that the lines were all going in one direction — downwards. He listened as Rob explained the financial forecast. Slide after slide, each was the same as the one before. Andy was only an intern, but even he understood one thing. Kett's of Norwich was deep in the shit. When Rob had finished going through the slide, an uncomfortable silence permeated the room. Andy had to stop himself from laughing as Rob half sat down, then got back to his feet when the CEO gave him a look that anyone from Norfolk would describe as 'proper mardy'.

'Right,' the CEO said, breaking the silence. 'That's not what I was hoping for.' It was stifling inside the boardroom, but Andy didn't think that was why the CEO's face was so florid. If Charles went down clutching his chest, the one thing Andy knew was that he would be at the back of the queue for mouth to mouth. There probably wouldn't be much of a queue, though. 'Please tell me you have a plan?' the Big Cheese asked, patting at his forehead with a red handkerchief that matched his face.

'Next slide please, Adam,' Rob said. Andy stabbed at the mouse with his index finger so hard he felt his fingernail split under the pressure. He looked up at the screen on the wall to see a new slide with the title 'Localised Marketing' on it.

'So,' Rob said, 'this is our latest marketing initiative.' He paused and looked around the room. One or two of the attendees nodded at him, which Andy figured gave Rob the courage to continue. 'Our USP, our unique selling point, is that we are proper local. Even the name only means anything to locals.' Andy had been born and bred in Norwich and had a vague memory of learning at school about some bloke called Kett being hung at Norwich Castle about a million years ago for stealing a loaf of bread or something. 'So, we build that into our product range,' Rob explained. 'We launch a new line, using only the best local produce. Nothing from Europe.' Just as well, Andy thought. Anything from over the channel would be three times the price anyway, thanks to the import duty that Brussels had imposed in the last few years. With Andy's help, Rob limped through the next few slides, all with graphs showing dotted upwards arrows. 'Minimal road miles, maximum profit margins. Nothing foreign. Nothing from outside Norfolk,' Rob continued. He paused, and Andy realised that was the grand finale of Rob's pitch. It was, Andy thought, just as well Rob wasn't in sales. All the heads in the room turned towards Charles and waited for his reaction.

'Yes,' Charles said a few seconds later. He thumped a chubby hand on the table, and the glasses that Andy had laid out earlier all trembled. 'Yes, I like it.' Rob's expression changed into a half-smile, half-grimace, and Andy thought for a horrible few seconds that he had just seen what his boss's come face looked like. 'So, where do we go from here?' Charles barked. 'We need a name for this, let's brainstorm it.'

Andy could tell from the way several of the meeting

attendees' shoulders drooped that this wasn't the first time they'd been put through this. Rob walked across to a white-board and grabbed a marker pen, taking the lid off with exaggerated enthusiasm. He looked around the room, avoiding Andy's eyes, and Andy watched as Rob waited for the magic to begin.

'Focus on local?' the thin woman on the other side of the room offered. Rob wrote it on the whiteboard in careful lettering, with a question mark after it.

'Locally focused?' the morbidly obese woman on the opposite side of the table countered. Rob recorded the offering as the two women looked at each other with hostile stares.

'Locally loved?' This was from a man at the end of the table who Andy thought worked somewhere in marketing alongside Rob.

'Loving it local?' Charles chipped in. The entire room nodded in agreement as one. 'Come on, keep going,' the CEO said. 'Don't just agree with the first thing I say.'

'Loving the locals?'

'Living it locally?'

'Local living?' Rob was struggling to write them on the whiteboard as the suggestions came thick and fast. Andy watched him as his boss broke into a proper sweat from scribbling on a whiteboard.

'Pride of Anglia,' Andy muttered under his breath.

'Loverly locally?'

'Local living?'

'Stop!' Charles slammed his hand back down on the table. The vibration shook the table so much that several of the board members reached for their glasses to steady them. 'Pride? Pride of Anglia? Who said that?' There was silence around the room as the group looked at each other.

Andy gave them a few seconds before slowly raising his hand.

'It was me, sir,' Andy said, almost in a whisper. The CEO looked at him, his forehead creased.

'Who the fuck are you?'

'He's one of my team, Charles,' Rob said, cutting off Andy who had just opened his mouth. 'That's Adam, one of my youngsters who I'm teaching. He's doing well, with my help and experience.' Andy was speechless, but only for a few seconds.

'I'm Andy, sir,' he said, looking at Charles. 'I'm an intern.' Andy shot a sideways glance at Rob as Charles glared at them both.

'Right, I've decided,' Charles said. 'I want that. Pride of Anglia. Perfect. Fucking brilliant.' He looked around the room, eventually settling on Rob. 'Why could none of you lot have come up with that? What was your name again?' Charles looked at Andy. 'Aaron was it?'

'Andy, sir. My name's Andy.'

'You. Marketing bloke.' Charles pointed a chubby index finger at Rob. 'Hire Aaron. I want him on the team.' The CEO started scribbling in his notebook, and Andy ignored the dark look that he knew Rob was shooting across the table at him. There was a silence in the room as everyone waited for Charles to finish his notes. Under the table, Andy felt a foot nudge against his leg. He looked at his neighbour, a man in a suit who had the expression of someone who'd seen it all before. Andy's neighbour, a grin fixed on his face, nodded toward the screen in front of Andy. On the screen, an instant message had popped up. According to the status bar, it was from Karen in Accounts.

'Andy. OMFG. Last night was something else. I can hardly walk.' Andy swallowed as he read the rest of the instant message. 'I'm never going to be able to look at

Charles' desk again. Not after that. Hope it's not too sticky.' A winking smiley face completed the message.

Andy gulped, his mouth like sandpaper. He looked up at the main screen in the boardroom where sure enough, the message was repeated in glorious technicolour. The only person in the room not staring at it was Charles who was still scribbling. Andy closed the message down as quickly as he could, before looking around the room. He was met with a mixture of expressions. Horror from the thin woman, outraged surprise from the morbidly obese woman. Shock from Rob, and undisguised admiration from pretty much everyone else. He looked over his shoulder, through the glass wall and caught his fellow intern Martin grinning at him from the desk where Karen in Accounts normally sat. Bastard.

6

Tom paced in the kitchen of the farmhouse, wondering where Frank was. The kitchen was only about ten steps across, and if it weren't for the flagstones, Tom would have worn a path in the floor. He reached the end of the kitchen, touched the wall with the palm of his hand, and turned to pace in the opposite direction. As he reached the large wooden table in the middle of the room, he paused and looked at the bottle of whiskey and tumbler on a placemat. When he'd grabbed the bottle less than half an hour ago, it had been unopened. It was now a third empty, but drinking it hadn't calmed Tom's nerves at all. If anything, it had made them worse. Tom stared at the bottle, nibbling at the skin by the side of his fingernails, trying to decide whether to have another nip before Frank came back. He knew that Frank would be annoyed to see that Tom had been drinking, especially as it wasn't even six o'clock in the evening, but given that there was a body in one of the pig sheds, Frank would be annoyed about a lot more than his brother having a couple of fingers of whisky. Leaving the bottle where it was, Tom set off toward the far wall. He could feel his heart thumping and really needed Frank to come home. He would know what to do, he always did. When they were younger, their mother had always said that Frank had the brains, and Tom had the brawn. It wasn't until he was a teenager Tom realised that Frank actually had both.

'Shit, shit, shit. Hurry up, Frank,' he muttered under his breath before touching the wall, turning around, and setting back again. He pulled his phone from his pocket to see if Frank had texted him or tried to call, but there wasn't any signal. The thick stone walls of the farmhouse saw to that. He wandered over to the kitchen window and held the phone out toward the glass, waiting for the single bar of reception he knew he'd be able to pick up there. Nothing. 'Shit,' he repeated, 'Shit, shit.' He thumbed at the screen of his mobile to start the 'Find Me' app. Both Tom and Frank had the same app that showed their locations. It was a safety thing, Frank had told Tom, just in case there was an accident on the farm. Well, there had been an accident, and the app wasn't much help now. According to Tom's screen, Frank was somewhere in the middle of the North Sea.

Several minutes and a few more fingers of whisky later, Tom jumped when he heard the familiar sound of Frank's Land Rover pulling up outside the farmhouse. He took a couple of large steps toward the table and managed to drink another couple of inches straight from the bottle before the door flew open and Frank burst into the room.

'What's going on Tom?' Frank said, the urgency in his voice making it tremble. He stared at Tom, who looked back at him with wild eyes. Frank noticed the bottle on the table, its contents still moving from when Tom had slammed it back down on the table. 'Jesus, have you been drinking? You have, you stupid man.'

'A…A…Accident,' Tom said, pointing with an index finger toward the general direction of the pig sheds. He stared at his fingernail, realising it was bleeding. 'There's b…b…been an accident.' Tom didn't stammer often, not since he'd been in school, but when he was really wound up it came back with a vengeance.

'Yes, you said that on the phone,' Frank said. 'Who's had an accident? You said someone died. Is that right?' Tom's head nodded up and down.

'Yes, yes, yes.' Tom stopped nodding, feeling nauseous.

'Who?'

'One of the w…workers.'

'What? One of the illegals?' Frank asked. Tom nodded again, less violently this time. His eyes followed Frank as his brother walked over to one of the cupboards and fetched another tumbler. Frank returned to the table and poured himself a generous measure. He looked up at Tom and raised his eyebrows.

'Yes please,' Tom said. 'Need a pee.' Tom heard Frank mutter something as he walked out of the kitchen.

A few minutes later, Tom returned and took a seat opposite Frank at the kitchen table. Frank was drawing his finger over one of the many scars on the table top. It was a proper farmhouse table, and Tom knew it would sell for a fortune on one of those artisan shite websites. He'd looked into it a while ago, but never done anything about it.

'So, Tom,' Frank said in a quiet voice. 'Why don't you have a sip of your drink and tell me what happened. Nice and slowly, okay?' Tom picked up his glass and took a delicate sip of the whisky just to prove to Frank that he could. He could have drained the glass in one go, but from Frank's expression, Tom knew this wouldn't be a good idea. Frank had got his 'calm' face on. It often preceded Frank's 'irritated' face, which almost always became

Frank's 'really fucking angry' face pretty soon afterwards. Tom put his glass down and crossed his hands on the table, willing them to stop shaking.

'Well, I was on the farm sorting out the pigs. Feeding them and that, you know?' Tom said. Frank just nodded in reply. 'They'd all had lunch, and then…'

'Hang on, Tom. Who had lunch? The pigs or the illegals?'

'Well, both. But I'm not talking about the pigs. I'm talking about the workers that Marko dropped off. Five of them altogether but four of them ran off. I was going to get to that bit,' Tom said.

'Okay, sorry. So, there's only one dead one then?' Tom nodded in reply to Frank's question.

'Yeah, just the one.'

'Oh, well that's okay then. Just the one dead illegal immigrant on our farm.' Frank frowned as he took a sip from his tumbler. Tom looked at him for a few seconds before continuing.

'So, they all had their lunch, the immigrants I mean, and I was about to load them up to take them to do the mucking out when a white Transit van appears. They all go bananas, start shrieking at each other and all that. Then they just turned around and did one toward the woods.' Tom paused, staring at his brother whose face was flitting between calm and irritated. 'Except one. The dead one,' Tom said.

'When did he die?' Frank asked, his frown deepening.

'He's not dead yet. He will be in a bit, but at the moment he's still running through the fields.' Tom thought for a second before putting his hand on the table. 'So here's the van,' he said, nodding at his hand, 'and here's the illegals.' He put his other hand down. 'The van's coming this way,' he moved one hand across the table before starting to move the other hand in the opposite direction, 'and they're all running this way, toward the woods, but the dead one's got a gammy leg and can't run proper.' Tom's eyes flashed around the tabletop as he wondered what he could use to demonstrate to Frank how far the immigrant who couldn't run had got.

'It's okay, Tom. I get it,' Frank said. 'I get it so far.' There was a pause. 'Who was in the van?'

'Your mate, Mick.'

'Mick?'

'Yeah, Mick.'

'Who the fuck is Mick?' Frank said. Tom sat back in his chair. He didn't like it when Frank swore.

'Er, Mick. He's the bloke what does the boars and gets their…' Tom's voice faltered. He wasn't quite sure how to explain it to Frank, so he made a masturbating gesture with his hand and wrist. 'You know, their stuff.'

'Mike. His name's Mike, not Mick. How long have you bloody known him for?' Frank said, nodding. Mike was one of the few mates Frank had in the area, and they had been friends for years. 'So, what happened to the one with the gammy leg anyway?' Frank asked.

'He'd fell over, so me and Mick, sorry, Mike, went to pick him up. Poor bloke had fallen arse over elbow right into the shit. He was covered in it, and none of his mates was anywhere to be seen. We got him cleaned up as best we could, and I left him by the tractor while Mike did the thing with Boris. You know.' Tom made the same gesture with his hand. 'Then Mike went off in his van with his jam jar, and I went into the shed to show the one with the gammy leg how to clean the pens out. But I told him not to open the door to Boris' pen. I did tell him, Frank.' Tom could feel his voice wavering.

'You told him?' Frank asked. Tom looked at his brother's angry face.

'Yeah, I told him three or four times not to open it.'

'How was his English?'

'Well, he was a foreign.'

'Did he speak any English at all, Tom?'

'No. Of course not. Like I said, he was a foreign.' At this, Frank groaned and put his head in his hands. 'So I went off to fill up the water, leaving Gammy Leg to do the floor. When I got back, well I thought he'd disappeared. Gone after his mates or something. Then I saw his foot. I think it was his normal foot, not the dodgy one. It was kind of, well, kind of sticking out from under Boris. I've never seen a boar smile, but I swear he was looking at me with a bloody grin on his snout. Anyhow, I went in there, whacked Boris on the arse to shift him, and pulled the poor bugger out.'

'He was definitely dead?' Frank asked Tom.

'Er, you've seen the size of Boris? Besides, I think Boris was maybe a bit peckish after his, well, after him and Mike had, you know.' Tom stopped speaking, and the two brothers sat in silence for a few seconds.

'What do you mean peckish?' Frank asked.

'He was hungry.'

'Jesus Tom, I know what the word means,' Frank said, rolling his eyes. 'What did Boris do?'

'He, er,' Tom pointed at his face. 'He had a bit of a nibble of the poor bloke's face.'

'He ate his face?'

'Yeah, Boris ate his face. Well, most of it,' Tom said. 'He left an ear.'

'Sweet Jesus,' Frank muttered, taking another sip of his whisky. 'Come on then,' he said as he got to his feet. 'Let's go and have a look.'

7

E mily stared at the screen in front of her, chewing at
the end of her pencil. She rapped her fingers on the
desk while she tried to think of something to type. Something that didn't make her look like a complete idiot. When
she'd finished the report on the 'Wong Way' episode, she'd
left the part about being chased off the premises by a little
Chinaman with a machete out of it. That part of the visit,
Emily had decided, wasn't that relevant to the food standards assessment. Seeing as Mr Wong hadn't mentioned it,
Emily couldn't see a reason for her to either.

The inspection Emily was trying to write up had been
of a mobile kebab van that was parked up the road from
Carrow Road, Norwich City's football stadium. It was only
ever parked there on match days when the local football
team, the Canaries, were playing at home. There had been
several reports over the last few weeks of fans having diar-
rhoea and vomiting after eating from the van, and the
Food Standards Agency had decided to investigate. It was
only after a local radio journalist from Canary FM couldn't
do the usual post-match phone-in as he couldn't get away

from the toilet that the Food Standards Agency got properly interested. They had tried the interview from the toilet, but it hadn't gone well. As the kebab van only had two people working in it, Mr Clayton had assigned it to Emily.

Norwich City's rise to the Champion's League, helped no doubt by the fact that most of their European players hadn't had their work visas extended after Independence Day, had been rapid and unexpected. The influx of young footballers from the rest of the world had propelled the Canaries upward and brought with it a much larger following. This, in turn, brought with it a lot of people determined to make money from them, such as the owners of Kevin's Kebabs. The van had started life as 'Kevins Kebabs', but a grammar pedant had added a possessive apostrophe with a marker pen the first time it had parked up. Thinking back, Emily wasn't sure which of the two swarthy North African looking men was called Kevin as she hadn't been in the van long enough to find out.

The visit had started out reasonably well. She'd gone to the van just as they opened up, introduced herself, and had begun working through the checklist. The two men had seemed nice enough, and to be fair to them, she didn't see a great deal wrong with their set-up. It wasn't the tidiest or the cleanest kebab van Emily had been in, but it was far from awful. Emily was waiting for her temperature probe to warm up so that she could measure the hot plate when her concentration was interrupted.

'Burger and chips, please pet. Plenty of onions.' Emily looked up to see a young man standing at the window of the van, a yellow scarf wrapped around his neck even though it was late summer. Yellow, Emily remembered, was the team colour.

'Oh, sorry,' Emily replied with a smile. 'I don't work

here.' She glanced across at the kebab van owners, who were both looking at her with deadpan expressions.

'Why are you in the van then?' the football fan asked. 'Come on love, I'm starving. Just give me a burger and chips.' Emily looked behind him. A few more fans were making their way toward the stadium, and a bright yellow queue was beginning to form. It was a pretty straight split of people with children and young men, the only thing uniting them their Norwich City colours. Emily removed her probe and walked all of two small steps across to the owners.

'Can you serve this lot, please?' she asked them. To her dismay, they both seemed to have lost their previous command of the English language. One of them shrugged his shoulders and looked at the other one who returned the gesture.

'Oi,' a loud voice came through the open window of the van. 'Oi. I want a hot dog.' Emily walked back to the window.

'I don't work here, okay?' she said.

'What's going on, Dave,' a man at the back of the queue shouted. The customer at the front turned around.

'Dunno mate. She says she doesn't work here.'

'What's she doing in the van then?'

'No idea.'

'But she's got a white coat and hat on and everything.' As the fan at the back of the queue shouted this, Emily heard a group of fans singing from up the road to her left. Almost as one, the fans in the queue turned to look in the direction of the singing. 'Here come the pizza eaters, boys,' the man at the back shouted, looking around with his fists clenched. 'Let's be 'aving you.' Emily watched, incredulous, as the fans separated into two groups. The ones with children ran down the road toward the stadium, the young men ran up the road toward the singing. As they disappeared from her view, Emily could hear them chanting 'Delia's Yellow Army' at the top of their voices.

As I attempted to complete the inspection of Kevin's Kebabs, a small episode of football hooliganism occurred in the vicinity of the catering van, Emily typed, her tongue between her teeth. *I was unable to complete the inspection due to the presence of opposing supporters, followed by riot police with batons and copious amounts of tear gas.*

'That'll do,' Emily muttered as she saved the report and grabbed her coat from the back of her chair.

By the time she walked into the Murderers Pub twenty minutes later, Emily had convinced herself that nothing would come of the report as far as the Food Standards Agency was concerned. It was hardly her fault that there'd been a massive punch up, and it was only when the police turned up on horses that things got really nasty. Fair credit to the Norwich fans, though. It was the only time Emily had ever seen fresh horse manure being used as a weapon.

Once she had got a drink from the bar, Emily walked around the pub looking for her flat mate, Catherine. The place had been a pub forever and was full of wooden beams, tiny alcoves with one or two seats, and some proper hardcore drinkers. Emily finally found Catherine huddled in a corner of the pub, nursing what looked like a tonic water. Knowing Catherine, as Emily did well, it wouldn't just be tonic water in the glass but also a significant amount of gin.

'Hello babes,' Emily said, dropping into a chair next to her friend. 'How are you?' Emily looked at Catherine, dismissing the flash of irritation that she always felt when she looked at her best friend. Emily knew that Catherine didn't regard her as an ugly sister, but that was how Emily felt. Catherine could wake up after a massive night out, stumble into their shared kitchen with smeared makeup, bedraggled hair, and the mother of all hangovers and still look amazing. Bitch.

'Hey you,' Catherine replied, offering her cheek for an air kiss. 'You're looking…' Catherine's eyes flicked over Emily's trouser suit, '…butch.' Emily laughed. 'So, what's new? Not seen you for bloody ages.'

Since Emily had started at the Food Standards Agency, she'd been getting up before Catherine and was in bed way before her flat mate had come back. To say Catherine was a bit of a night owl was an understatement. Not seeing each other was one of the reasons why they'd arranged to meet in the pub, to catch up properly.

'Yeah, so far so good I think,' Emily said. 'I'm doing my own inspections, anyway.'

'Really?' Catherine replied, looking at Emily as she took a sip of her drink. 'How are they going?' Emily looked at Catherine, who was wearing a completely blank expression, and spent the next few minutes telling her about the visit to the Chinese takeaway. When she got to the bit with the machete, Catherine's jaw dropped. They sat in silence for a few seconds before Catherine's face creased up. 'Sorry, I'm so sorry,' she said, putting her hands across her face and rocking with laughter. Emily sat back in her chair and folded her arms, watching her friend's shoulders jerking up and down.

'Who have you been talking to?' Emily asked.

'I can't say,' Catherine replied, her voice muffled by her hands. 'I promised I wouldn't say a word.' Despite herself, Emily felt a smile creep onto her face. Catherine's laughter was infectious.

'What have you heard?' Emily asked.

'Honestly, I can't say,' Catherine replied, removing her hands from her face and waving them in front of her eyes.

'Let me get you a drink, though. Same again?' Catherine pointed at Emily's half-empty glass.

'Go on then,' Emily replied.

'Do you want anything to eat?' Catherine asked. She paused for a few seconds. 'Kebab maybe?' It was Emily's turn to laugh.

'Piss off and get me a vodka and Coke.'

Emily was checking her phone a good ten minutes later, wondering where Catherine had gone, when her flat mate returned with their drinks. She put them down on the table with a thump, and Emily looked at her friend. Any laughter on her face had long since disappeared. If anything, Catherine looked very pissed off.

'What's up, mate?' Emily asked. 'Who's upset you?' Catherine nodded in the general direction of the bar.

'I was waiting at the bar, standing next to a couple of blokes, and while I was waiting to be served I kind of over-heard their conversation,' she said.

'Which ones?' Emily asked, craning her neck so that she could see past her friend.

'Don't stare, for God's sake,' Catherine said. 'Middle of the bar, one in a nasty red check shirt, one in a cheap suit. You see them?' Emily nodded.

'Yeah, I've got them. Red Check has got his back to us, but Cheap Suit looks okay.'

'No, they're both twats,' Catherine replied.

'How come?'

'Cheap Suit was having a go at his mate about a message that Red Check had sent. Apparently, it was in the middle of a really important meeting, something to do with Kirsty or something. In Accounts.' Emily looked at the two men at the bar, neither of whom were looking back at them. Catherine had a habit of sticking her nose into other people's conversations, and it didn't always go well.

'So what?' Emily asked.

'Well, the message wasn't from Kirsty, or Katie, or whatever her name was. It was from Red Check pretending to be her. He'd got onto her computer and sent Cheap Suit a message thanking him for giving her a good seeing to, and it popped up in the middle of some meeting.'

'Oh, right,' Emily said, looking again at the two men. 'Well, that is kind of funny.'

'It bloody isn't, Emily. That's proper rude, that is. Imagine if that was you?'

As Emily considered her reply, the young man in the cheap suit glanced across in their direction and she got a good look at him for the first time. She took in his boyish good looks, tousled hair, and vaguely bemused expression.

'I should be so lucky,' she muttered under her breath as she took a large sip of her drink.

8
———

F rank looked across at Tom sitting in the passenger
seat of the Land Rover as it bounced across the farm
tracks toward the pig sheds. The light was just beginning to
fade, but the shadows couldn't hide the uncertainty on
Tom's face from Frank. It had been that way since they
were children. Tom wasn't able to hide his feelings in the
slightest. If he felt something, it was obvious. This wasn't
helped by the fact that Tom had never been the sharpest
tool in the box, something recognised by pretty much
everyone who came into contact with him. If it weren't for
the fact that the brothers had gone to the same school,
Tom would have been a constant target for every bully
north of the Suffolk border. As it was, there were a few
who had tried, but thanks to Frank they'd only done it
once. Frank didn't mind using his fists when he had to, and
he wasn't afraid of the sight of blood. This was one of the
reasons why he became a butcher.

He turned his attention to the current problem. A dead
illegal immigrant. That situation presented a number of
issues, which Frank was sure Tom knew about even if it

was in an abstract sense. When Frank had asked him why he hadn't called the police, Tom had just shrugged and mumbled something about getting into trouble. That was the understatement of the year, without a doubt. Employing illegal immigrants was bad enough, but Frank knew they didn't have a choice on that one. Dead illegal immigrants raised things to a whole new level of trouble. The farm would be closed for sure. Tom would end up in prison, Frank as well.

For a few moments, they travelled in silence while Frank contemplated the inevitable Health and Safety investigation if the whole incident was uncovered. How many of the rules had they managed to break? Illegal workers, no safety equipment anywhere in sight, and a randy boar named after the Prime Minister. The press would have a field day, and Frank had to stop himself making up headlines for the Eastern Evening News. 'Boared to Death by Boris' was his personal favourite. Frank shivered as he thought about being squashed by a post-orgasmic boar who then gets the nibbles and starts to chew your face off. He hoped to God for the poor bloke's sake that he was already dead by the time Boris felt like a snack.

Frank drew into the yard outside the pig sheds and brought the Land Rover to a shuddering halt. The brothers got out of the vehicle, and Frank followed Tom toward the door of one of the sheds.

'He's in this one. It's empty,' Tom said. 'I thought I'd better hide him out of the way just in case all the other illegals came back.' Frank was sometimes surprised by Tom, and this was one of those times. At least his little brother had managed to think something through today. Tom swung the door open, and Frank could see the outline of a body lying on the floor in the gloom. There was a familiar smell in the air inside the shed, only subtly different to the smell of newly slaughtered pigs. Once he had managed to find the switch on the wall, Frank turned the lights on and the overhead fluorescent tubes flickered into life. He took a step toward the body and leaned over to examine it.

'My God, Tom,' Frank said with a sharp inhalation of breath. 'You weren't kidding about Boris being peckish.' The man's face was gone, the only things left that were recognisable as being human were his staring eyes and grinning teeth. And an ear.

'So w…w…what are we going to do, Frank?' Tom said. Frank turned to him.

'Tom, calm down. There's no point getting upset. We just need to think this through.' Frank ran his fingers through his hair, something he always did when he was trying to work something out. He tapped a foot on the concrete floor a couple of times before making a decision. 'Right, first things first. We can't leave him here. Let's move him into one of the fridges until we've worked out what we're going to do. It's not as if there's much in the way of meat in them at the moment, is it?'

Once he had instructed Tom to take the immigrant's feet, Frank knelt and hooked his arms under the man's armpits. Between them, they manhandled the body across the yard and toward the fridge shed.

'Blimey, he's heavy, isn't he?' Tom said, breathing hard. Frank would have replied, but he was just as out of breath as his brother. They put the immigrant down by the shed door, and Frank waited while Tom went into the shed and opened up one of the fridges. Once they had manoeuvred the body into the fridge, Tom closed the door and flipped the main switch on the wall to turn it back on. 'That's not been used for about a year, that fridge,' Tom said. That much had been obvious to Frank just from the musty smell inside it. 'It should be okay though, they're pretty solid them ones. Made in England, so they are.'

The brothers sat in silence as they drove back to the farmhouse. Frank was turning things over in his head, working through various options. He glanced across at Tom in the passenger seat, but he was examining his fingernails. As Frank watched, Tom worried at one of them with his teeth. He wasn't fussed about washing his hands after moving a dead body then. Frank sighed and turned his attention back to the matter at hand. By the time they got back to the farmhouse, he had the beginnings of a plan in his mind. All he needed to do now was to persuade Tom that it was the only option they had left. It would be even better if it was Tom's idea.

Back at their seats in the kitchen, Frank made sure Tom had a generous helping of whisky in his glass. He topped his own glass up and went to the cupboard to get another bottle. This could be a long night.

'We need to chat, Tom,' Frank said. Tom looked at him, his eyes already tired. 'Think it through, work out the best way forward. Just like Mum used to say.' Tom's eyes widened at the mention of their mother. She wasn't talked about that often. Their father was talked about even less, and even then only when they drove past an Eddie Stobart lorry. 'Don't you think?'

Tom nodded his head in reply. 'Guess so,' he said, staring at the glass in front of him. 'We can't leave him in the fridge, can we? The bloody thing eats electricity, that does.'

'So, we need to do something,' Frank said. 'How about calling the police?' Tom's startled look told Frank he'd hit a nerve.

'But we'd get in trouble,' Tom said, his voice wavering

like it had used to do back in the playground when he was threatened. 'Proper trouble as well.'

'You're right, Tom,' Frank replied, choosing his words carefully. 'The farm would probably be closed down. We'd be in prison for, well, I don't know,' Tom's eyes widened a fraction further, and Frank realised that Tom hadn't thought about prison. He decided to press the point home. 'Years, I guess. They don't put family in the same prison, I don't think, so we'd be in different ones. You're a good-looking lad as well, didn't Mum always say that? You know what happens to good looking lads in prison? You won't be making sausages, you'll be playing hide the sausage.' Tom grabbed his glass off the table with a trembling hand and took a large slug. Frank watched him wince as he swallowed and felt a twinge of guilt which passed about as quickly as Tom's heartburn would.

'No,' Tom put the glass down hard on the table, rattling the bottle of whisky. 'No, not doing that.'

'So, we need to think of something else, Tom,' Frank said, picking up the bottle and refilling Tom's glass. 'What do you think?' They sat in silence for some minutes, Frank waiting for Tom to come up with something. Anything.

'We could, er, I guess we could get rid of it?' Tom said, breaking the silence.

'What, get rid of the body?'

'Yeah,' Tom replied, taking another sip. 'Get rid of it.' Frank wondered if Tom had got any ideas about how to get rid of a body. 'Dump it somewhere,' Tom offered in a quiet voice.

'It'd be found, though. Then the police would trace where it came from. Then…' Frank left the sentence hanging but made sure Tom saw his ominous look toward the door as if the police were going to burst in any moment. 'Same if we buried it. Sooner or later, it'd be found. We need to find a way to get rid of it so that it can't be found. Ever.' Frank got to his feet and made his way to the toilet, leaving Tom staring into his whisky. As he washed his hands, Frank wondered how he could steer Tom toward the obvious. The risk was that he'd fall asleep before coming up with the plan, and Frank knew that the only way to get Tom to carry it through was to make him think that it was his idea. Tom might not have inherited much from their father, but he had inherited his stubborn streak. Returning to the kitchen, Frank saw that Tom had refilled both their glasses almost to the brim. That was a lot of whisky.

'Have you got any ideas, Frank?' Tom asked his brother. Frank took a deep breath before replying.

'Not really, Tom,' he said. 'I mean, we need to get rid of the body completely. So that it can never be found. It's the only way we can save the farm.' Tom looked up, and Frank knew that he didn't have long before Tom was asleep on the kitchen table. 'I mean, how is it possible to get rid of a body? You're a farmer, I'm only a butcher. What would we know about getting rid of a body?' Frank paused, watching his brother think. Time for a prod. 'On a pig farm?' Tom's eyes half closed and for a second Frank thought he was about to fall asleep, but he was concentrating.

Frank could see the exact moment that Tom put it all together. First, he jumped in his chair, eyes widening. Then he shook his head from side to side and looked at Frank for a second. Tom's mouth opened an inch, then closed again. He frowned for a few seconds before picking up his whisky and almost draining the glass.

'Frank,' Tom whispered. 'I've got an idea. I don't think you're going to like it very much, but I've got an idea.'

9

F rank watched Tom get drunker and drunker, helping him out by topping up his glass when Tom got anywhere near emptying it. The original bottle had run out a while ago, and Frank had been forced to get his emergency bottle from his bedroom. Half an hour after Tom had told Frank all about his idea, Tom was fast asleep on the table. For a moment, Frank thought about leaving Tom where he was while he did what needed to be done, but decided against it. He didn't want Tom waking up and stumbling in on him, although it was unlikely.

'Come on mate,' Frank said, rocking Tom's shoulder. 'Time for bed.' Frank had to do this a couple of times before Tom woke up enough for Frank to manhandle him to his bedroom. By the time Frank had taken Tom's shoes off and thrown a blanket over him, his little brother was snoring like a baby.

After washing their glasses in the kitchen, Frank went to one of the cupboards and pulled out their father's old set of butcher's knives. They were rolled up in an oilskin wrapper which Frank unrolled on the kitchen table. He looked at the knives for a few minutes, remembering his father wielding them back when they used to slaughter their own animals on the farm. He had taught Frank well, and by the time he was twelve, Frank could kill, skin, and process a whole pig in under three hours. He'd not butchered a pig properly for a few years now, as they paid the commercial slaughterhouse they had to use an extra few pounds to cut their pigs into the prime sections. All Frank did these days was slice the prime cuts into the best joints, but butchery was like riding a bike. You never forget, Frank thought as he picked up a cleaver from the roll of knives. The kitchen light glinted off the lightly oiled blade, and Frank ran his thumb over the cutting edge. He knew it would be sharpened to exactly forty degrees. Their father didn't really take care of much in his lifetime, but he did look after his knives. Frank considered using a whetstone to brighten the blades a little, but decided against it. They didn't need it for what he was going to use them for. He rolled the knives back into their oilskin, grabbed his coat from the back of the kitchen door, and slipped the rest of the whisky into his coat pocket.

As Frank drove down the track to the pig sheds, he thought about his brother. In a sense, Frank felt bad about manipulating Tom into thinking that what Frank was about to do was all his own idea. But Frank knew that it was the only way Tom's silence was guaranteed. Tom had always been quick to try to get out of trouble, and if there was any way he could make something someone else's fault, he would. It was only when the blame fell squarely on Tom's shoulders that he would just retreat into himself and say nothing. He'd been that way since the pair of them had been children.

When he got to the sheds, Frank made his way to the old abattoir. It was a low building, standing on its own away from the other sheds, and had been one of the original buildings on the farm. There were no windows, just a green wooden door with flaking paint, and it had stone walls just as thick as the ones in the farmhouse. Flicking the light switch, he was relieved when the old fluorescent bulbs spluttered into life. The building wasn't used that often, and the only things in that were used were the mincing machine and bone grinder. He looked around the interior of the building, taking in the butcher's table, the railing and hooks on the ceiling, and the drain set into the middle of the floor. It smelt unused and musty but was still in good shape. After checking that the hose still worked, he left the abattoir and walked over to the shed with the fridges.

Twenty minutes later, Frank stood in the abattoir in shirtsleeves, having long since discarded his coat. Moving a body was hard work, and he mopped his brow with a discoloured handkerchief as he regarded the man hanging upside down in front of him. The hardest part had been getting him onto the rail. Slipping the nooses over his ankles had been easy enough, but when Frank tried to haul him up, one of the pulleys had stuck. It had taken all of his strength to unstick it, and by the time he'd managed to get the body where he wanted it, Frank was sweating profusely. He was regarding the body through professional eyes, working out in his head how he was going to complete this task when he remembered the half empty bottle of whisky in the Land Rover.

'Dutch courage,' he mumbled as he left the shed and went to retrieve it. He stood in the yard, unscrewed the bottle top, and took a large swig, silhouetted in the light of a full moon. Screwing the cap back on, Frank walked back into the shed and selected a small knife from the roll on the countertop before expertly slicing through both the carotid artery and jugular vein of the hanging man. As he watched the blood flow from the wounds, Frank unscrewed the bottle for a top up.

He hadn't done proper butchery for a while, and even though he'd never butchered a human being before, once Frank started all the old movements came back to him. Once he'd made the first large incision and unzipped the man's abdomen, it wasn't that different to a pig. It took him almost an hour to reduce the immigrant to his constituent parts, and then another forty minutes to strip the flesh and put what he could in the mincer. The bones were ground down to meal, and the only recognisable thing left was the head. Frank regarded it now, wondering what the best thing to do with it was. He left it on the butcher's block for the time being and lifted the large plastic tub that was full of mince. Frank was surprised how heavy it was. There had to be a good 25 to 30 kilograms in there, and not much of it was fat. The pigs would have a field day, he thought as he carried the tub out to the shed with the fridges in. The red tub with the offal in it could stay where it was until Tom got a chance to take it to the rendering plant. It was absolutely indistinguishable from pigs' innards, and Frank knew that it would be rendered along with everything else. The single remaining tub with the bone meal could be spread out on the vegetable patch behind the farmhouse, or he could always take it into the shop and sell it to the local allotment owners for a few quid. When he returned to the abattoir, Frank looked again at the head. If he was going to feed it to the pigs, he'd need to get rid of the hair and teeth first. Frank opened a drawer and got a thick black plastic bag out to put the head in so he could take it back to the farmhouse.

Once Frank had finished hosing down the abattoir and cleaning the knives and machinery, he looked at his watch.

It was almost two o'clock in the morning, and they were expecting a meat delivery from the slaughterhouse first thing in the morning. Grimacing at the thought of only getting four hours' sleep, Frank swung the bag containing the head over his shoulder and flicked off the lights in the abattoir as he left to go to bed.

10

Tom opened his eyes and immediately wished he hadn't. He had an absolute bastard of a headache behind his eyes which was an unwelcome reminder of why he rarely drank whisky. He got himself into a seated position on the edge of the bed and sat still for a few minutes waiting for the nausea to subside. He realised that Frank must have put him to bed last night, but couldn't remember it at all. He'd not even woken up this morning when Mike had collected Frank to take him to work. Tom slowly got to his feet and shuffled to the bathroom for a pee.

Ten minutes later, Tom was feeling a bit better having drunk the best part of a litre of milk. He sat in the kitchen in his usual place and waited for the kettle to boil. There was a note Frank had left in the middle of the table as he usually did when he got up before Tom. *Gone to work. Put stockpot on at four. Mince in the fridge shed.* The slaughterhouse must have dropped their meat off while Tom was still sleeping. At least that would keep Frank happy, Tom thought. Frank always took the prime cuts into the shop so that he could slice them just how the customers wanted them prepared, and Tom imagined him now talking to one of his little old ladies about which piece of belly she wanted for her tea. Next to the large stockpot on the stove, the kettle whistled as it came to the boil. Tom took it off the stove and made himself a cup of tea, drinking it by the kitchen window. He looked at the grey skies and rain outside, knowing that he would be spending most of his day in it, and sighed.

Once all the pigs were fed, Tom went to the main pig shed to see if the sows had come into heat yet. He gave Boris a sideways look as he walked past the enormous boar, but the sows weren't quite ready. He pressed a hand down on their backs and had a quick look at their rear ends which were the only female genitalia that Tom had ever seen in the flesh. Maybe tomorrow would be Boris's day, he thought as he wandered over to the shed with the fridges in. He got the large tub of mince that the slaughterhouse had dropped off and lugged it back to the tractor. At least he could spend a couple of hours in the kitchen where it was warm and dry.

Back in the kitchen, Tom assembled everything he needed, humming to himself as he arranged the herbs and spices on the kitchen table. He loaded up the sausage making machine with the casings and added what he knew was just the right amount of rusks to a mixing bowl. Then he added some mince, herbs, spices, and finally a generous helping of freshly ground pepper. The next part was the bit that he enjoyed most. Tom plunged both hands into the mixing bowl and set to work mixing the ingredients together.

He worked quickly, almost on auto-pilot, and within three-quarters of an hour had a long string of sausages that curled its way around the kitchen table. He snipped them into batches of eight, and packaged them into Frank's own branded wrapping, making sure that the text 'Frank's Butcher' was front and centre on each one. By the time he had wrapped all of them, he had over fifty packs of sausages stacked up on the kitchen table.

'That's a good job, that is,' Tom said to himself as he looked at his handiwork. He went outside to get a large plastic tray from the back of the Land Rover, running through the pouring rain as quickly as he could. When he had the sausages stacked on the tray, he carried it to the car and got in to head off to Frank's shop.

When Tom arrived at the butcher's shop, the small car park was full, so he parked on the double yellow lines outside, putting his indicators on to ward off any rogue traffic wardens. Like it would actually make a difference. Frank was deep in conversation with a customer when Tom carried the tray into the shop. There were three or four other customers milling about, which was a good sign.

'Hey Tom, that's great timing,' Frank said with a broad but fake smile. 'I was just telling Mrs Timmings here that I've been expecting a sausage delivery, and here you are.' Mrs Timmings looked at Tom over the top of a pair of half-glasses. She had to be ninety if she was a day. 'Isn't that right, Mrs Timmings?'

'What?' she replied.

'I said, I was just telling you about the sausages,' Frank repeated, this time much louder.

'Oh, yes. Sausages,' she said. Tom glanced at Frank who still had his fake smile on before he headed back to the door.

'I'll see you later, Frank,' Tom said. 'Pot goes on at four. I've not forgotten.' The bell above the door tinkled as Tom opened it, and he stepped back outside to see a traffic warden regarding his Land Rover.

'I've only been there for about twenty seconds, mate,' Tom said, trying not sound too annoyed.

'Can't park there,' the traffic warden replied from underneath his peaked cap. 'They're double yellows, they are.'

'I know. Look, I'm sorry. I won't do it again.' The last thing Tom could afford at the moment was another parking ticket.

'I'll tell you what,' the traffic warden said, his pen poised over his pad of tickets. 'You sort me out with a pack of them sausages I've just seen you carrying into the butcher's, and I might forget all about a ticket.' Tom wasn't quick at the best of times, but it didn't take him long at all to work that one out.

'Deal,' Tom said before rushing back into the shop.

11

'How can I sodding well turn left when it's a field?' Emily swore at her sat-nav as it suggested, yet again, that she take the next turning on the left. With a quick glance in her rear view mirror to make sure there wasn't anything behind her, she stopped the car and looked at the paperwork on her passenger seat. She had got the right postcode, but for some reason, the sat-nav didn't have a clue where she was. Still swearing under her breath, she put the car in gear and carried on down the lane, peering through the windscreen wipers for a turning on the left. It was just beginning to get dark, and she if she didn't find the place in the next ten minutes or so, she was going to head back to Norwich.

About two hundred yards past the spot where the sat-nav was so insistent she turned left, Emily saw a thin rutted track with a wooden sign that said 'Hill Top Farm'. She looked around at the flat landscape. There wasn't a hill in sight. She edged the car into the lane and drove as fast as she dared up the track, wincing as the car rocked from side to side as the wheels hit large potholes. Through the wipers, she could see a farmhouse at the end of the track in front of her, but she still couldn't see any sign of a hill.

When Emily got to the farmhouse, she parked the car and ran through the rain across to the door with her paperwork tucked underneath her coat. There were a couple of lights on, so she knew someone was home. Emily looked at the door but couldn't see a doorbell so she knocked as hard as she could.

'Ouch,' Emily muttered, flexing her fingers. It was a pretty solid door. She stood in the rain, waiting, but there was no response. She gritted her teeth and knocked again. This time, through the door, she heard someone shout something. 'Oh, come on,' Emily said. 'How big is your bloody farmhouse?'

The door opened about eight inches, and a face peered through the gap. Emily smiled at the man looking at her. She would have put him in his late twenties or early thirties, and he had the complexion of a man who spent most of his time outside.

'Hello,' she said, smiling even though she didn't really feel like it. The man just stared back at her. 'Are you the farmer?' As soon as she said this, Emily realised what a stupid question that was. Of course he was the farmer. Why else would he be living in the farmhouse?

'Yep,' the man said after thinking for a few seconds.

'Oh, good. I'm from the Food Standards Agency.' He didn't reply but just carried on looking at her. 'Can I come in? It's raining,' Emily asked, shaking her hair in case he'd not noticed she was soaking wet through.

The door opened fully, and the man stepped back to let Emily in. She walked through the door and was hit by a wave of warm air and the most fantastic smell of cooking. Emily looked around the kitchen, taking in the minimalistic look. It was functional and lived in, but there wasn't much of a personal touch in the slightest. It certainly didn't have a woman's touch, and Emily thought for a few seconds about what she would add to it if she lived here. 'Wow, something smells good,' she said, looking at the large stockpot bubbling on the stove. Her stomach grumbled, and she realised that she'd not eaten anything since lunchtime. 'What are you cooking?'

'Dunno,' the man replied. 'My brother cooks. I just heat it up. Soup, maybe.' Emily looked at the man, able to see him properly for the first time. He was definitely a farmer. He had jeans and a check shirt on, was well built, and Emily noticed that his hands were like shovels. Emily got the paperwork out from under her coat and looked at the front page.

'You must be Tom Pinch?' He nodded in reply. 'I'm Emily Underwood. Like I said, I'm from the Food Standards Agency.' She watched as Tom processed this information. A few seconds later, he replied.

'Right.' A man of few words then, Emily supposed.

'I've got some paperwork for you to look through before your annual inspection. It's due in the next few weeks. There's a copy of your last report, and a self-assessment to fill out so that your visit goes as smoothly as possible.' Emily was determined that this visit was going to be absolutely spot on. She couldn't afford any more problems, so she turned on the charm even more. 'We're really keen to help you out with the inspection, so if there's anything you need help with, just ask.' Emily noticed that Tom hadn't even looked at the paperwork, and she wondered if he could actually read.

'I'll have to wait for my brother,' Tom said. 'He does things like that, see.'

'Okay, no problem. My number's on the paperwork.'

This time, Tom did glance down at the file Emily had put on the table. Emily suddenly realised something. 'Is your brother the butcher in the village?'

'Yep,' Tom replied.

'I met him the other day,' Emily said. 'Nice chap.' She looked at Tom, but there was no reaction from him at all. Emily tried a grin, but still nothing. She looked again around the kitchen. It wouldn't take much to brighten it up. Maybe a lick of paint on the walls, and a new sink. Even just a bunch of flowers in the middle of the table would work wonders. She walked over to the stove and sniffed as her stomach gurgled again. Whatever was in that pot really did smell amazing. Emily turned back to face Tom. 'Can I have a look inside?' She pointed at the pot.

'No.'

'Oh, okay then. Well, I guess I'd better be making tracks. Things to do, people to see. You know how it is.' She paused and looked at him. Maybe he didn't. 'Right then, I'll be off.'

'Okay,' Tom replied, walking over to the kitchen door and opening it for Emily. 'Bye.'

Emily tried not to laugh as she walked over to the door. Tom really wasn't very good around people, that was obvious. She fought the urge to kiss him on the cheek as she walked past him and through the door, just to see what he would do.

'Just ask your brother to call me if he's got any questions,' Emily said as Tom closed the door in her face. At least it had almost stopped raining. She walked over to the car, laughing to herself. 'What a strange chap,' she mumbled.

As Emily opened the car door, she paused. If she wasn't mistaken, she'd just heard a loud scream from inside the farmhouse. She waited for a second, unsure whether she should go back and knock on the door to make sure that Tom was okay. She didn't hear anything else, so shook her head and got in the car.

'Weirdo,' she said as she started it up and drove back down the track.

12

Andy sat back in the oversized beanbag and waited for the other meeting attendees to arrive. He was in what was known as 'The Thought Factory', a windowless room full of black beanbags on the top floor of Partridge Towers. According to one of the women Andy worked with, it had been plain old 'Meeting Room 3' until a couple of months ago. The table and chairs had disappeared, to be replaced by the large beanbags, and a new sign had appeared on the door. There was a flip-chart in the corner of the room with the words *THIS IS WHERE THE MAGIC HAPPENS* in large blue letters. Andy doubted it very much.

One by one the rest of the marketing team arrived, each sinking into their own beanbag. Last to arrive was Rob from Marketing who took the beanbag nearest the flip-chart. There were only six of them in the room. Kett's of Norwich didn't have a very large marketing department.

'Andy, would you do the honours with the flip-chart please?' Rob asked. Andy struggled to get to his feet, sighing as he did so. He should have known that as the intern, he'd be in charge of the flip-chart. At least Rob had got his name right. That was progress of sorts. Andy stood next to the chart and picked up a blue pen. He took the lid off it, and sniffed deeply, enjoying the intoxicating smell. Rob frowned at him before turning his attention to the rest of the room.

'Ladies, Gentlemen, thanks for coming to this breakout session,' Rob said in his trademark reedy voice. Andy hadn't realised he had a choice in the matter. 'I've got the results in from the 'Famous Face' competition we ran on the intranet site. Some really good suggestions here.' The competition had been to identify a famous person with a connection to Norfolk that Kett's of Norwich could hire as a front man or woman for the Pride of Anglia competition. 'So,' Rob continued. 'Drum roll please.' He looked around the room with his eyebrows raised, but there was no response. Andy flipped the front page of the flip-chart over to a clean page and raised his pen, ready for action. 'First, I'll go through the unsuccessful nominations, which Andy will write up on the board. Then at the end, I'll reveal which local celebrity we've hired as the face of the competition. You ready, Andy?'

'Yep,' Andy replied in a tired voice. 'Born ready, Rob.'

'That's my boy,' Rob laughed, but no one else joined in. 'Right then, in first place in terms of votes, we've got Horatio Nelson.' Several of the people in the room looked at each other with bemused expressions. 'We had quite a lot of votes for him in fact, but obviously he's not available. Next up was Delia Smith, but she wasn't available either.' Andy knew that wasn't strictly true, as he'd been the one to phone up Delia's agent to inquire whether she might be interested. Andy had got as far as telling the agent which supermarket firm was running the competition when the man on the other end of the line just laughed and hung up. 'Stephen Fry was next, but he's now living in Los Angeles, so he's out.' Rob shuffled his notes as Andy wrote Stephen Fry's name on the board. 'Next was Mylene Klass, but it turns out she's gone vegan. Then we tried Hannah Spearritt, but we couldn't find her.'

'Who?' a bald man in the corner asked.

'Hannah Spearritt. She's an actress,' Rob replied.

'No, she's not, she's a singer,' a rather large lady who Andy recognised from the board meeting replied. 'She was in some band, S Club wasn't it?'

'She acts as well. Didn't she do that thing with the dinosaurs in it?' someone else replied from deep within a beanbag. This prompted an argument between two of the marketing department about whether or not Hannah Spearritt had also been in *Doctor Who*. Andy listened to them going back and forth, wondering when Rob was going to shut them up. It was only when the two of them started arguing about which Doctor Who had been the best one when Rob finally stepped in.

'Gents, I know that this room is for the free expression of ideas, but we're going in a slightly different direction here. Can we re-baseline back to the primary objective?' Andy blinked a couple of times as he tried to work out what Rob had just said. 'Back to the nominees. A few votes for Alan Partridge, but Charles ruled him out on the grounds that most people in Norfolk think he's a wan…, er, don't like him. I'm not convinced myself, but Charles is the big cheese.' Andy had a sudden vision of Steve Coogan's character chasing after someone with a large piece of Stilton and couldn't help but grin. 'Something to add, Andy?' Rob asked.

'Smell my cheese,' Andy replied before thinking about it. That was what Alan Partridge had been shouting as he waved the Stilton around, but from the blank expressions, Andy realised that he was on his own with that one.

'Good, thanks,' Rob said, scribbling a note. 'That might work as a slogan for the dairy section of the competition. Nice one.' Several heads in the beanbags nodded, so Andy wrote 'Smell my cheese' on the flip-chart as he tried not to laugh. 'Right then, they were the nominations. There were a few others, but we couldn't find a connection to Norfolk, so we had to thin those ones out. So, I'm pleased to announce that the famous face of the Pride of Anglia competition is Tina Lovett.' Andy looked at the faces in front of him. It was obvious that no-one had got a clue who Tina Lovett was. Neither had Andy until he'd googled her name, and even then he only found out who she was when he got to the fourth page of the search results. 'She does the weather on ITV Eastern,' Rob explained.

'Does she? I thought that was Lucy Cambridge? The one with the squashed face?' the bald man piped up again.

'Lucy Cambridge does the daytime weather,' Rob replied. 'Tina Lovett does the night-time one. She comes on at midnight. Anyway, she's agreed to do it, so the decision's been made. Good, right then, that's a wrap. Thanks, team.' He paused for a few seconds, looking at each face in turn. 'Let's get back out there.'

Rob got to his feet and strode to the door. As he walked past Andy, Rob muttered. 'Follow me. Let's do this.' Andy put the lid back on the pen and followed his boss through the door. He glanced over his shoulder as he left the room to see two of the marketing department trying to help the large lady out of her beanbag. Andy wasn't optimistic about their chance of success.

They reached Rob's desk in the corner of the large

open plan office, and Rob threw himself into his chair. 'I think that went well, don't you?'

'Yeah, it was awesome,' Andy replied. 'You could see the fire in their eyes.'

'Really?'

'Oh, definitely.'

13

F rank whistled to himself as he closed up his butcher's shop for the day. What a day it had been as well. He'd taken more by lunchtime than he had done in the last week. On a whim, he popped into the off-licence over the road from his shop and picked up a bottle of Prosecco to celebrate. His pockets bulging with cash, he was still whistling as he walked to his car.

On the drive back to the farm, Frank thought about their finances. He'd sat down a couple of evenings ago and gone through them with a fine tooth-comb. To say they were depressing reading was an understatement at best. He'd tried various ways of rearranging the figures to make the numbers go upwards, but hadn't been able to come up with anything. Buying Boris had been a gamble, and if he was as fertile as he was supposed to be, then they could have some more pork that actually belonged to them in a couple of months' time. Until then, they were going to have to live off the profits of one of the boar's byproducts and as much cheap meat as he could repackage. At least the money in his pockets would see them through the next couple of weeks if they ate frugally.

'Good evening, Thomas,' Frank called as he walked in through the front door. His brother was only ever Thomas when Frank was in an excellent mood. To Frank's surprise, Tom was sitting leaning back on one of the kitchen chairs, arms and legs crossed, and a face like thunder.

'What's up with you, Tom?' Frank asked, his good mood forgotten for a few seconds. Tom never got angry for more than about five minutes at a time. It just wasn't in his nature, and the idea that Tom had been sitting there stewing and waiting for Frank to come home was a foreign one. Tom didn't reply to Frank's question but nodded at the stockpot on the stove.

'You could have told me what was in that,' Tom said, his jaw clenched. Frank looked at the pot. 'One thing I was not expecting in the stockpot,' Tom continued, 'was a fucking head.' It wasn't like Tom to swear, Frank thought. The last time that had happened was after a particularly nasty accident when they were teenagers. The saddle of Tom's bike had detached as he'd gone over a ramp, and the result had been bloody.

'Oh, sorry. I thought you'd have worked it out. I've taken the teeth out and ground them down, but I needed to soften up the hair so that I could scrape it off properly.' Frank looked at his brother's face and couldn't help himself. He started laughing. 'I'm sorry, mate,' Frank said with a broad grin. 'Did it make you jump?'

'Just a bit,' Tom said, relaxing and leaning forward. 'I nearly shit myself. It wasn't just me though, some woman was round from the Food Standards Agency earlier. She wanted to look in it, said it smelled lovely she did.'

'Now, that wouldn't have been good,' Frank said, his smile faltering. 'What did you tell her?'

'I said it was soup,' Tom replied. This time, they both laughed and continued laughing until Frank was almost crying. He couldn't even begin to imagine what would have happened if the woman from the Food Standards Agency had looked in the pot, but it wouldn't have been good.

When they had calmed down, Frank turned to Tom.

'Have you got the paperwork she left?' Tom walked over to the sideboard and picked up the thin file, passing it to Frank. He looked at it carefully, reading the card stapled to the top corner of the papers. Frank fished in his pocket to get the card that he'd been given earlier in the week. Sure enough, it was the same woman. Emily Underwood. 'Did she say much?'

'Not really.'

'She didn't say when they were coming back for the inspection, then?' Frank asked.

'No,' Tom replied. Frank was pretty sure that Tom wouldn't have had an extended conversation with her, anyway. He leafed through the paperwork, noting all the things the farm had been marked down for at the previous inspection.

'I think we've got most of these covered, Tom. Besides, there's not a lot for them to inspect at the moment anyway. Same in the bloody butcher's.' Frank looked at the stockpot on the stove. 'Of course, there's always the chance they might find something new to moan about.'

The two brothers sat in silence for a few moments before Tom pointed at the bottle of Prosecco on the kitchen table.

'What's that for?' he asked Frank.

'Nearly forgot about that. We're celebrating, little brother.' Frank smiled and pulled wads of banknotes out of his coat pockets, spreading them on the kitchen table. 'Look at this lot.'

'Blimey,' Tom said. 'Did you get lucky on the horses or something?'

'Nope. Sausages,' Frank replied. 'Sold the bloody lot. At one point, there was a queue out of the door for them.' Frank watched Tom's eyes widen. 'I've never known them to shift that fast. Mrs Timmings bought some for her lunch and then got on the blower to a bunch of her mates once she'd had them. They came out of the woodwork like no-one's business. I've even sold all the bonemeal to that weird bloke who runs the allotments. He'll probably sell it on at a profit, but he's happy and we're happy.' As Frank walked over to the fridge to put the Prosecco in, there was a knock at the door. 'Can you get that, Tom?' he called to his brother. Tom disappeared, and a few seconds later Frank heard him call his name.

'Frank?'

'Yep, coming,' Frank replied. It was probably the bloody woman from the Food Standards Agency again. Frank was sure that Tom would have told her to come back later once he was back from the butcher's. Paperwork wasn't Tom's strongest point. Frank got to the door to see a man in a white coat standing on the doorstep. Frank didn't know his name, but he recognised the delivery man from the slaughterhouse. At least it wasn't the Food Standards Agency woman, but there was no reason for him to be here in the evening unless there was some sort of problem. Frank wondered for a second whether the delivery man's visit was connected to the woman visiting earlier. The last thing Frank needed was some sort of problem with the slaughterhouse. He'd heard of farmers going under when the slaughterhouses they used got closed down because of tainted stock from over the channel, or something like that.

'I'm really sorry, Mr Pinch,' the visitor said. Frank started to get a sinking feeling in the pit of his stomach.

Whatever the delivery man was here for, it wasn't to deliver good news. 'The bloody van broke down.'

'Sorry, what?' Frank was confused. 'What's that got to do with me?'

'Your delivery,' the delivery man replied, 'that's why it's late.'

'No, it's not.'

'Er, yes it is.' The man from the slaughterhouse was wringing his hands together. 'It's in the back of the van.' Frank could feel his heart start to thud in his chest. He was starting to get really worried. 'I couldn't deliver the meat this morning because the van was knackered.'

'Are you sure it's my delivery?'

'One hundred percent, Mr Pinch.'

'Can you just leave it in the yard, please? We'll get to it in a minute,' he said in a quiet voice before he closed the door in the face of the delivery driver. Frank turned to Tom and spoke in a fierce whisper.

'Tom, if the meat wasn't delivered this morning, what did you make the sausages from?'

'I thought it had been delivered, and that you'd taken the prime cuts off like you normally do,' Tom replied, his bottom lip quivering.

'Christ, you realise what we've done, don't you?' Frank asked Tom, even though he knew the answer. 'If they didn't deliver the meat this morning, what did you make those sausages out of?' Tom glanced across at the stockpot on the stove, the colour draining from his face.

'Oh crikey,' Tom whispered. 'I feel sick.'

'You and me both, Tom. You and me both.'

14

‘What are we going to do, Frank?’ Tom asked his brother from the passenger seat of the Land Rover. Frank didn't reply straight away. He had a peculiar look on his face which Tom knew meant he was thinking hard. The car bounced down the track to the pig sheds, the meat that the slaughterhouse had just delivered bouncing around in the back of the car. It normally went in the trailer, but Frank had loaded the trailer up with some farm machinery, so they'd put the meat on the back seat.

‘We're not going to do anything, Tom,’ Frank replied a few seconds later, his jaw set firm. The brothers looked through the windscreen at the sun setting on the horizon. ‘Nothing at all.’

‘Won't we get in trouble, though?’

‘Not if we don't get found out, we won't.’ Frank looked across at Tom, and Tom felt reassured by the look on his face. If Frank said they weren't going to get into trouble, then that was that. ‘We were going to feed him to the pigs anyway. Then the pigs were going to be turned into sausages.’ Frank paused before continuing. ‘All we've done is cut out the middleman. Or the middle pig.' Tom smiled at Frank's joke.

'We can't get found out, can we?'

'No, Tom. We can't get found out. Just a few more little things to sort out, and then we're home free. Can't have the Food Standards Agency finding anything here.'

'Okay,' Tom said. 'That's okay then. I don't want to get into any trouble.'

'You won't, Tom. Don't worry. It's only meat,' Frank said. 'We've not done anything wrong, not really. Just a little mix-up, that's all.'

Tom thought about this as Frank drove on in silence. Tom could feel the beginnings of an idea at the back of his mind, but he couldn't quite work out what it was. It would come, Tom knew. He quite often had ideas, but they took a while to come to fruition. Their father used to say that a good idea was like a good whisky. The longer you waited, he'd said, the better they were. Seeing as old Farmer Pinch never used to have whisky in the house for more than a day or two before it was gone, it had taken Tom a while to work out what he was talking about.

The Land Rover jolted as Frank drove over a deep rut in the road, and the object in a bin liner in the footwell bounced and hit Tom in the shin.

'Ouch,' Tom said. 'That bloody hurt.' He kicked the bin liner hard, and the object rolled away. Frank laughed as Tom massaged his leg. 'I didn't know heads were that bleeding hard.'

'Should have turned it into soup after all,' Frank said, and they both laughed. He parked the Land Rover by the sheds. 'Right, you go and check on the sows, and I'll get things set up here.'

Tom walked into the main pig shed. Although it was getting dark outside, there was still enough light for him to see. He nodded at Boris who was staring at him with half-closed eyes and what looked like suspicion. Tom went over to the sows in a pen at the far end of the shed and pressed his hand down hard on one of their backs. The sow stiffened straight away, standing stock still.

'Oh, you cheeky little piggy,' Tom muttered. 'I think you're ready to get to know old Boris.' He checked the other two sows who responded the same way. As he walked back to the door of the shed, he winked at the large boar. 'You might want to freshen up a bit, Boris,' Tom said. 'Tonight's your lucky night, you old bugger.'

Outside the pig shed, Frank had got the machinery down from the trailer and pointed it toward the main outside area that the few pigs they had left used.

'Tom, do you want to get the head?' Frank asked. Tom walked over to the Land Rover and retrieved the bin liner from the footwell.

'Them sows are ready,' he said to Frank as he walked back toward him. 'All three of them. Boris is just changing into his lucky pants.' Tom didn't know what lucky pants were, but he'd heard Frank mention a couple of times that he was wearing his. He only wore them when he was heading out for an evening in Norwich, so Tom knew they had something to do with sex. Frank laughed as he started up the log chipper.

'Get him in there, Tom,' Frank shouted over the noise of the machine. Tom emptied the contents of the bin liner into the hopper. The large machine rumbled and coughed a couple of times before a fine red mist spurted out of the chute. It was followed by a spray of white chunks that spattered across the pig pen. Tom saw a fleshy chunk sailing through the air and pointed it out to Frank.

'Look, an ear,' Tom shouted. Seconds later, a large seagull swooped out of the darkening sky and grabbed it

mid-air before flying away followed by several other seag-
ulls. Frank flicked a switch to turn the machine off.

'There we go, job done,' Frank said, slapping the metal
casing of the log chipper. 'I'll give it a good clean in the
morning. Once Boris has done his thing with the sows,
we'll let him out in the pen. He'll make short work of all
that mess.'

Tom and Frank manhandled the meat out of the car
and into the fridges before they turned their attention to
Boris. This would be a two-man job, Tom knew. They got
the sows into the pens and tied them up, Frank happy for
Tom to coordinate things. There wasn't that much that
Tom was good at, but pigs were one of them.

'Right then, you ready?' Tom asked Frank. They were
standing either side of Boris' pen, each grasping a thick
rope that was attached to the boar's harness. When Frank
nodded, Tom kicked the door of the pen open and the two
men braced themselves. They needn't have bothered.
When Boris took off across the floor to get to the first of
the sows, both Tom and Frank lost their footing and were
dragged across the floor. Boris leapt onto the first sow
whose legs buckled under the strain, and there was a loud
scream from the pen. Tom wasn't sure whether it was a
scream of delight from Boris or a scream of horror from
the sow. It could well have been both, Tom thought as he
got to his feet and brushed himself down. The two men
watched as Boris did what he had been bought to do,
Tom's hand covering his mouth.

'Dear God, that's brutal,' Frank said under his breath.
Tom discovered that he couldn't speak, so he just nodded
in reply.

15

E mily Underwood shuffled in Mr Clayton's uncomfortable visitor's chair. She was in his office, waiting for him to come back from the canteen with a cup of coffee. The offices of the Food Standards Agency in the centre of Norwich only had one canteen, and it was on the bottom floor. Her boss's office was on the fifth floor. She wriggled, smoothing a non-existent crease from her trousers. Today was the dark purple business suit. It was Emily's least favourite of the three, but it was also the one that made her look the most professional. At least, that was what the article she'd read in Cosmopolitan promised. Purple equals power, the article had said. Emily wasn't convinced, but she figured that the writers in Cosmopolitan knew more about fashion than she did.

When Mr Clayton had e-mailed Emily first thing to ask her to pop up to his office after lunch, she'd not thought anything of it at first. The more she thought about it throughout the morning, the more concerned she became. Why had he summoned her to his office, instead of coming to see her on the shop floor? Mr Clayton was, by his own admission, a 'people person' who made a point of being seen in the large open plan offices. She remembered him during the interview for the post. It was only a few weeks ago but felt like months. He'd mirrored her body language exactly from start to finish during the interview, and been so obvious it was hysterical. Emily crossed her legs, he crossed his. She leaned forward, so did he. At one point, Emily had to fight the urge to scratch her arse just to see if he would scratch his. By contrast, the other interviewer, who Emily later found out had been drafted in at the last minute to cover staff sickness caused by a rogue piece of salmon, spent most of the interview gazing out of the window.

Emily looked at the thin brown file on Mr Clayton's desk. Even though it was upside down, she could see her name on the top and knew it was her personnel file. When he'd left to get a coffee, Emily had seriously considered opening it and looking through the few pages inside to see what the interview was about, but decided against it. She jiggled her leg up and down, wondering if she had time now to have a peep in it or not. Just as she decided that she did have time, the door behind her opened and Mr Clayton breezed in.

'Emily, I'm so sorry to keep you,' he said as he walked around his desk and took a seat in his plush leather chair. 'There was a horrible queue in the canteen.' Her boss was dressed in his usual dark suit and cream shirt. He wore a blue and white tie that was the source of much amusement behind his back as they were the same colours as Norwich City Football Club's arch-rivals. Mr Clayton either didn't realise or didn't care. As he sat down, he smoothed his hair over his head. It wasn't quite a combover, but would be in a couple of years. Especially, Emily thought, if he kept worrying at it like that.

'That's okay, Mr Clayton,' Emily replied, her voice as sweet as she could make it without feeling sick. She watched him pick up her personnel file and open it, keeping it angled up so that she couldn't see what was inside.

'So, thank you for coming up to see me,' Mr Clayton said with a smile that lasted for about three seconds. 'I just wanted to do a quick performance review now that you've been flying solo for a couple of weeks.'

Emily frowned. She had a performance review already booked for her three-month point, but that was still at least six weeks away.

'Okay,' Emily replied, suddenly unsure of herself. She tucked a strand of hair behind her ear and fidgeted again in her chair before sitting upright with her hands on her knees.

'So, how do you think you're getting on?' Mr Clayton said, closing the file and putting it back on the desk.

'I think I'm doing quite well, all things considered,' Emily said with a weak smile. 'I mean, there's been a couple of hiccups, but nothing serious.'

'Hmm, hiccups,' Mr Clayton replied, echoing Emily's words. 'Such as what, do you think?'

Emily paused for a few seconds before replying.

'Well, there was the kebab van at the football. That one didn't go very well, but that wasn't my fault.' Mr Clayton laughed, but again, any sign of humour was short lived.

'Yes, you could say that. I read your report and the various newspaper articles,' he said, 'and I agree, there wasn't much you could have done about that.' Mr Clayton paused for a second. 'How about when you visited the Cathedral Tea Rooms? How do you think that inspection went?' Emily scrunched up her forehead and tried to remember what had gone wrong on that visit, but she couldn't think of much. She'd written about it in her diary, but that wasn't much help to her now.

'I thought that went rather well,' she replied with a wan smile. 'Is there a problem?'

'How many stars did you give them?'

'Er, four I think,' Emily replied. 'Yes, I remember now. It was four.' She tried to put as much confidence in her voice as she could as she said this.

'Why only four?' Mr Clayton asked, picking up the file and opening it.

'The scones.'

'Was there a problem with the scones? The Cathedral Tea Rooms have always had excellent results from our inspections.' Mr Clayton looked at Emily over the file.

'Yes, there was a problem with them,' she replied. 'Way too much flour. They were disgusting. I tried one and my tongue got stuck to the roof of my mouth.'

'Emily,' Mr Clayton sighed. 'You can't take stars off because you don't like the scones.'

'Oh,' Emily said. 'Okay, sorry.'

'It wasn't just that, though. Do you remember having an argument with the proprietor?'

'Vaguely.' Emily thought back to the inspection. She remembered having a bit of a barney with the old chap who was running the place. 'Yeah, now you come to mention it, we did have a few words.' Mr Clayton glanced at the file before continuing.

'Did you call him a pompous old arsehole?' he asked her. Emily looked in her lap. She had called the old fart that, and worse, so she just nodded her head in reply. 'Do you remember his name?'

Emily looked up at the ceiling. What was the man called? Something to do with a chess set. When she remembered his name, she blurted it out.

'Yes, it was Mr Bishop.'

'No, Emily. Not Mr Bishop.' Mr Clayton put air quotes around the word 'Mister' with his fingers. 'He is The Bishop. The Bishop of Norwich.'

'Ah,' Emily replied. There wasn't much she could say to that. 'Oh dear. I probably shouldn't have said that, should I?'

Mr Clayton didn't reply, but continued reading the file.

'It's not just one complaint though, Emily. There's quite a few for someone so new to the department,' he said, looking at her. 'Mr Wong submitted a complaint. He said you were racist toward him.'

'Bollocks was I,' Emily retorted, ignoring Mr Clayton's startled expression. 'He chased me with a machete!'

'Did he?' Mr Clayton replied, leafing through the papers in the folder. 'That's not in your report, and if it's true, do you not think it's worth mentioning?'

They sat in silence for a few moments, Emily seething. This wasn't fair, none of it. She took a deep breath and let it out through her nose.

'Emily, listen,' Mr Clayton said. 'I like you, I really do. There's something about you that's quite captivating.' Emily frowned, not sure why he'd chosen that particular word. She hoped he wasn't about to proposition her. There'd been an article in the Eastern Daily News about workplace perverts the other day, which had advised women to report them straight away. Straight after a swift knee to the testicles, Emily had thought at the time. 'But this can't go on, Emily. So I'm sorry, but I'm going have to give you a formal warning.'

Emily felt tears start to prick at her eyes. A formal warning? After three weeks on the job? That would mean she could be chucked out at her three-month review unless she showed, what was it, significant and sustained improvement. Something like that if she remembered the contract right. She blinked, determined not to cry in front of this man.

'Try to think of it as a development opportunity,' Mr Clayton said. 'A chance to prove yourself. Okay?' Emily knew full well that it was far from okay, and with the words 'a chance to prove yourself' ringing in her ears, she got to her feet and fled from his office.

16

Andy leaned back in his chair to try to avoid Rob's fetid breath without him noticing. Either his boss was terrified of vampires, or he had been mainlining garlic all weekend. Either way, it was gross. Rob was perched on the edge of Andy's desk, dishing out instructions. The rate Rob was going with what he wanted doing, Andy would be lucky to get the weekend off.

'So, get together with this woman Jessica at the Forum, make sure that they know what they're doing,' Rob said as Andy scribbled in his notebook. The Forum was a large building in the centre of Norwich that housed the city library, the local media, and a variety of other organisations. It was also going to be the venue for the Pride of Anglia ceremony. 'They all work for the council, that lot. I don't trust them as far as I can throw them,' Rob continued. 'The competition presentation can't go wrong. You've got my brief, yeah?'

Andy nodded in response. It wasn't really Rob's brief. Andy had written it. The plan for the presentation evening had taken him hours to finish, but when he'd submitted it to Rob all his boss had done was change the signature block on it and hand it into Charles the Big Cheese. Andy had watched Rob simpering and soaking up the glory as Charles told him what a fine piece of work it was.

'Now, the other job is to get the products together for the competition. We've not really had the response we expected from the Eastern Daily News promotion, so we need to get out there and source them for ourselves,' Rob said.

'What sort of a response did we get?' Andy asked.

'Minimal,' Rob replied, waving his hand as a waft of garlic accompanied the gesture. 'We got some carrots from a woman who runs a greengrocer in Ludham, and an amusingly shaped parsnip.' Andy stifled a smile at the mention of the parsnip. He and Martin had been in Morrison's down on the riverside the other day buying some beer when Martin had spotted a parsnip that looked very similar to a full set of male genitalia. They'd bought it with a crate of Kronenburg and Martin had entered the parsnip into the competition under a false name. 'So, what we need is local produce. I don't care what it is, as long as it was produced in Norfolk. Focus in on meat, though. That's got the best markup if we flog it in bulk. You got that?'

'Sure,' Andy nodded. 'Any ideas where to start?'

'Hmm.' Rob crossed his legs, rested an elbow on his knee and put his fist to his chin. That must be his thinking pose, Andy thought. It made him look like a bizarre version of Bruce Forsyth. 'How about seeing if there's some sort of local butcher's society? Start with that.'

'What, like the Freemasons?' Andy said, an image of a bunch of men in red striped aprons lined up with their trouser legs rolled up and sausages draped around their necks in his head.

'No, more like a directory or something. Just get on the internet and sort something out,' Rob replied. 'Now go, champ. Be careful out there.' He punched Andy on the arm, which triggered another wave of garlic.

'Can I take someone with me, Rob?' Andy asked.

'Who?'

'Martin, the other intern.'

'Who does he work for?' Rob asked.

'He's in sales. Is it Doug, the manager there?'

'Oh yeah, Doug the Divot we call him,' Rob laughed. Andy frowned, no idea at all what Rob was talking about. 'I play golf with him. No problem, I'll fix it,' Rob said as he launched himself from Andy's desk. Andy held his breath, not wanting to get another mouthful of Rob's left-over garlic.

A few minutes later, just as Andy had given up trying to find a secret society of Norfolk butchers and settled on a list of local shops from Google, an instant message from 'Martin the Intern' popped up on his screen.

ROAD TRIP!!! the message said.

Oh yes, Andy typed. *Meet me out the front by the Alan Partridge statue in 10 minutes.* He printed out the list, shut his computer down, and went downstairs to wait for Martin. The statue of Alan Partridge was wearing a traffic cone on its head as usual, and an elderly security guard was trying to clean some obscenities that were spray-painted on the base. When Martin arrived, they made their way down to the garage to where Andy kept his pride and joy — a bright yellow MG sports car called 'Delia', although he kept the fact he'd named his car to himself. Ignoring Martin's standard comment about it being a hairdresser's car, Andy gunned the engine as he left the garage.

'Hairdressers,' Andy said to Martin when they got onto the dual carriageway, 'do not drive MG Trophy 160s.'

'So, your boss Rob then,' Martin said a few minutes later. 'What's he like?'

'He's a bit of a knob, but he could be a lot worse I guess,' Andy replied.

'Have you met his wife?'

'No,' Andy said. 'Have you?' He looked across at Martin.

'Not exactly,' Martin replied. 'I've seen a few pictures of her though, on Facebook and that.'

'Really?' Andy said, surprised. 'You friends with her then?'

'No, a friend of a friend. You know how it is.' Andy didn't use Facebook, so he had no idea how it was. 'Safe to say though,' Martin continued. 'Rob's a feeder. She's a big girl.' Andy started laughing.

'So, you're stalking my boss's wife on Facebook?' Andy asked.

'Not stalking, Andy,' Rob replied. 'Just observing from a distance.'

They drove in silence for a few moments, looking for the next butcher's shop on Andy's list. So far they'd visited five or six, and had several carrier bags full of all kinds of meat in the boot. The next place on the list was a place called 'Frank's Butcher's' in a small village halfway between Norwich and Ipswich. According to the sat-nav, it was somewhere on the road they were driving down.

'There it is,' Martin pointed through the windscreen at a tired looking butcher's shop with a couple of old ladies milling about outside it. Andy pulled into the kerb.

'Mate, do you want to run and in and see what they've got? There's double yellow lines, and I think there was a sodding traffic warden hiding behind a bush just back there.'

'Yeah, I saw him too. Sneaky bastard.' Martin got out

of the car and Andy waited, his eyes fixed in his rear view mirror on where the traffic warden had been. He drummed his fingers on the steering wheel for a few seconds before he got his phone out of his pocket and fired up Twitter. Pleased with the fact he had four new followers, which took his total to just over a hundred, he was just about to follow them back when there was a loud thump on his windscreen. Andy jumped and took his eyes off the phone to see a yellow parking ticket on the screen and the traffic warden walking away from the car. Andy rolled his window down, muttering under his breath. The bastard had snuck up on him when he wasn't looking.

'Hey,' Andy called out to the traffic warden's retreating back. 'Hey, I'm not parked. I'm still in the car.' There was no response from the traffic warden. Not even a glance over his shoulder. Andy reached through his open window and was peeling the ticket from his windscreen when Martin got back into the car.

'He got you then,' Martin said with a grin.

'Never bloody saw him coming,' Andy replied. 'That's forty quid that is. Do you think I can claim it as a business expense?'

'Good luck with that. At least you got something to show for the visit though,' Martin said. 'That butcher's rubbish. He's only got three pork chops, and they're imported from Suffolk so they wouldn't be eligible for the competition. He said to come back in a few days. They should have something in then.'

Andy drove back to Norwich in silence, still fuming from the parking ticket. That would be almost a week's wages down the drain if he did have to pay the fine. He parked in the underground garage below Partridge Towers, and they both got out.

'Mate, I need to go and find some woman called Jessica

in the Forum,' Andy said as he got the carrier bags out of the boot of his car. 'Can you take this lot and put it in the fridge in Charles' office? He's worried it'll get nicked if it goes in the fridge in the staff room.'

'Sure, no worries. You want me to come to the Forum with you?'

'No, don't worry. I've got it covered.'

Pleased to be out of the car and in the fresh air, Andy sauntered toward the centre of Norwich enjoying the pale sunshine. He was walking past the office of the Food Standards Agency when he saw a homeless man sitting on the pavement, not far off his own age. Andy dug into his pocket and pulled out a couple of pounds, dropping it into the forlorn cup the man had set out in front of him. The homeless man was just thanking Andy when a young woman came flying out of the main doors of the Food Standards Agency and half-walked, half-ran down the steps onto the pavement. Andy glanced at her, noticing she was wearing a particularly florid purple business suit. She also appeared to be in floods of tears. The young woman was only a few feet away from Andy when her heel got caught in a crack in the pavement and she started to stumble over. Instinctively he put his hands out to break her fall and she crashed into him. To his horror, Andy realised that as she'd stumbled, she'd put her arms out to her sides and his hands were on her chest. He was standing with an unexpected helping of side boob in each hand.

'I'm so sorry —' he started to apologise as he tried to remove his hands from her breasts.

Andy never saw the knee coming. He lay curled up in a foetal position on the pavement, trying not to be sick, as the homeless man wandered over and put a sympathetic hand on his shoulder.

'Are you okay, mate?' the man said. 'That looked nasty,

that did.' Andy couldn't even reply, he was too busy trying to gulp air. The last thing he remembered before the excruciating pain between his legs was the young woman's tear-stained face close to his.

'You fucking pervert,' she had said before she ran off as he crumpled to the pavement.

17

Frank looked at the clock on the wall of the butcher's shop for the third time in as many minutes. He'd not had any customers through the door since he'd opened up after lunchtime. It was that, and the fact that he didn't have a great deal of meat left to sell to any customers who did walk in that made his mind up for him. It was time to close up.

Thursday was often a slow day and closing early wasn't unusual. Besides, he had a night out in Norwich planned that evening with Mike, so an early finish wasn't a bad idea. It would give Frank time to get back to the farm without rushing around. He walked to the till and opened it, emptying it of the meagre takings from the day. He'd be lucky if he had fifty quid altogether. Still, it was enough for a few beers with Mike, so Frank wasn't complaining. As long as Tom had a bottle of wine to keep him company, he'd be happy for the evening. Frank made a mental note to pick up a bottle of cheap white wine for his brother on the way back.

As he walked to where his Land Rover was parked

around the back of the butcher's shop, Frank thought about money, or rather the fact that they didn't have much of it at all. If anything went wrong with the Land Rover, which given its age and condition was quite likely, they'd be buggered. When he got back to the farm, he would have another quick look at the books. The few hundred quid they'd got from their unexpected windfall had proved very useful, but the arrival of a larger than expected electricity bill that morning had made the bonus short-lived.

Along with the bill, there'd been a flyer from a local solar energy farm offering to install solar panels on their farmland. They promised a secure, long-term income, especially with the price of energy from the other side of the channel being so expensive. It was a tempting idea, and if their father hadn't sold off so much of the farm Frank would have seriously considered it. The problem was that they needed the land for the pigs. It was just there weren't many pigs at the moment. Boris, for all his enthusiasm, wasn't proving to be the most fertile boar in East Anglia. Frank was still thinking about getting the solar panel firm over for a visit to see what was what as he pulled into the track leading to their farm.

'Hey Tom,' Frank said as he walked in through the front door of the farmhouse. 'How're tricks?'

'Frank,' Tom said from his position at the kitchen table, the Eastern Daily News spread out in front of him. 'Good day?'

'Not brilliant, but not awful. You? Any news?'

'Nah, not really. Mike came by, wanted to know if you're still up for tonight?'

'Okay, cheers,' Frank replied. He'd forgotten to text Mike to confirm the arrangements for the evening. 'I've got you a bottle of vino for while I'm out. It's in the car.'

'Nice one.'

Frank bustled around the kitchen for a few minutes, tidying up after Tom. For some reason, although Tom was quite capable of feeding himself, he was incapable of cleaning up after he had done so. Frank had long since given up on trying to get him to tidy up after himself.

'So, d'you get many customers today then?' Tom asked.

'Loads of customers, but not as many sales.'

'How come?'

'They all came back for more of those bloody sausages,' Frank laughed. 'I had to tell them that we'd run out of that particular recipe.'

'Really?' Tom replied, a half-smile on his face. 'We should have put them in the competition I've been reading about.' Tom pointed at the paper on the table.

'Yeah,' Frank said. 'It's a shame your man wasn't a bit fatter.' He saw Tom's smile falter. 'You okay, Tom?'

'Just thinking, that's all.'

'What about?'

'What we did,' Tom said. 'Can I ask you a question?'

'Course you can, Tom,' Frank said, sitting at the table opposite his brother. Tom looked worried, and Frank knew that was never a good sign. 'What's up?' They sat in silence for a moment, Frank knowing better than to press Tom. It would come out, whatever it was.

'What you said the other day, about your man? The one that we…' Tom paused. 'Well, that one?'

'What about him?'

'Well, you said he was just meat. Did you mean that?' Tom said, a deep frown on his face. 'It's just I've been thinking…'

'Tom,' Frank cut him off. 'You don't need to worry. We've done nothing wrong, and yes I did mean what I said.' The last thing Frank needed was Tom going off on one about the whole thing. He reached out and took Tom's hand in his, squeezing his fingers. 'So don't worry about it, okay? It was an accident.'

They sat in silence for a few moments before Tom looked at Frank and smiled. With relief, Frank could see that Tom's concern had disappeared just with a few words. What else were big brothers for, Frank thought as he got to his feet.

'Right then Tom, I'm going to get ready. I'm supposed to be picking Mike up in an hour or so, so I need to make myself beautiful for the ladies.'

'Don't forget your lucky pants,' Tom said with a grin.

'Yeah, when we've got a bit more money I might buy some new ones,' Frank returned Tom's smile. 'The ones I've got aren't working very well.'

Three hours and three pints later, Frank and Mike were propping up the bar in the Murderers pub in the middle of Norwich. The pub was half full, but still busier than the other pubs they'd been to earlier in the evening. Frank looked around the pub while Mike bought another round.

'Bit quiet in here, isn't it?' Frank said. Mike, who was wearing one of the most horrible shirts Frank had seen in a long time, turned to face him.

'Yeah, is a bit,' he said. 'It'll liven up though. The band's about to start.' Thursday night in the Murderers was a live music night. Frank couldn't stand the music, but it certainly drew an interesting crowd. Depending on the band, more often than not there was an influx of young-sters from the University of East Anglia. A couple of years ago, Frank had enjoyed the company for a couple of hours of a young media studies student called Julie, who for some reason was wearing a onesie. She was way too large to be wearing a onesie in public, but Frank hadn't minded. Even now he still couldn't pass the deserted car parks by Anglia Square without smirking.

In a very drunken conversation a few months ago, Mike had told Frank that they made the perfect sexual predators. In Mike's opinion, fuelled by several pints of strong beer in a pub called the Belgian Monk, he was the alpha male, the lion of the pack who just went straight in for the kill. Frank, by contrast, was the cheetah who ran around the pack picking off the weakest ones in the herd. Frank hadn't said anything at the time, but he was more than happy with that analogy. If it was reality though, then they were both starving and on the point of extinction, Frank only slightly less so than Mike. He had Anglia Square to thank for that.

'Come on mate, let's grab a seat and see what's what,' Mike said, picking up two pints of lager from the bar. 'Follow me.'

They sat in one of the alcoves in the pub, far enough away from the band not to be deafened once they'd started, but still with a good view of the bar.

'Cheers fella,' Mike raised his glass, and Frank did the same.

'Chin chin,' Frank replied, and they both sat back on the wooden benches.

Almost an hour later, just after Frank had refilled their glasses, Mike nudged him on the arm. Frank moved his arm to avoid spilling his drink on the table. He looked at his friend, who was nodding in the direction of the bar.

'Oi oi, saveloy,' Mike said. Frank had never quite understood that phrase, other than in Mike's world it meant 'look over there'. He did as instructed. 'At the bar, just being served now. You see them?' Frank looked at the two women Mike was nodding towards. He squinted, trying to make them out through the gloom. A few minutes earlier, the lights in the pub had been turned down to get the atmosphere going for the band.

'Yeah, I see them,' he said.

'What do you think?' Mike replied. 'Mine's on the left.' Frank paused, looking at the young women. Truth be told, either of them would do nicely. Mike licked his lips and got to his feet. 'Come on, mate,' he said. 'Let's go hunting.'

18

'Catherine, would you bloody well hurry up in the bathroom?' Emily shouted at her flat mate through the closed door. 'I need to get ready as well.' There was a muffled reply which Emily didn't catch, but knowing Catherine it was something rude. Emily sighed and walked into the kitchen of their flat to pour them both a gin and tonic. While she waited for the bathroom to become free, she scribbled some notes down in her diary. When Emily had turned thirteen, her grandmother had bought her a moleskin journal and encouraged her to write in it every day. According to her grandmother, when she was older, having a journal would be 'an amazing way of looking back at how far she'd come'. Emily hadn't been convinced at first, but to humour her grandmother, had started writing about stuff that happened. There was now a pile of moleskin diaries hidden away in her cupboard, never to be read by anyone else.

About ten minutes later, Catherine came into the kitchen. Emily closed her journal and looked at her flat mate as she handed her the drink. Catherine was dressed in a pair of skin-tight Dolce and Gabbana jeans, with a loose chiffon blouse that gave just the slightest a hint of a lacy bra underneath. 'Jesus, Catherine,' Emily said. 'You going out like that? I thought we were just going for a couple of drinks and to watch the band.'

'We are,' Catherine replied, winking at Emily over the top of her glass. She took a sip of the gin and tonic. 'My God,' she said, grimacing. 'How much gin have you put in this?' Emily was about to reply when Catherine grabbed the dark green bottle of Gordon's from the kitchen worktop and filled up her glass.

'Not nearly enough, obviously,' Emily muttered as she walked into the bathroom. When she walked back out again a few moments later, Catherine was halfway down the glass and had topped up Emily's.

'Right then, my turn,' Catherine said. 'Are you going out like that?' Emily looked down at her baggy sweatshirt and jeans.

'Er, yeah,' she replied. 'What's wrong with this?'

'What bra have you got on?'

'What do you mean, what bra have I got on?' Emily said, frowning.

'Is it one of your grey ones?' Catherine asked. 'That's gone all fluffy from being washed so many times?' Emily pulled the top of her sweatshirt away and peeked inside.

'It might be,' she replied.

'Matching knickers?'

'Might be,' Emily said. 'Listen, Catherine, all I want to do is go out for a few drinks. That's all. I'm not going out on the pull.'

'But you never know, Emily,' Catherine said. 'Mr Right could be sitting there in the pub right now, just waiting for you to walk in. One thing he won't be expecting is grey fluffy underwear.' Emily was saved from having to think up a reply by a car horn sounding outside.

'Come on, the taxi's here,' she said. Catherine downed the rest of her gin and tonic in one large gulp.

'Up to you, Emily. But don't say I didn't warn you if you do end up dragging some poor lad back here.'

Twenty minutes later the two women were sitting in a dark corner of the Murderers Pub, both sipping at their drinks and waiting for the band to start.

'So, how come today was so shit then?' Catherine asked Emily.

'Oh mate, where do I start,' Emily sighed. 'Well, first off, I got put on a written warning this morning.'

'What?' Catherine said, her eyebrows shooting up. 'What on earth for?'

'A few too many complaints, apparently.'

'How many's a few too many?'

'More than one.' Emily took a sip from her drink. 'The problem is one of them was the Bishop of Norwich.'

'Oh my God, you're joking,' Catherine laughed. 'Let me guess, you called him something un-bishoplike?'

'I didn't even know he was a bloody bishop, did I?' Emily said. 'It wasn't like he was in his long purple dress and the weird hat.'

'Mitre.'

'What?'

'They're called mitres,' Catherine said. 'Bishop's hats.' Emily stared at Catherine for a few seconds. How on earth did she know that? 'I used to do a lot of pub quizzes when I was at Uni,' Catherine explained. Just as Emily was about to reply, the band started warming up, and they both listened for a few minutes. Catherine leaned into Emily and shouted in her ear. 'So, what happened when you left work, then? You said you had an argument with some bloke?'

'Well, it wasn't an argument. He assaulted me.'

'He what?'

'He assaulted me,' Emily shouted. 'I ran out of the office, and almost fell over. I was upset, crying.' Catherine nodded. 'My heel got caught in the pavement.'

Emily finished off the story, but from the way Catherine shook her head, it was obvious that she'd not heard.

'What did you say?' Catherine shouted. Emily took a deep breath.

'I said,' she replied at the top of her voice. 'I said, then he grabbed my tits.' The second part of the sentence came out just after the band stopped warming up and the pub had returned to silence. Several people looked over at Emily, whose cheeks had started to flush. One woman sitting just to their right stared before kicking her husband, who was also staring. The husband was smiling though, which Emily assumed was the reason for the kick. 'Oops,' she whispered to Catherine. 'Do you think anyone else heard that?'

'Only about half the pub,' Catherine smiled. The two of them carried on their conversation in much quieter voices, and Emily listened as Catherine tried to tell her that it sounded like an accident. Emily looked into her drink as Catherine explained why she thought this, trying to remember the exact sequence of events that had led to her kicking the bloke in the bollocks when she realised Catherine had gone quiet. Emily looked up at her flat mate to see her looking over at the bar.

'What's up?' Emily asked.

'Don't look now, but there's a couple of blokes at the

bar taking an interest in us.' Emily sighed. This happened most times she went out with Catherine. No matter where they went, Catherine always seemed to think that one of them, usually Catherine, was the centre of someone's attention. The real problem was that she was often right.

'Catherine, not tonight,' Emily said. 'I'm really not in the mood for your games.'

'I'm not messing mate, they're definitely interested. One's dressed normally, the other one's got an absolutely horrible shirt on. Have a discrete look.' Emily risked a swift glance over her shoulder and saw the two men standing at the bar. Catherine was right; the two men were deep in conversation and looking over at their table. She was also right about the shirt one of them had on.

'Oh God, I know one of them,' Emily said. 'The one on the left, dressed normally. He's a butcher. I met him the other day when I took some paperwork to his shop.'

'So which one do you want, then?' Catherine replied. Despite herself, Emily laughed.

'Catherine, I don't want either of them. I just was to have a few drinks and listen to the band.'

'Too late for that, mate,' Catherine replied. 'They're coming over.'

Emily groaned. This was not what she had wanted at all. She kept her head down until the two men were standing by their table.

'Hello, ladies,' the one in the nasty shirt said. 'Do you mind if we join you?' Emily was trying to come up with a reason as to why they did mind when Catherine replied instead.

'Of course you can,' her flat mate said. 'Emily, budge over a bit and let the boys sit down.' With a daggered look at Catherine, Emily moved up the bench she was sitting on to let one of them sit down, and the butcher took a seat next to her.

'Hi, I'm Frank,' he said. 'I think we met the other day? You work for the food standards lot, don't you?' Emily glanced up at him.

'Yes, I do,' she said, hoping that her tone and look would give him the message that she really didn't want to talk.

'Emily is it?' his friend said. 'That's a lovely name. We've not met, though.' He put his hand out for Emily to shake. 'I'm Mike.' She shook his hand as he sat down on a stool next to the table. He sat there, staring at Emily with a grin plastered on his face. 'So, Emily.' He punctuated her name with a raise of his eyebrows. 'What is it you do at the Food Standards Agency, then?' Before Emily could reply, Catherine cut in.

'Hi, I'm Catherine,' she said with a broad smile.

'Hi,' Mike replied, glancing across at Catherine for a second before returning his gaze to Emily. 'Let me guess, Emily. You must be in sales or marketing?'

'Er, no,' Emily replied. 'Why do you say that?'

'Well, with a face like yours you must be customer facing,' he said with a look that turned Emily's stomach. 'They wouldn't hide someone like you behind the scenes now, would they?' Emily felt Catherine nudge her leg under the table, but she didn't look at her friend for fear of bursting out laughing.

'What is it you do then, Mike?' Catherine asked. Emily saw Frank start to grin. Mike turned to look at Catherine, almost as if he'd only just noticed her.

'Oh, I work in agriculture,' he replied. 'Same as Frankie boy here, just in different areas.'

'That's a pretty big field,' Catherine said, smiling at her own joke. 'What do you do in agriculture? It must be something…' Emily watched Catherine run her eyes over Mike's arms. 'Something manly?' Behind Mike, Frank's grin broadened. Emily waited, fascinated. This could be interesting, she thought.

'In fact, I'm a porcine fertilisation specialist.' Emily wasn't sure, but she thought that Mike had flexed his biceps as he said this. Catherine leaned forward and put her elbows on the table. For a second Emily thought she was going to stroke the man's upper arm.

'So what does a porcine fertilisation specialist do then, Mike?' Catherine said with an exaggerated blink, her voice almost a purr. Mike opened his mouth to reply when Frank cut him off. He leaned forward and shot his eyes at the two women.

'He wanks off male pigs into a jam jar. For a living.'

Emily felt Catherine grab her forearm hard and dig her nails in.

'Emily, I'm just nipping to the toilet,' Catherine said. 'Come with me, would you?'

19

———

Tom sat on the elevated seat of his tractor and looked out at the sunrise over the farm. It was beautiful, he thought, but ominous at the same time. 'Red sky at morning, shepherd's warning' was the saying, and it was true enough. The blood red sky told of an approaching weather front, perhaps later on that day, more likely tomorrow at some point. Tom didn't need a weather forecast to tell him that.

He'd crept around the farmhouse that morning, careful not to wake Frank up. Tom wasn't sure what time he'd come in, but he knew it was pretty late and from the angle the Land Rover was parked at outside the farmhouse, it had been a good evening. Not as good an evening as Frank would have liked, Tom was sure. If that had been the case the Land Rover wouldn't have been there at all, but that hadn't happened for a long time. Every time Frank left for one of his nights out, he'd call out to Tom and tell him not to wait up as tonight could be his lucky night and he might not be back at all. Tom couldn't remember the last time that had happened, though.

The last thing Tom had done before he left the farmhouse was put the coffee pot on so that there would be fresh coffee ready for Frank when he woke up. Then Tom had left, preferring to sit on the tractor and watch the sunrise than wait for Frank to stumble out of bed in a bad mood.

Tom was waiting for Marko, the gangmaster. They'd spoken on the phone last night about getting some more help in, and Marko had said that he would be by in the morning just after sunrise with a few more illegals. There was a lot to do today, and Tom wouldn't be able to do it all on his own. The other option was to wait until tomorrow and try to persuade Frank to help out, but that was something Tom wanted to avoid if he could.

The distinctive sound of a woodpecker echoed across the fields from the woods. Tom tilted his head to one side and listened. 'Forty pecks a second,' he whispered to himself. He was proud of himself for knowing that, and also the fact that woodpeckers couldn't sing. A few years ago Frank had taken Tom to a pub quiz in the village, but Tom had been disappointed at the lack of woodpecker related trivia questions and had told the quizmaster as much at the end of the quiz. Tom and Frank's team hadn't won, and Frank hadn't taken Tom to any more quizzes. The sound of the woodpecker was replaced by the coughing of an engine, and Tom pulled his beanie hat down over his ears before getting off the tractor. Marko was on his way.

Tom waited by the tractor as Marko's beaten-up blue Transit van rounded the corner of the track. Tom wondered for a second if he should have arranged to meet Marko further toward the road so that his knackered van wouldn't wake Frank up, but it was too late now. The van coughed to a halt, and the driver's door opened.

Marko was a small man, much smaller than Tom and Frank, and he was what Frank called a 'shifty looking bugger'. True to form, as he walked toward Tom, Marko's eyes shot right and left as if he were expecting to be attacked by something at any moment. Good job Boris was secure in his shed, Tom thought. The two men shook hands.

'Tom,' Marko said. He always pronounced it 'Thom', no matter how often Tom corrected him.

'Marko,' Tom replied. 'How're things?' Marko just regarded Tom with cold, black eyes. There was nothing wrong with his English when he was on the phone. He just wasn't much of a conversationalist face to face. To an extent, that suited Tom.

'Got one for you,' Marko said as he walked round to the rear of the van.

'Just one?' Tom asked, following him. 'I need more than one to get these pigs ready for slaughter, Marko.' Marko stopped and wheeled around. Tom halted and took half a step backwards when he saw the look on Marko's face.

'Got one. Okay?'

'Yeah, sure,' Tom replied. 'One's fine. More than enough, in fact.' He knew his voice was trembling but couldn't do anything about it. For some reason, Marko scared the shit out of him. 'Thanks, Marko.'

Marko ignored him and carried on to the back of the van. He opened one of the doors and barked something in a foreign language. There was a shuffling noise, and Tom watched as a young man got out of the van and squinted in the light. He was maybe mid-twenties, not very big but he looked fit enough. Marko slammed the door of the van and said something else to the man who had got out. Tom couldn't understand what Marko was saying, but the way the gangmaster pointed at his watch and then pulled his hand across his neck was a pretty obvious message about timekeeping.

'Five o'clock, yes?' Marko said, looking at Tom who just nodded in reply.

Tom waited for the van to limp back down the track, leaving a trail of black smoke as it did so before he turned to take a closer look at the man Marko had dropped off. The first thing Tom noticed was how hairy he was. He had a mop of black hair, several days' growth of a thick beard, and bushy eyebrows that almost covered his eyes. A large tuft of chest hair poked out from underneath a grey t-shirt. Tom pointed at his own chest.

'Tom,' he said to the man, tapping his finger on his sternum.

'Thom?'

'No, Tom.'

'Ah, sorry. Thom,' the man said. Tom sighed. It looked like he was going to be 'Thom' for the day. The immigrant pointed at his own chest. 'Kyle,' he said.

'Kyle,' Tom repeated, nodding his head.

'No, Kyle.'

'That's what I said, Kyle,' Tom said. From the look on the man's face, he didn't understand. Tom watched as he frowned, shook his head and then looked at Tom and smiled. Kyle had the straightest teeth he'd seen in years. Wherever this man was from, he had a damn good dentist. 'Okay, hop in the trailer and let's get to work.' Tom pointed at the trailer hitched behind the tractor and Kyle nodded and walked toward it.

For the next three hours, the two men worked hard to get the pigs sorted out. Kyle, despite his lack of English, was a quick learner. He was also a hard worker, and Tom was surprised how much they'd got done between them. They'd been working for an hour when Tom heard Frank's Land Rover starting up, and Tom wondered if Frank had had some coffee, or if it would still be sitting in the pot when he got back to the farmhouse. By the time they sat down for lunch outside the pig sheds, the troughs were all full of food, the water replenished, and the pigs ready to be let out of the sheds. Tom had thought they'd struggle to get all that done before the end of the day, let alone done by lunchtime.

As he munched on his sandwiches and Kyle ate the ones Tom had given him, Tom wondered if he could come to some sort of arrangement with Marko to have Kyle on a more permanent basis. He was one of the most useful workers that Marko had provided in months. Tom had tried that once before with a similar lad who was an absolute workhorse, but Marko was having none of it. 'Too difficult, too difficult,' he'd said at the time. Tom couldn't see what was so difficult about it. Maybe Frank could have a word with him if he got back from work before Marko came back? Tom sighed, knowing that it wouldn't make any difference. Marko hated Frank. Tom knew that from the way he looked at him.

'You done, Kyle?' Tom asked, even though he could see that Kyle had finished his sandwiches. 'Come on, we've got work to do.' Tom walked toward the main pig shed to let the pigs out into their pen in the field. Once he had let them out, Tom leaned on the railings of their pen and watched them for a few minutes. Kyle stood next to him. 'Three weeks, mate,' Tom said. 'Three weeks and then they'll be ready for market. Do you have markets in your country?' Kyle didn't reply, but just smiled, showing off his straight teeth again. Poor bloke hadn't got a clue what he was talking about, thought Tom.

Tom's phone buzzed in his pocket. He pulled it out and looked at the screen. It was a message from Frank to let him know that he'd be back early from the butcher's shop. According to the text, Frank felt like shit and didn't have anything left worth selling, so he was going to sack it for the day. Tom looked at the time on the phone and realised the butcher's would have only been open for a couple of hours. That wasn't good. If the shop wasn't open, that meant there wasn't any money coming in, and even Tom knew they needed money. Only a few days ago, there'd been a line of customers out of the shop door. Tom frowned, thinking hard.

He walked over to the door of the shed and picked up one of two shovels that were leaning against the wall. It was heavy, with a solid steel blade and mahogany shaft that reflected the light. Tom could see his distorted reflection in the wood. A fine piece of craftsmanship, even though it was only a shovel. Tom hefted it in his hand, feeling the weight of the thing. The business end was shiny, with just a few flecks of rust. One thing Tom's father had been really particular about was looking after his equipment, and both Tom and Frank had inherited that trait. Tom knew just how keen the blade of the shovel was as he sharpened it himself, without fail, every month. His frown deepened for a few seconds before he made up his mind and forced his face to relax. No point giving the game away just yet.

Tom pointed at the other shovel and raised his eyebrows in Kyle's direction. Kyle got the message and grinned, picking it up.

'Right, Kyle,' Tom said. 'We need to get rid of all this shit on the floor. Understand?' From the look on Kyle's face, the answer was no. Tom started to scoop up the excrement and a few seconds later, Kyle joined in. Within twenty minutes, the floor was clean and Tom pointed to the door of the shed. 'After you mate,' he said. 'One more shed to clear.' Kyle grinned and started walking toward the door. Tom picked up his shovel and set off after him.

20

Frank grimaced as he tried to swallow the Paracetamol without any water. He had an absolute bastard of a headache behind his eyes which even the coffee Tom had left out for him this morning hadn't helped with. Frank swore, not at anything in particular, but at pretty much everything. He managed to get the tablets down his neck with the help of a rancid energy drink he'd bought from the corner shop in the hope that it would help ward off a hangover. It hadn't helped in the slightest, but what did he expect for fifty pence?

He looked around his shop, which for a butcher's shop lacked the one thing it was supposed to have. Meat. Not for the first time, he wondered how much longer he could keep it open. When he was buying the energy drink on his way in, there'd been a headline on one of the newspapers about more directives from Brussels to keep European meat in Europe. He'd not bought the newspaper, but he knew that it would also say that part of this strategy was to keep British meat out of Europe. That was what was killing local farms and businesses. It wasn't about subsidies, it was about markets. Since Brexit, there was no market for British meat. The only market Frank had was a bunch of old ladies who bought just enough to feed themselves. Tom had told him that the next round of pigs they could slaughter were at least three weeks away. That was a long time to keep an empty butcher's shop open.

Frank flipped over the sign on the door to 'Closed' and made his way to his Land Rover after locking up the shop. Large spots of rain were starting to fall from the sky, so he broke into a jog to avoid getting too wet. Frank put the vehicle in gear, and made his way down the High Street, only pausing to flick a quick 'V' sign at the traffic warden trying to hide behind a bright red post box half way down the High Street. There were parasites, and there were traffic wardens. Parasites would win in Frank's internal popularity contest any day of the week.

About a mile away from the farm, Frank drove past a battered blue Transit van which he knew belonged to Marko. As he slowed down to let the van past, he waved at Marko but got nothing back in return. The other man didn't even look at him, but just stared straight ahead and ignored Frank. Muttering to himself about what a rude little bastard Marko was, Frank tried not to let his good mood slip. When he pulled up to the farmhouse ten minutes later, he'd all but forgotten about Marko.

Tom's tractor was nowhere to be seen, so Frank opened up the app on his phone to see where he was. The small blue dot on the screen was over the top of the pig sheds, and Frank was surprised that Tom was still working. It wasn't as if he had that many pigs to look after. Humming to himself, Frank let himself into the farmhouse.

'Bloody hell, Tom,' Frank said as a wall of warm air hit him as he walked into the kitchen. 'Why is the bloody heating on?' He crossed to the boiler and turned the radiators off before turning his attention to a stack of letters on the table. Several of them had ominous looking red lettering across the top of the envelopes. 'Final Demand' seemed to be pretty popular. Frank knew what was in the letters, as he'd been ignoring them for months. He sat at the table and opened one of them, tutting as he read through it. The letter was from the electricity company, and if they didn't pay £240 by the end of the month, they'd be cut off. Frank didn't think they weren't allowed to do that, but he was also sure that he didn't want to call their bluff. They probably had enough left in savings to cover that bill, but it was one of many. He leafed through the other letters, recognising the logos on the envelopes. One from the gas board, one from the water people, and another one from the solar panel firm. Frank threw the letters back onto the table and walked back outside to his Land Rover. It was time to have a proper chat with Tom.

Just as Frank ground to a halt outside the sheds, it started to rain again. He could see Tom at the door to the main shed, so made his way over to him. As he approached, Frank saw Tom's wide grin.

'Hey Frank,' Tom said. 'Busy day?' Frank was disconcerted by Tom's smile, and pushed past him into the shed to get out of the rain.

'Not bad, Tom,' he replied. 'Bit quiet. How about you?'

'All good,' Tom said. 'Got some good news for you.' He pointed at the sows in the far corner of the pig shed. 'I'm pretty sure that good old Boris has come through.'

'What, they're pregnant? Already?'

'Well, two of them are. I'm pretty sure. Not so sure about the third one, but she might be.'

'Boris, you dirty old boar,' Frank said with a glance at

the sleeping giant. 'How do you know they're pregnant though, Tom?'

'Their thingies are sticking up. Two of them are anyway.'

'What thingies?'

'Their lady thingies,' Tom said. 'Down the back end. Surest way of telling, that is.'

Frank wasn't sure what Tom meant by 'lady thingies', but he had to give it to his brother. He did know far more about pigs and if he thought they were pregnant pigs, then they probably were. 'So timing wise, when are we looking at?' he asked.

'Three, three, three,' Tom answered, obviously pleased to be asked his opinion on something. 'Three months, three weeks, three days. Then a couple of months for fattening up, and we'll be laughing all the way to the slaughterhouse.'

'That's great news, Tom,' Frank said. It was great news, but it wasn't going to help them through the next few months. The cash from milking Boris, for want of a better term, wasn't going to make much of a difference to their cashflow. 'We do need to talk about money though, Tom.'

'Oh, okay,' Tom replied.

'We've got more going out than we've got coming in,' Frank said. He saw Tom frown as he worked out what this meant.

'So we need more money, is that what you mean?'

'Yep, that's what I mean,' Frank replied. 'How far off are the next pigs we actually own from slaughter?'

'Three or four weeks, I guess. I mean we could do it earlier if we're desperate, but if we wait for a bit longer then we'll get much more for them.'

'We might not have a choice, Tom,' Frank sighed. He thrust his hands in his pockets and looked over at the sows

in the corner for a few seconds. When he looked up at
Tom, he saw a broad smile playing across his brother's
face. 'What's so funny, Tom?' he asked him.

'Got something to show you,' Tom replied, walking
toward the door of the pig shed. Frank followed him,
wondering what he was up to.

They made their way across the courtyard between the
sheds. At least the rain had eased up a bit, Frank thought.
Tom reached the door of the abattoir and turned to
face Frank.

'I had an idea, Frank,' Tom said as he opened the door.
Frank looked inside the dark interior. The first thing he saw
was a shovel lying on the floor near the door, the business
end of it caked with something dark and sticky. As his eyes
adjusted to the gloom, he saw what Tom had brought him
here to see. Hanging by his ankles from the rail that looped
round the ceiling of the room, stark naked and quite
clearly dead, was a man who Frank didn't recognise.

'Frank, meet Kyle,' Tom said.

'My God, Tom,' Frank gasped. 'What on earth have
you done?'

21

A ndy sat at his computer, fiddling with a PowerPoint presentation that Rob had asked him to put together.

'Make it snappy, make it sharp. Big visuals,' Rob had told him. 'I want colour, I want a presentation that will hit the board members in the bollocks and make them wince. Figuratively speaking if they're female, obviously.' Andy hadn't said a word to anyone at Kett's of Norwich about the incident with the woman outside the Food Standards Agency, except for Martin, so he was sure Rob was just being his usual self. Which meant that, in Andy's opinion at least, he was being a cock.

It took Andy the best part of twenty minutes to get the animation for a flying packet of sausages how he wanted it. He looped through the presentation on his screen and watched the sausages swoop in from the left side of the screen before shuddering to a halt on the other side. Perfect. Not quite a kick in the bollocks, but well on the way to it. He was just about to start on the text that he wanted to go with the sausages when an instant message popped up on his screen. Rob from Marketing had something to say.

How's the presentation going? the message read.

Working on it now, Andy typed. He added the word 'boss' as an afterthought.

I need it by eleven o'clock.

Okay, no problem. Andy looked at his watch. It was almost quarter to ten, and he'd spent ages on the bloody flying sausages. He would need to get a shift on to have something for eleven. Andy was sure that the Board wasn't meeting until after lunch, and he'd planned on working through his break to finish it off.

The presentation was the final brief for the board meeting on the forthcoming Pride of Anglia competition. Rob's plan was to go through it with them, and no doubt take all the credit despite the fact Andy had done the bulk of the work for it. Andy frowned and picked up his notes to leaf through them. He would have to prioritise what was going into the presentation or he had no chance at all of getting it finished, and he was trying to work out what to leave out when an envelope fluttering down onto his desk distracted him.

'Post,' a man's voice said from behind him. Andy turned to see the Kett's of Norwich postman, known only as 'Postie', standing behind him. Andy had asked several people what his real name was, but no one seemed to know. Even his name badge just said 'Postie' on it, and that was the name he gave when anyone asked what he was called.

'Thanks, Postie,' Andy said. He watched the man walk over to another desk and throw some envelopes onto it, shouting 'Post' at the woman behind the desk as he did so. She jumped, spilling tea down her blouse, but Postie just wandered off to frighten some more unsuspecting victims.

A few minutes before eleven o'clock, Andy had the presentation close to where he wanted it to be. He opened up his messenger window and typed a message to Rob to let him know that the presentation was done. A few seconds later, Rob replied with a message that he didn't need it until half twelve now.

'Oh, for Christ's sake,' Andy muttered. Still, on the plus side, that gave him enough time for a cheeky pint in the Murderers. He tapped out a message to Rob to let him know that he was going to head into the city to speak to the woman at the Forum, but didn't mention going to the pub. What Rob didn't know wouldn't hurt him.

Great plan, go get her, Rob's reply popped up on Andy's screen.

The Forum was a large glass-fronted building in the middle of Norwich, and for some reason had a permanent collection of depressed looking teenagers dressed mostly in black loitering outside it. Andy navigated his way through them and walked through the revolving doors at the front of the building. Crossing to the reception desk, he asked the pale looking lad sitting behind it where he could find Jessica.

'Who?' the receptionist replied.

'Jessica?' Andy repeated himself, wondering if one of the goths from outside had just wandered in and sat behind the desk. 'She's something to do with events, I think.' The lad behind the desk just shrugged his shoulders and pointed toward a door to the side of the room. Andy looked at it and saw a sign saying 'Events' on the door. 'Mate, thank you so much,' Andy said. 'You've been so helpful, I'm just overcome with gratitude.' He looked at the receptionist, who was just staring at the screen in front of him. He obviously wasn't into dripping sarcasm, Andy thought as he left him to it and walked toward the door. He raised his hand and knocked on it, pushing the door open when he heard a male voice shout 'Come in' from behind it.

Andy pushed the door open and looked around it into an open plan office. There were maybe ten desks inside, only one of which on the far side of the room was occupied. He looked at the man sitting behind it, and immediately felt inadequate. It was obvious, even from this distance, that the occupant spent much more time in the gym than Andy did. He didn't look that tall, even though he was sitting down, but there was no getting away from the fact that he was built like a brick shithouse.

'Er, hi?' Andy said. 'I'm looking for Jessica?' The man got to his feet and started lumbering his way across the room towards Andy. As he got closer, Andy could see the raw anger in his face and he took half a step backwards but with the door right behind him, he couldn't go any further.

'You looking for Jessica, are you?' the man said, almost in a growl. The tight polo shirt he was wearing emphasised his enormous arms. 'Why are you looking for Jessica?' He stopped right in front of Andy and leaned forward so that their foreheads were almost touching. Andy's mouth had gone very dry, and he swallowed. The man's next sentence came out in a loud bark, almost a shout. 'Are you Dave?' He was so close to Andy that he was out of focus. 'Are you Dave?' the man repeated, his voice much quieter and full of menace.

'No,' Andy replied, ashamed that his voice had just gone up a couple of octaves. 'I'm Andy. Andy, not Dave.'

'You look like Dave,' the man whispered. 'I've seen your pictures on her phone. You're Dave.'

'I'm not Dave, I'm Andy. From Kett's of Norwich.' Andy's fingers trembled as he grabbed his identification card that hung round his neck on a lanyard. 'Look, there, that's me. Andy. It says so right there.'

The man peered at the photograph on the identification card and looked at Andy. He took a step backward and unclenched his fists much to Andy's relief.

'Right, Andy,' he said. 'You do look like Dave, though.' Andy had no idea who Dave was, or what he had done to this man, but he wouldn't want to be in his shoes when the two of them finally got together.

'Well I'm not. I'm Andy.'

'Yeah, got that.'

'So, er, is Jessica about?'

'Nope, she's at lunch,' the man replied. 'Have a seat if you want, she'll be back soon.' Andy looked at the empty desks around the room, wondering where he should sit. He decided on a desk near the door, just in case the current occupant of the office reconsidered whether or not he was in fact Dave. Andy sat at the desk, glancing at his watch. He'd give it ten minutes, and if Jessica hadn't come back from her lunch break, he'd head back to the office.

Andy watched as the man who'd just threatened him lumbered back across the office, and pulled his phone out of his pocket to pass the time until Jessica got back. Andy glanced up as a shadow flashed across the screen of his phone. Mr Muscle was back, with a tray of French Fancies in his oversized hand.

'Cake?'

'Oh, that's very kind of you,' Andy replied, reaching out for the tray.

'Not the pink ones. They're her favourite.'

'A yellow one is fine,' Andy said. 'I prefer them, anyway.' He picked a cake out of the tray and ate it slowly, not daring to look back at his phone until the other man was back on the far side of the room.

22

———

Tom muttered to himself under his breath as he pulled up on the tractor outside the pig sheds. It was still dark, but he'd always been more of a morning person than Frank. He didn't think Frank would be up for a while anyway. Tom had still been awake when Frank had gone to bed, and from the way his brother had been thumping around in the farmhouse, he'd had a fair bit to drink. It had been almost two in the morning, so just over four hours ago, but as Tom walked into the main shed and opened the fridge doors, he could see why Frank had been so late.

Neatly stacked on the shelves in the fridge were joints of meat. Lots of meat. There were leg joints, shoulder joints, stacks of ribs as well as a couple of fine looking joints of rump. On the floor of the fridge was a bucket full of mince, and another bucket next to it full of blood. Kyle had done well. Tom had heard the stump grinder firing up as he'd lain in bed, unable to sleep. At least this meant that he wouldn't find a head in the stock pot again.

There was a saying in the pig farming community,

'everything but the squeal'. Their father had explained it to Tom and Frank when they were both small. It meant that when a pig was slaughtered, every bit of it was used somehow. None of went to waste. Everything 'but the squeal' got used somehow or other. It looked to Tom as if that was exactly Frank had done with Kyle. There was more mince in the bucket than there had been with the previous body, so Frank had been a lot more frugal this time round.

Tom couldn't work out why Frank had been so annoyed with him last night. After Tom had shown him Kyle, Frank had stomped around the pig sheds for ages, calling Tom all the names under the sun. Eventually, Frank disappeared back to the farmhouse and returned a while later with a bottle of whisky and two glasses. They'd sat in the abattoir with Kyle in silence for a while before Frank had broken the silence.

'Why'd you kill him, Tom?' Frank had asked when they'd both had a couple of glasses. Tom had told Frank that it was an accident, but Frank had just laughed.

'No it bloody wasn't. You smacked him round the head with a shovel,' Frank said.

'No I didn't.'

'Then why are there bits of blood and hair on the shovel then?'

'It was more of a jab than a smack,' Tom had replied. 'With the sharp end. But he kept on wriggling on the floor.'

'So, what did you do?'

'Well, smacked him with the flat end until he stopped wriggling.'

'Do you not think that's wrong, Tom? I mean, the other one was an accident. I get that. But him?' Frank looked toward the man hanging up by the ankles. 'That's no accident.'

'It's just meat, Frank,' Tom had replied. 'That's what you told me.'

'Don't you dare go blaming this one on me, Thomas Pinch.' Tom didn't reply, recognising the use of his full name for the warning it was. They sat in silence for ages, twenty minutes or maybe even longer, before Frank eventually continued. 'Next time though...'

'Next time what?'

'Next time,' Frank said, with a look at the upside-down Kyle. 'Next time, can you choose one without quite so much hair?' He took a large sup of his whisky. 'That's going to be a bugger to scrape that lot off.'

By the time Tom had finished loading up the trailer with the trays of meat, he was sweating even though it was still chilly outside. Tom left the buckets of mince and blood where they were. He could sort them out later, once Frank was at work. Sausages and black pudding. Tom ran through the ingredients of black pudding in his head. Blood, oatmeal, salt, onion, milk, pepper and spices. And of course, the magic ingredient, fat. Frank had even left a tray in the fridge with neatly trimmed cubes of fat on it. Although Tom would never touch the black pudding he was going to make, he was sure it would taste fantastic. Kyle hadn't looked particularly fat, but he obviously had enough for Frank for carve off enough for a decent black pudding.

Tom hopped back on the tractor and drove to the farmhouse. There was no light in Frank's window, so he must still be asleep. Tom parked up and transferred the meat into the Land Rover. When he'd finished, he walked into the kitchen to put the coffee pot on for Frank when he woke up.

Forty-five minutes later, Tom heard the toilet flush and knew that Frank was up and about. While he waited for his brother to come out of the bathroom, Tom poured them both a mug of coffee and added two sugars to Frank's. Just how he liked it.

'Morning Tom,' Frank said as he walked into the kitchen. 'That coffee smells good.'

'Here you go,' Tom said, putting a mug down in front of his brother. Frank stretched his arms above his head and yawned.

'Thank you, Tom.'

'I've loaded the Land Rover for you. It's all good to go, and I'll sort out the sausages and black pudding later and bring them in.'

'Nice one,' Frank said. 'But this has to be a one off, you understand? Regardless of what I said last night, there won't be a next time. Okay?'

'I get that.'

'I mean, this will get us out of the hole we're in at the moment. But once we're back on track...' Frank left the sentence hanging.

'I get that too, don't worry,' Tom said. 'It won't happen again.' Frank looked at him, and Tom knew from his expression that he was silently asking him if he was telling the truth. 'I promise. Are you still angry with me?' Frank shook his head, and Tom knew that everything was cool.

'A bit, yes. But not as much as I was last night. I didn't realise just how much meat you could get off one person if you put your mind to it,' Frank said, draining half his coffee mug with a single gulp. 'We're going to make a fair bit from young Kyle, but it has to see us through until the pigs are ready.'

'Okay, cool,' Tom nodded and grinned at his brother.

'We're not out of the woods just yet, Tom. What if Marko gets suspicious that another immigrant has disappeared from our farm?'

'He won't,' Tom said. 'He told me the other day that they disappear all the time. Not just from here, but from all over the place. He's put it in his business, er what was the word? Begins with 'S'.'

'Strategy?'

'Yeah, that was it. He told me he'd put it in his business strategy for the year.'

'Good God,' Frank said. 'A gangmaster with a business strategy. Whatever next?' Frank finished his coffee and put the empty mug on the table. 'Right, I need to get off. When are you going to bring in the sausages?'

'I'll do them now if you want?' Tom replied. 'The black pudding will take a bit longer, but I can bring the sausages in while the pudding's in the oven. Should be lunchtime at the latest.'

'Perfect, see you in a bit then.' Frank got to his feet and walked over to the door. 'See you later.'

Tom waited until he heard Frank's Land Rover pull away from the drive before he washed up their cups and headed out himself to go and get the buckets. As he drove toward the pig sheds, he tried to work out how many sausages and how much black pudding he'd be able to make out of Kyle, but maths had never been his strong point, so he gave up.

'I'll find out soon enough,' he mumbled under his breath before starting to whistle one of the songs from Snow White and the Seven Dwarfs, which was his favourite film of all time.

23

Emily chewed the end of her biro while she tried to work out what she was supposed to be filling out on the form in front of her. It was a Laboratory Request Form, not one she'd filled out before. In a sealed plastic bag on the desk in front of her was the sample of meat from the visit she'd just done. That bit had been simple. It was a case of using the small blue plastic spoon attached to the lid of the sample pot to dig out some meat from the sausage, shove it in the pot and tighten the lid. There were a few details to put on the label on the outside of the pot, but it was easy enough. The form was a different matter completely, though. Emily had only got as far as filling out her details, and the details of where the sample had come from, but now she was completely stuck. A bizarre list of tests and analyses was written on the form, and she didn't have a clue which ones she was supposed to ask for.

She was on the verge of admitting defeat, and speaking to Mr Clayton, when she saw a phone number for the lab printed on the bottom of the form.

'Thank God,' she muttered as she reached for the

phone. The last thing she wanted to do was to ask her boss how to fill out a bloody form. She stabbed at the numbers on the phone and sucked the biro while she waited for someone to pick up.

'Hello?' a deep male voice said, sounding almost surprised.

'Oh, hello,' Emily replied. 'Is that the lab?'

'Yes, it is. How can I help you?'

'Ah, er, yes. My name's Emily Underwood and I'm an Food Standards Agency officer. I've got a sample here that I need to send off to you guys, and to be honest, I'm a bit confused about the form.' The voice at the other end of the line laughed.

'Now, you're not the first person to say that. I've been trying to get it changed for ages, but nothing doing. What did you say your name was again?'

'Emily Underwood.'

'What a lovely name.' Emily almost looked at the receiver. She'd not been expecting that reply. 'Did you do 'Under Milk Wood' in English when you were at school?'

'Er, no,' Emily said. She'd never even heard of Under Milk Wood. 'We did Macbeth and some obscure Russian bloke who wrote about women staring out of windows, whining about ducks going to Moscow.' There was a pause at the other end.

'Sounds like Anton Chekov to me.'

'Could be. I wasn't very good at English.'

'What was your favourite subject, then?'

'Ooh, let me think,' Emily said. She nibbled at the pen, trying to think of something funny to say. The voice at the other end of the line was quite intriguing. 'Probably the one I was best at was Biology.'

'Oh tut tut, Emily. That's not what I asked. Of course you were good at Biology, you're an Environmental Health

Officer. I asked what your favourite subject was, not what you were good at.'

'Geography, then.'

'Why Geography?' the voice said. Emily paused before replying. She wasn't sure how to answer that one. The reality was she'd loved Geography because she'd had a crush on Mr Greenmore, the Geography teacher, since she was in Year 11.

'Er, I liked volcanoes.' Mr Greenmore had shown them an experiment with a plastic erupting volcano that shot lava all over the desk in the Geography lab. It was only when Emily was a few years older, and a bit more grown up, that she'd realised how erotically charged the whole experiment had been. Not something she could discuss with the voice at the other end of the line though, and Emily felt stupid as she waited for a reply. The voice was quite something, and Emily realised that she liked the sound of it. There was something about the way the man spoke that was intriguing and, Emily had to admit to herself, quite sensual.

'That's cool,' the voice said, but from his tone, Emily thought it probably wasn't.

'So, anyway,' Emily said. 'What's your name? I mean, you know mine, you know what I did for English at school, and my favourite subject. But I don't even know your name?'

'I'm Gary,' the voice said. 'I run the lab.'

'Well, hello Gary.'

'Well, hello Emily.' Yep, there was definitely something about Gary's voice that piqued Emily's interest. 'I'm sorry if I'm being nosey, but we don't get many phone calls down here, especially not from young women who sound as nice as you do. How can I help you?'

Emily was thrown by Gary's last comment, and stalled for a second or two before replying.

'Er, I'm stuck on the form.'

'Oh yes, the form. Just tick the first three boxes in the column on the left-hand side. That's it.'

'That's it?'

'Yep.'

'Oh.' Emily was disappointed at such a simple solution. 'Right, okay then. I'll do that.'

'Was there anything else, Emily?'

Emily paused for a second, remembering what Catherine had told her about throwing caution to the winds every once in a while. Sometimes, according to Catherine, the best things come out of the smallest hunches. Emily was sure Catherine had read that in Cosmopolitan or somewhere like that, but what if she was right?

'Well, actually, I was wondering. I'm quite new to the Food Standards Agency, and am still finding my feet. Could I maybe come and have a look round the lab at some point?'

'Well of course you can. I'd be delighted to show you round. Come down now if you want. The kettle's just boiled, all you need to bring are some biscuits.'

Emily looked at her watch. It was almost an hour until lunchtime, and the lab request was the only thing she had to do. She could swing by the canteen and pick up a packet of biscuits.

'Sure, okay,' she replied before she realised that she had no idea where the lab was. 'Where are you based?' There was a deep laugh on the other end of the line.

'Where else? We're in the lower basement,' Gary said. 'There's no lifts though, you'll have to get to the ground floor, walk round to the back of the building and down the ramp to the car park. They've hidden us away from everyone else. Not exactly sexy, laboratory work.' Emily was tempted to disagree with him, but decided against it.

'Nice one. I'll be down in twenty minutes. Any particular type of biscuits?'

'Surprise me.'

Emily spent at least fifteen minutes in the toilet before making her way down to the lab. The first thing she did was fire off a text to Catherine. *Just going to meet a man with the SEXIEST voice I've ever heard.*

While she waited for a reply from her flat mate, Emily redid her hair, made sure her makeup was holding up, and checked for bits of food in her teeth. She was looking at herself in the mirror, wondering whether or not to open the top button of her blouse. Knowing Catherine, if it was her, she would have her blouse unbuttoned so far that Gary would be able to see her belly button piercing, but that wasn't Emily's style. Plus, Emily didn't have a belly button piercing. Her phone buzzed just as Emily decided that opening her top button was taking things a bit far. If he was as nice as he sounded, she didn't want to come across as too much of a tart.

You go girl, knock him dead. Emily smiled at Catherine's reply. This was, she had to admit to herself, verging on the ridiculous. Getting excited about meeting a man just because she liked the sound of his voice. A few minutes later, she was waiting outside the door of the lab, wondering if the doorbell was working or not. She'd pressed it twice, and not heard a thing.

When the door opened, Emily took one look at the man standing there and could only think of one thing. Please be Gary, please be Gary. The man in front of her was tall, broad shouldered, a chiselled face like a model from an underpants advert, and a tight white lab coat that fitted him very well indeed.

'Hi, I'm Gary,' he said. 'You must be Emily Underwood? Come on in.'

Emily followed Gary through the door, a packet of chocolate hobnobs in her hand. She'd stopped off at the shop and spent ages trying to decide between ginger nuts or bourbons before eventually deciding to go all in and buy some chocolate hobnobs. Sod the price. As she watched Gary stride confidently down the corridor, she knew she'd made the right decision on the biscuits.

'Do you want a cup of tea?' Gary said as he led Emily into what looked like the staff room. He walked over to the sink and grabbed a couple of mugs before flicking the switch on the kettle. 'Did you bring biscuits?'

'Yes, of course,' Emily replied. 'Chocolate hobnobs.'

'Ooh, I knew I would like you.' Gary looked at Emily and smiled. As she offered him the packet of biscuits, she wished she had undone her top button, just in case. He was something else.

Gary made them both a cup of tea and spent the next thirty minutes giving Emily a guided tour of the lab. He obviously wasn't in any hurry at all as he showed her round, taking time to explain all the various bits and pieces of equipment. Emily tried to understand what he was telling her, but she kept getting distracted by the look of the man. By the time they got back to the staff room after the grand tour, Emily had forgotten most of what he'd told her. She sat in one of the armchairs while Gary crossed the room to the sink, their empty cups in his hand.

'So how come you never come up to the main building, then?' Emily asked him as he rinsed the cups.

'How'd you mean?' he replied.

'Well, I've never seen you in the canteen or around the

building. I'm sure I would have noticed you.' As soon as the words were out of her mouth, Emily regretted them. That hadn't sounded at all how she'd wanted it to, but Catherine would be proud of her.

'I certainly would have noticed you,' Gary replied with a broad smile that made Emily want to take a deep breath. Was he flirting with her? They looked at each other for a few seconds before he finally turned his back on Emily to make the tea. Emily flapped a hand over her face, hoping that she wasn't blushing. 'So, did you bring that sample with you?' he asked over his shoulder.

'I did, yes,' Emily replied. She pulled the sample pot and paperwork out of her coat pocket, smoothing the form on the coffee table in front of her. Gary walked across and put two cups of tea on the table before crouching down next to Emily. She caught a faint smell of aftershave or deodorant coming off him as he pointed at the relevant boxes on the form.

'You just need to tick those three boxes, Emily,' he said. Emily looked at him, their faces only inches apart, and wondered what she would do if he leaned across and kissed her. What would he do if she leaned across and kissed him? What about if… 'Are you okay?' Gary asked.

Emily blinked a couple of times, snapping herself out of her daydream.

'Yeah, sorry. I'm fine,' she said.

'You looked a bit far away for a moment then?'

'I was. Bad habit of mine. Sorry again.'

'Hey, no problem,' Gary said as he stood up. He walked round the table and sat in the chair opposite, and the moment was gone. 'So, do you want to leave that with me? I should be able to process the sample this afternoon, seeing as you've made the effort to come down here and ask in person.'

'That would be great, thank you,' Emily replied. That would mean she could get the report finalised and in Mr Clayton's in-box by the end of the day. Finishing the report that quickly wouldn't hurt at all. 'My boss is really on my case at the moment, so the sooner the better. I'll make it up to you.' She chewed her bottom lip, which according to Catherine, was a sure-fire way to get men going when it was done right.

'I'll hold you to that,' Gary said. 'How about you give me your phone number and I'll text you the minute it's done?' Emily paused for a second before grabbing her bag to get a pen. She forced herself to calm down and try to look nonchalant as she pulled a pen and piece of paper out of her bag.

Emily left the lab a few minutes later, managing to thank Gary for the guided tour and express service without touching him. She stood outside the door of the lab and fired off a text to Catherine. *Call me if you're free?* She was half way across the car park when her phone rang.

'Catherine? Listen, you are not going to believe what just happened!'

24

A ndy groaned as he saw Rob walking across the office toward him with a determined look on his face, a large black bin liner clutched in his hand. The last thing he needed this early in the morning was Rob on his back.

'Andy, could we have a chat in the breakout space?' Rob said as he reached Andy's desk.

'Sure, Rob,' Andy replied, getting to his feet. 'I'd love to.'

The two of them settled themselves into the large beanbags a few minutes later. Andy tried to make himself comfortable, distracted by the noise of the polystyrene balls. When they'd both managed to get comfortable, and the noise had subsided, Rob looked at Andy over steepled hands.

'Grasshopper, we need to have a chat,' Andy's boss said. 'Three things my friend, there are three things we need to discuss.'

'Please, do continue,' Andy said, wondering for a moment why he was being called a grasshopper, and also wondering what was in the bin liner that Rob had dumped in the corner of the room.

'Okay, number one,' Rob said, shifting in the beanbag so that he was almost, but not quite, leaning toward Andy. 'The details for the event at the Forum still haven't been finalised. Number two, the presentation for the board isn't done. And three, we've not got enough meat.'

Andy paused before replying. He had an answer for all three of those accusations.

'Rob,' Andy said. 'Number one, Jessica wasn't in when I visited there last week, but I've got an appointment with her later on this morning.' Andy wondered for a moment whether to tell his boss about the steroid munching bloke who'd threatened him on the basis that he looked a bit like someone called Dave, but he thought better of it. 'Two, I have finished the presentation.' Technically true, but there was a small lie in there as it was Martin who'd finished it off last night after they'd got back from the pub. Andy still needed to go through it to make sure that Martin hadn't included any Easter eggs for the Board, but it was one version of the finished product. 'What was three again?'

'Meat.'

'Oh yeah, well I'll go out this afternoon and get some more.'

'We don't have long, Andy. There're only a couple of days until the main event at the Forum. You need to be on top of this.' Andy wasn't sure why he — the intern — was the one who had to be on top of this as opposed to Rob who was the marketing manager, but he let it go. 'Right, anyway,' Rob continued. 'We had an internal meeting yesterday, and we decided that we need some localised marketing efforts to leverage consumer engagement in the parochial channel.'

'Sorry, what?'

'Strategic marketing content,' Rob replied, reaching for the bin liner. 'The intent of our focus groups suggests that we need to reinforce this with visuality, and emphasise the end state.'

'Rob, sorry but I am only an intern. I'm not sure what you're talking about? Could you explain it to me?' Andy was quite pleased with himself for not swearing.

'You need to hand out leaflets advertising the event,' Rob said.

'Okay, no problem.'

'In fancy dress,' Rob said, placing the bin bag between them.

'Okay,' Andy replied. 'I think.'

Twenty minutes later, Andy walked up to the Forum with the bin liner clutched in his hand. He walked through the revolving doors, ignored the lanky depressed teenager behind the desk, and went straight to the door marked 'Events'. After he'd knocked on it, he took a large step backwards and waited. A few seconds later, the door swung open and one of the largest women he'd ever seen in his life stood in front of him.

'Are you Andy?' the woman said. 'I'm Jessica. Come on in.'

Andy stepped through the door, looking around the inside of the office for the previous occupant who was nowhere to be seen. Reassured that he wasn't there, Andy dropped the bag off by the door and walked into the office.

Jessica and Andy spent the next twenty minutes going over the plans for the Kett's competition. As he sat there and fended off cakes, biscuits, and something that looked a bit like a disabled gingerbread man, Andy realised that Jessica was all over the whole thing. He started to relax, realising that despite Rob's misgivings, everything that should be in place already was.

'Have you got any questions, Andy?' Jessica said after they'd been through the entire plan several times.

'I have got one question,' Andy said. 'It's not about the competition, though.' Andy paused while Jessica polished off a pink French Fancy, one of several piled up on her desk.

'Go for it,' she replied, crumbs spilling onto her more than ample bosom.

'Who's Dave?'

Jessica looked at Andy, open mouthed, for a few seconds. Andy was hoping she would close her mouth and hide the half-eaten cake when she started laughing. Andy had to admit that the way her whole body rippled as she laughed was impressive, even if it was in a bizarre sense.

'Oh dear, has Steve had a go at you?'

'Steve?'

'Steroid Steve,' Jessica pointed at a desk in the far corner of the room. 'Sits over there. Bless him. I met a bloke called Dave on the internet on a speciality site for plus size ladies and the men who love them. Steve saw some of the pictures that we sent each other. Some of them were quite, er, adult.'

Andy grimaced but tried not to let it show on his face. This was getting into a world that not only did he have no interest in, but was one he was happy knowing nothing about. He reached for the bin liner between them.

'Could I ask you a favour? I've been given this fancy dress costume. Could you give me a hand getting into it?'

A few minutes later, Andy was standing outside the Forum in his fancy dress. It had taken him and Jessica a while to get him into the costume and through the doors of the building. The costume was made of foam, extended Andy's height by a good two feet, and was completed by a pair of yellow tights and boots. It was a hot dog outfit. He was now a seven-foot-tall hot dog. Andy had a stack of leaflets in his hand, and he waddled his way toward a mother with a small child.

'Would you like a leaflet?' Andy asked the child. She was dressed in pink and stared at him, open mouthed. Andy had no idea about children, but the girl couldn't have been more than three years old. Andy glanced at the mother, whose expression mirrored her daughter's. The girl's mouth opened wider, and she started to scream. Her mother turned away, a look of disgust on her face, and hurried her daughter away from Andy.

Andy was looking in dismay at the retreating mother and child when he realised there was a teenager standing next to him taking a selfie. The teenager was dressed in black and had more metalwork in his face than a car crash victim.

'Do you mind, mate?' Andy hissed at him. 'I'm trying to work here.' The teenager said nothing, but laughed and walked off to join a small crowd of similar looking goths. Andy ignored them as he had spotted a couple walking toward the Forum, arm in arm. The woman was wearing a long flowing skirt with a multi-coloured blouse. She looked to Andy as if she was stuck in the Seventies even though she was only his age. The man who she was hanging off had blonde dreadlocks, a nose ring, and bright red trousers that almost matched the colour of his companion's dyed hair. Andy walked across to them and thrust a leaflet in the man's hands.

'Local produce competition here, mate,' Andy said. 'Loads of local meats, dairy products, the works. You guys up for it?' The man looked at the leaflet, his hands shaking, taking a few seconds to read it. He looked up at Andy with ever so slightly yellow eyes.

'Meat is murder, man,' he said, jerking his forehead

toward Andy who recoiled at his fetid breath. The woman with him pawed at his arm.

'Leave it, Rupert. Come on, just leave it. He doesn't understand.' Andy was trying to work out what that meant when he realised there was a small mob of goths around him, phones in hands.

'Would you lot stop the bloody photos?' Andy said.

'Why?' one of them answered. 'It's not every day you see a man dressed as a giant penis.'

'I'm not dressed as a giant penis. It's a hot dog costume.'

'That's what you think, mate. Have you seen yourself?' the goth next to Andy asked. 'Where's Veronica? She's seen more cocks than the rest of us put together. Get her over here.' Andy watched as a heavy set young woman lumbered her way toward him, all in black and with more tattoos than a sailor.

'Veronica, cock or hot dog?' a voice said.

'Oh, that is a cock,' Veronica said. 'That is definitely a very large phallus. Can I get a pic, come on someone?'

'Oh fuck off, the lot of you,' Andy muttered as he retreated toward the revolving doors of the Forum.

A few moments later, Andy was staring through the plate glass of the revolving doors watching the security guard on the inside of the building. The guard lifted his radio to his mouth.

'Yeah, Micky, could you come down to the foyer and give me a hand?' There was a burst of static on the radio that Andy couldn't understand. The guard in front of Andy continued. 'Totally stuck mate, I need some help to free the doors. Some bloke in fancy dress, completely buggered the doors.' There was a silence on the radio, followed by another burst of static. 'Yep, he's dressed as an enormous penis.'

25

F rank eased the Land Rover into the car park behind
his butcher's, and backed it up against the rear doors
that led into the shop. He hopped out of the vehicle and
opened the doors. Ten minutes later, all the trays of meat
that Tom had loaded into the Land Rover were in the
main store. He parked the car and walked back into the
shop, feeling happier than he had for a long time.

He hadn't used the main display counter behind the
window for a long time, deciding that it was better to leave
it empty than sitting there with a solitary sausage or pork
chop in it. Besides, just turning on the chiller and lights ate
into his electricity bill. Most of his customers were local,
and he didn't feel the need to advertise for passing trade.
Not that there was much passing trade in the village,
anyway. Today would be different, Frank thought as he
wiped down the dusty surfaces and flicked the switch to
turn the display cabinet on.

By the time Frank was ready to open the shop, the
display was full and there was enough meat in the main
fridge to restock the cabinet several times over. For a

reasonably skinny guy, Kyle had gone a long way, and there were still the sausages that Frank hoped would be in the shop by lunchtime. Then, this afternoon, black pudding. Not something he'd been able to offer for a while.

He flipped the sign on the inside of the door to 'Open', and unlocked it. Smoothing his hands over the front of his red and white striped apron, Frank stepped out onto the pavement to have a look at the display cabinet from the outside. He nodded, happy with the way it looked, and went back inside to make himself a cup of tea. The kettle hadn't even finished boiling when his first customer walked in. A sour looking old woman whose name he couldn't remember for the life of him.

'Good morning, my dear,' Frank said, plastering a smile on his face. 'Well aren't you out and about early this fine day?' The woman didn't reply, but sauntered over to the counter.

'Got any chops?' she asked in a high-pitched voice which suited her perfectly.

'I most certainly have,' Frank replied. 'What sort of chops would you be looking for?'

'Pork chops. I want one for me tea.'

'Yes, of course,' Frank said. His smile slipped for a second before he hiked it back up again. 'Pork chops. Now, would you like a fat one, thin one, on the bone, boneless, fatty, lean? I've got them all today.'

'A pork one.'

'Jesus H. Christ,' Frank muttered under his breath as he reached into the counter and pulled out a deboned slice of Kyle's upper thigh. He slapped it down onto the cutting board on top of the counter. 'Now this,' he said to the old bag. 'This is a pork chop that I think is perfect for you. What do you think?'

A moment later, the old woman shuffled out of Frank's

shop with the chop wrapped in greaseproof paper, and six pounds forty pence less of her pension money. Frank put the kettle back on, but was disturbed again by the sound of the bell over the door as another customer walked in.

'Good morning, I'll be out in a second,' Frank called out as he threw a tea bag into his cup. He looked up to see the customer's reflection in the mirror. It was an old chap called Bertie, who had to be in his nineties if he was a day. One of Frank's better customers. Bertie had a dog, some sort of daschund, who Frank thought ate better than Bertie did. 'Hey Bertie, do you want a cup of tea?' The old boy was pleasant enough to talk to and had a few good stories to tell. Mostly about shooting Germans down over the English Channel. Frank had heard them all several times already, but would quite happily listen to them again if it meant Bertie bought something.

'Yes please, Frank,' Bertie replied. 'That'd be magic. Two sugars please, old boy.' Frank smiled. Being called 'old boy' by a man almost three times his age was something else. Twenty minutes later, Frank had another twenty quid in his till, and Bertie had a fine loin of Kyle for him and his sausage dog to share.

The next couple of hours saw a steady trickle of customers come into the shop. There were never more than one or two customers at a time waiting, and the money was pouring in. By the time Frank heard Tom come in through the door at the back of the shop, he was more than ready for lunch.

'Hey Tom,' Frank said after flipping the sign over to 'Closed'. 'You got the sausages?'

'I have, yes. Black pud's not quite ready, though. I wasn't sure whether to bring the sausages now and the black pudding later, or bring them all at the same time.' Tom put a tray full of sausages on the counter.

'Don't worry, Tom,' Frank said. 'That'll be fine. There's a couple of customers coming back later for sausages, so I'd rather have them than the black pudding anyway.'

'Okay, cool.'

The two brothers spent the next few minutes arranging the sausages that Tom had delivered. There were a few gaps in the main display that Frank was quite happy to fill with sausages. He was in the middle of arranging the links of meat so that they looked perfect when he looked up and noticed two black Range Rovers with tinted windows pull up outside. The passenger door of the one in the front opened, and a large man in a black suit got out. He walked over to the door and rapped on it.

'We're closed,' Frank called out. He looked at the man standing outside the door who was staring back him with his eyebrows raised. 'Oh, for God's sake,' Frank muttered as he walked over to the door. Cracking it open a couple of inches, he spoke to the suited man outside. 'We're shut for lunch. Can you come back later?'

'Can you un-shut please?'

'What?'

'Can you open back up?'

'Well, not really,' Frank replied. 'We're busy.' The man outside the shop glanced over his shoulder at the second Range Rover.

'Please?'

There was something in the man's look that made Frank think that opening the shop up might not be a bad idea. It wasn't that he was threatening. He was, but that wasn't what convinced Frank. The Black Range Rovers outside were brand spanking new. Top of the line models. Whoever was inside them had some money, that much was for sure.

Frank opened the door to the butcher's, and stepped

back as the passengers in the second Range Rover climbed out. There were two of them, a couple from the way they were hanging off each other. A tall ginger haired lad with a scruffy beard, and a thin brunette. They walked in and examined the product in the counter. Frank stayed silent and watched them as they pointed at the meat on display. The woman's wedding ring had a stone in it the size of a small marble, and Frank was sure it wasn't cubic zirconia.

'What do you think?' the ginger man said in a cut glass accent, pointing at some of the sausages that Tom had just put in the display. His female companion nodded and turned to him with a wide smile. Perfect teeth, and not a wrinkle in sight. 'Hey, could we take two packs of those sausages please?' he asked. This was definitely someone who went to posh school.

'Of course,' Frank replied, reaching for some grease-proof paper to wrap the sausages in. 'That'll be eleven quid.' The customer looked confused for a second before the bodyguard, at least that was what Frank assumed he was, stepped forward and opened his jacket. As he reached into his inside pocket, Frank could see the black metallic handle of a gun in a holster. A gun? In England? His eyes widened at the sight, and he looked again at the young couple who were both smiling back at him.

'There you go mate,' the bodyguard pressed a twenty-pound note into Frank's hand. 'Keep the change.'

'Thanks very much,' Frank replied, looking at Tom with a grin. 'Very kind of you.'

As the customers walked toward the door of the shop, the woman turned to her companion.

'Your Granny is going to love these when she comes over this weekend,' she said, her broad American accent obvious. 'I can't wait for her to try these sausages.'

As the black Range Rovers pulled away from the kerb,

Frank saw a hand throw a screwed up yellow piece of paper out of one of the driver's windows. The number plate of the second Range Rover was a personalised plate — HRH 6 — and they weren't bothered about parking tickets.

'Frank?' Tom asked.

'What?'

'Was that Ed Sheeran?'

'No, Tom,' Frank sighed. 'I don't think it was.'

26

E mily shifted into third gear as she rounded the corner. It was the first time this year she'd been able to put the roof down on her Mini, and it reminded her why she'd bought a convertible in the first place. Her phone buzzed on the passenger seat, distracting her for a second. She glanced at the phone to see an incoming text message, and when she looked back up to the road she was hurtling toward a large black Range Rover coming the other way. She shoved the wheel to the left, narrowly missing the Range Rover which was braking hard, and flew past it. There were two of them, in a convoy, and as she passed the second car she flipped a 'V' sign with her hand at the tinted rear windows.

'Wankers,' Emily shouted at the top of her voice before laughing as she accelerated away.

She was still chuckling as she slowed down at the entrance to the village, mindful of the speed camera that might, or might not, be working. Thumbing at her phone, Emily saw a text message from Catherine. *Any news from the lab man?*

No, nothing, but give it time, Emily tapped out her reply as she pulled into the car park behind the butcher's shop she'd come to inspect. She pulled into a space in between a dented Range Rover and a tractor and got out of her car.

Emily walked through the car park to the front of the butcher's and got to the front door just as the man inside flipped the sign back over to 'Open'. Perfect timing. She pushed the door open and walked inside.

'Mr Pinch?' Emily asked. 'I'm here to do your inspection.'

'Oh, does it have to be today? I've been really busy for the first day in ages.'

'It won't take long, I promise,' Emily smiled sweetly at the butcher. 'It's Frank, isn't it? We met in the pub, do you remember?'

'I do,' Frank replied, not returning the smile. 'You and your friend buggered off to the toilets and then never came back.' Emily kept the smile hiked on her face as she replied.

'Sorry, my friend Catherine got taken ill so, we had to go,' she said before dropping her voice to a conspiratorial whisper. 'Women's problems.'

'Right, okay,' Frank said. He didn't look convinced, but Emily wasn't bothered. She followed him over to the counter and waited for him to get round to his side of it. 'Do we have to do this now?'

'I'm sorry, Frank,' Emily replied. 'But it won't take long. Half an hour, tops, especially if you went through the pre-inspection paperwork.' A proper inspection should take about three times that long, but Emily wanted to keep Frank on side. Hopefully, he'd appreciate it and put some decent feedback in to the Food Standards Agency to offset all the others. Frank sighed theatrically as he walked back over to the door and flipped the sign back to 'Closed'.

'Half an hour, then,' he said. 'I'll hold you to it.' Emily saw the ghost of a smile on his face and knew that she'd won him over. Catherine was right after all. Sometimes a little feminine charm never hurt anyone. A few minutes after she started, she saw the butcher's brother drive past on his tractor. He turned to look at Emily, but didn't return her wave.

Exactly thirty-three minutes later, the inspection was done and dusted. Emily sat in the back room of the butcher's, completing the paperwork and sipping a cup of tea that Frank had made her. In fairness to him, there was very little for Emily to comment on. Everything was as it should be, and he certainly had more stock than the last time Emily had been in his shop. It was all properly displayed, at the correct temperatures, and in the right place. The only thing that stuck out was the price. Frank Pinch's shop was a bit on the expensive side, but judging by the queue of customers that were waiting outside his door when he reopened the shop, this didn't seem to be putting them off.

The only awkward moment was when Emily had asked for a sample of meat for testing. This wasn't a new thing — the Food Standards Agency sampled about ten per cent of all products — but it seemed to throw Frank completely when Emily had asked for one.

'Why?' he'd asked her. 'I've not been asked for a sample for testing before.'

'It's just a routine test,' Emily had replied. 'It's since the horse scandal a few years ago. You know, when there was a load of horsemeat in the food chain, and loads of people got really upset about it.' It hadn't bothered Emily in the slightest. She hated horses, and wouldn't have had any problems eating one, but rules were rules.

'But this is all my stock,' Frank had complained. 'I can't give it away.'

'I'll give you a receipt, and the Food Standards Agency will reimburse you. There's an online form for it.'

They'd stood facing each other and Emily was just wondering how hard to push the issue when Frank disappeared behind the counter. She heard rustling, and he reappeared a few seconds later with some sausages wrapped in greaseproof paper. He put them onto the counter between them with a wry smile.

'There you go,' Frank said. 'Will they be okay? They're my emergency sausages for if I sell out.' Emily picked at the paper, glancing at the sausages. They weren't the same as the ones in the display cabinets. These were much paler, fattier looking, and nowhere near as appetising as the others. Hence the reason for them being emergency sausages, Emily guessed.

'They'll be fine,' Emily had said.

As she filled out the paperwork, Emily came to the receipt for the test sample. Frank had told her that he sold them at the same price as the ones in the display — almost two pounds per sausage. It was obvious to Emily that the sausages she'd been given weren't sold for that price, but what the hell, she thought. It wasn't her paying for them, and if Frank Pinch wanted to screw over the Food Standards Agency for a few quid over some manky looking pork sausages, she wasn't going to argue with him. Emily signed off the rest of the forms and walked back into the shop where Frank was just in the middle of finishing a deal over some pork belly.

'Just remember my dear,' Frank said to the little old lady he was serving. 'When you cook these, they need to be treated like a man should treat a woman. Take a couple of hours to get them properly warmed up.' He paused, and Emily saw the pensioner lick her pale lips like a lizard before he continued in a stage whisper. 'And then devour them.' The old lady's face lit up, and she dug into her handbag for her purse.

'Jesus wept,' Emily said under her breath. She was no prude, but even that was taking it a bit far. Catherine had been right to insist the two of them escape out of the fire door the other night.

Emily waited until the pensioner had left the shop and handed Frank the paperwork. She flinched as he brushed his hand against hers, but he didn't seem to notice.

'Thank you, my dear,' Frank said with a smile that sent a shiver down Emily's spine. Time to go.

'You just need to sign here, and here,' she said, pointing at a couple of areas on the page. Frank signed the paperwork with a well chewed biro. If Emily had noticed it earlier, she might have commented on it in her report, but it was too late now. He handed the papers back to Emily, and she managed to take them off him without touching him. 'Thank you so much,' she said with as bright a voice as she could manage. 'I think everything will be fine, but I'm sure the agency will be in touch with you if there is anything else.' Emily paused for a few seconds, considering asking Frank to fill out a customer satisfaction survey, but she thought better of it.

As she walked over to the door, another customer walked through it. The young man took a step back, standing underneath the dinging bell over the door and holding it open for her. Emily mumbled 'thank you' as she brushed past him, grateful to be back in the open air. She wasn't quite sure what to make of Frank, but she was quite happy not to be in the same room as him anymore.

27

'Are these local, mate?' Andy said to the butcher behind the counter. 'These sausages here?' He pointed to a bundle of sausages in the display counter. 'They're from round here, yeah?'

'Yes, they are. Very local,' the butcher replied. 'The meat in them sausages hasn't even been to Suffolk, let alone anywhere foreign.'

'They're a bit on the expensive side, aren't they?'

'You get what you pay for, sunshine.' Andy looked at the butcher with a critical eye as he said this. It wasn't his money that he was spending, but even so, two quid for a sausage was taking the piss just a little bit.

'Have you got any sausage meat?'

'Yes, I have. How much do you want?'

'Er, not sure. Medium size bag?' Andy replied. 'And eight sausages.'

'No problemo, compadre. Coming right up.'

Andy watched as the butcher wrapped a bunch of sausages for him and put them on the counter with a bag of what he assumed was sausage meat. No problemo?

Compadre? All a bit weird as far as Andy was concerned. Even though Andy didn't have any children, he knew one thing for certain. He wouldn't let this man babysit if he did.

'How much is that, then?' Andy asked.

'Well,' the butcher replied, extending out the word with his tongue. 'That should be twenty-five quid, but seeing as you're a new customer, I'll do it for twenty.'

'Bargain,' Andy said, not even trying to hide the sarcasm in his voice. 'Can I get a receipt though?'

'Course you can.'

Andy waited for the butcher to fill out the receipt. As he was putting the sausages and bag of sausage meat into his bag, Andy heard the bell over the top of the door tinkle. He turned to see the woman he'd just held the door open for walk back into the shop.

'Is that your yellow sports car in the car park?' she said. Andy looked at her. She was pretty, that was for sure. Very pretty. And also familiar, but Andy couldn't work out where from.

'Er, yeah, it is. Sorry. Am I blocking you in?' he said.

'Just a bit.'

'I'm just buying some sausages. Can I have two seconds?' Andy looked at the butcher who had stopped writing the receipt and was looking at the new arrival with a crooked smile. The woman didn't reply, but just fixed the butcher with a withering look. Andy looked at her, trying to work out where he knew her from.

A few minutes later, he was following her into the car park. She stood by her Mini, arms crossed, looking at him with an annoyed expression. He definitely knew her from somewhere. Andy blipped the remote, unlocking his car, and decided to take a chance. The young woman was very attractive, so he decided to throw caution to the winds. He twiddled his MG Owners Club key ring in his hands to hide his nervousness.

'Look, sorry, I know this sounds like a line. But do I know you from somewhere?'

'Don't think so.'

'Oh, okay, sorry. It's just you look really familiar, that's all. I'm sure I've seen your face somewhere before though.'

'Yeah, now that is a line.'

'It wasn't meant to be,' Andy said, glancing at the ID card around her neck. 'Sorry.'

'Don't be. Maybe if you could just shift your car, though?'

'Oh God, sorry,' Andy said. 'Of course.' He walked toward his car, thinking. He definitely didn't know anyone called Emily Underwood, the name on her ID card. Nor did he know anyone at the Food Standards Agency. As he reached the driver's door of his car, he turned to look again at the woman and the penny dropped. 'Oh fuck, it's you.'

'What?' the woman said as she took a step toward him. Andy had never before experienced his testicles involuntarily retracting, but the sensation made him wince. He fumbled at the door of his car, throwing it open. The sound of the engine starting reassured him, but not as much as the sensation of speeding away from the car park. He looked up at the rear view mirror to see the woman who'd floored him with a knee to the groin staring after him, hands on hips.

Andy thought back to that day, when he'd accidentally assaulted her before she'd quite deliberately assaulted him. Before he pushed the thought that she had rather nice breasts to the back his mind, considering how he'd come by that information, he grinned. Emily Underwood. What a shame they'd not met under different circumstances.

Three hours and several butcher's and farm shops later, Andy had managed to fill the boot of his MG with various types of local produce and spend every penny that Rob had given him. Everything from Frank Pinch's sausage meat to ostrich eggs. Well, one ostrich egg from a farm near Cromer that had an ostrich. He'd not actually seen the bird itself, but where else were they going to get an ostrich egg from? The farmer, an old boy who looked like he belonged at the helm of a lifeboat instead of a tractor, had thrown in a carrier bag full of Cromer crabs for nothing. Andy had some bad memories of Cromer crabs having been mauled by one when he was younger. Except that wasn't even in Cromer, it was in Swaffham.

Andy turned the radio on to take his mind off both the crabbing incident and Emily's breasts. He was just in time to hear an advert for the forthcoming competition. Set to some nasty background music that belonged in a lift, a nasal sounding woman's voice droned on in an unsuccessful attempt at excitement.

'This Saturday, live at The Forum, Kett's of Norwich are launching their new competition to find the Pride of Anglia. Winners in each category will get an exclusive contract through Kett's of Norwich to supply the whole of the fine city.' The woman paused and took an audible deep breath. No expense spared in a recording studio then, Andy thought. 'So come along for a fun-tastic time at The Forum with Kett's of Norwich. This Saturday, starting at ten. See you there.'

Andy laughed to himself, repeating the phrase 'Come along for a fun-tastic time at The Forum.' That had Rob written all over it. He was still chuckling when he pulled into the underground car park under Partridge Towers. Once he'd unloaded the contents of the boot of his car, he made his way to his desk and logged in to his computer to check his emails. He only had one e-mail, and that was for a product that a man his age shouldn't need just yet. He bookmarked it anyway, just in case, as an instant message popped up from 'Martin the Intern.'

Wassup….? Really, Andy thought as he typed a reply.

Hi mate, just back from shopping. What's occurring?

Not a lot. We've got to go to the Waterfront tonight though. The Waterfront was a live music bar, run by the University of East Anglia, that was a popular spot for students. It was also a popular spot for people like Martin who tried to prey on them, usually unsuccessfully.

Why? Andy typed.

There's a good band on, but it's also someone's birthday and that's where they're celebrating.

'Who?'

'Guess.'

'I don't know. Who?'

It's only, Martin's message showed him still typing, so Andy waited. *Karen from Accounts.* The message was finished with three smiley faces and some ASCII art that Andy had to turn his head to one side to see properly. It was crude, but pretty effective. Only Martin would know how to make a penis out of a bunch of dashes and colons.

28

Tom sat at the kitchen table after lunch, a copy of the Eastern Daily News open in front of him. He always bought the paper on a Friday because that was when the classified advertisements were printed. Ever since he left school, his treat to himself on a Friday was the newspaper and the classified ads.

Wiggling a pencil between his fingers, he scanned the ads line by line. He wasn't looking for anything in particular. It was more a case of just looking until he found something he wanted.

'One bucket,' he mumbled to himself. 'Small hole in bottom. 50p.' Tom wasn't sure, but he was fairly certain he'd seen buckets for sale in Homebase a few days ago for 50 pence, and they wouldn't have holes in the bottom. He put a small cross next to the advert to mark it as read. That way, if he came back to the paper later on, he'd know that he'd already seen this one. The next advert was for a canoe. No mention of a hole in the bottom. 'Hmm,' Tom said before spending the next ten minutes or so considering whether or not a canoe would be useful. The farm wasn't that far from the Norfolk Broads, and he'd seen people canoeing along them when he'd been out walking alongside the river. They looked as if they were having fun, if he remembered correctly. The only thing wrong with the ad was that it didn't say what colour the canoe was. He hoped it was blue, or green at a push. A red one would just look silly. Tom carefully drew a box around the advert so that he could speak to Frank about it later on when he got back from work.

Tom made himself a cup of tea and decided to read the rest of the newspaper before coming back to the rest of the classified ads after supper. If he read them all in one go, he reasoned, he'd have nothing to look forward to after he'd eaten. He turned the newspaper to see a full-page infomercial for the 'Pride of Anglia' competition. Tom's eyebrows went up as he started reading the article. His eyes flicked up to a picture of a woman who, according to the caption, was off the telly. He couldn't remember seeing her on the television though, but as he read the small text under her picture he realised why. It was because she did the weather, and he never watched the weather. Why would he need to when he was a farmer? He could predict the weather better than any skinny blonde woman on the television. Tom leaned toward the picture and examined it. Maybe he should start watching the weather forecast, after all? She was, what was the phrase that Frank used? Fit as fun. That was it, Tom thought, or at least it was something like that.

Tom thought back to one evening just after his birthday a few months ago. Frank had bought him a lovely new pair of slippers, and Tom had gone off to bed leaving Frank watching the television. When he'd got to his room, Tom saw the slippers and decided to put them on to show Frank. When Tom shuffled his way back to the lounge,

Frank was watching the weather forecast and, from what Tom could see, itching his leg furiously. Frank had been really, really annoyed when Tom startled him by asking him what he thought of the slippers.

'They're lovely, Tom,' Frank had said, so angry he looked as if he was about to throw something at Tom. 'Now bugger off and let me watch the weather in privacy.' At least Frank would enjoy going to see the weather lady, Tom thought.

The Pride of Anglia competition looked like it might be quite entertaining. There were different sections for different types of produce, the only thing linking it all together was the fact that it was all from East Anglia. There was a cheese competition, a sausage competition, even an egg competition. Tom wasn't sure how an egg competition worked, but Frank was very partial to a nice bit of cheese, so he'd enjoy that bit even if the egg competition was rubbish.

Tom finished reading the article, and after checking what was on the other side of the page to make sure there were no unread classified ads, carefully ripped down the centre of the page to remove it from the rest of the paper. He used the pencil to print 'Frank — what do you think?' across the top and put the article on the kitchen table for his brother to read.

Getting to his feet, Tom glanced out of the kitchen window to see if a coat would be needed for going down to check on the pigs. Clear blue skies. It looked like it was going to be a lovely day. Tom was going to have to walk down to the pig sheds as they were almost out of red diesel for the tractor. Frank was supposed to be picking up a couple of jerry cans full on his way back, and as the Land Rover was almost out of diesel as well, Tom knew Frank wouldn't forget as they needed the red diesel for both vehicles even though they weren't supposed to use it in the Land Rover. Something to do with tax, Frank said.

By the time he got to the pig sheds, Tom's teeth were chattering so much they hurt. He rubbed his hands together as he walked into the main shed. It was marginally warmer in there thanks to the heater in the corner. Tom was going to turn it off, as it was only supposed to be on at night, but he decided to leave it on for a bit longer.

'Morning, Boris,' Tom called to the boar in his pen. 'You dirty old goat.' Boris looked back at him with barely disguised hostility. 'You've got a visitor this afternoon mate, know what I mean? Nudge nudge, wink wink and all that.' Boris didn't answer. Tom walked over to the three sows in their pens and checked their water trough. 'Morning, ladies,' Tom said, giving one of them an affectionate scratch behind the ear.

Tom spent the next hour or so pottering around the pig sheds, tidying stuff up and talking to the pigs. He was just about to start walking back to the farmhouse when his mobile phone rang.

'Hello?'

'Tom, it's Frank.'

'I know,' Tom replied. 'It comes up on the screen.'

'If you know, why not start with 'Hello Frank' then?' Frank sounded annoyed, but Tom didn't think it was his fault, so he didn't say anything. 'Are you there?'

'Yep, I'm here,' Tom replied.

'The Range Rover's on the blink again. I was going to nip out and get some diesel, but the bloody thing won't start. Can you come and collect me later?'

'Sure, what time?'

'Half five okay? We'll put the jerry cans on the back of the tractor and get some diesel on the way back.'

'Okay,' Tom said and ended the call. Just as he did so,

he remembered that he'd forgotten to say goodbye, which was another thing Frank kept going on about.

Tom hurried back to the farmhouse with a smile on his face. It wasn't very often that Frank needed his help, but he needed it today.

29

E mily opened the door to her flat and threw her bag down in the hallway. Thank God today was over, she thought as she walked into the kitchen.

'Catherine?' Emily called out to her flat mate. 'You in?' She heard a muffled shout from the bathroom. Walking over to the kettle, she flung a sorry-looking bunch of flowers on the table.

When she'd got back to the office after finishing the inspection at Frank Pinch's butcher's, Mr Clayton had called Emily into his office for yet another 'chat'. It was part of the formal warning that they regularly discussed her performance, at least it would be for the next few months. The discussion had started off okay, with the two of them talking about some of the visits that she'd done over the last week. Emily had been ultra-careful not to wind anyone up, and on more than one occasion she'd bent the rules a fair bit to help people avoid fines or worse.

There was a kebab shop on Prince of Wales road, one of the most popular streets in Norwich on a Friday and Saturday night, that by the letter of the law should have been closed down a long time ago. When she'd inspected it earlier in the week, Emily had pointed out several infringements to the owners before popping out for half an hour. By the time she got back, the infringements had disappeared, and she was able to give them a relatively clean bill of health. Emily doubted they would display their two stars for food hygiene in the window though.

'So, Emily,' Mr Clayton had said. From the expression on his face, she knew the conversation was about to go downhill. 'Tell me about your visit to the Food Hall at Jarrolds?'

'Er, the visit to the Food Hall, or what happened afterwards?' Emily replied with a sinking feeling in her stomach.

'Start with the Food Hall.' Emily told Mr Clayton about the inspection. Jarrolds was one of the largest department stores in Norwich, and known as being 'a bit posh' by most of the locals. Emily suspected that the majority of the customers who shopped there were from the North Norfolk coast, where all the rich second-homers hung out, but she'd not been able to fault the Food Hall.

'I did the paperwork, handed it over to the Food Hall supervisor, and gave them their five star rating. The supervisor seemed quite happy with it, Mr Clayton.'

'Oh, she was,' Mr Clayton replied. 'Very happy indeed. She filled out the feedback form and was full of praise for you.' Emily managed a weak smile. She knew what was coming next. 'So how about what happened after the inspection?'

'Well, Mr Clayton, that was a genuine mistake. I'm not quite sure what happened, it must have been as I was walking through the lingerie department on the way out. I didn't steal it.' Emily looked at her boss, imploring him to believe her. 'It must have got stuck to me somehow.'

When Emily had tried to leave the department store, the shop's alarms had gone off and she'd been surrounded by security guards in seconds. There was an item of clothing, complete with the security tag, attached to her bag.

'You nearly got arrested for shoplifting, Emily,' Mr Clayton said with a sigh.

'But I didn't, Mr Clayton, did I?' Emily replied. 'I explained what must have happened, and they let me go. I didn't even know that you knew about it.'

'Emily, when a member of the Food Standards Agency's staff is stopped trying to leave an up-market department store with an expensive item of clothing, how do you think we would not get to hear about it?' Mr Clayton stared at Emily, and she felt herself withering under his intense gaze. 'We had a report sent in from the manager down there.'

They sat in silence for a few seconds. Emily couldn't think of anything to say in her defence that she'd not said already. Mr Clayton leafed through some papers on his desk.

'What was it that you tried to nick, anyway? Sorry, what was it that got stuck to your bag?' he asked. 'All it says in the report is lingerie.'

'It was a bra and pantie set,' Emily replied. 'The bra was a forty-four double G, and the pants were a size twenty. Not my size by some distance, and they were bright pink as well. Not my colour, either.' Mr Clayton looked at Emily, and for a horrible moment she thought he was about to ask her what her size and favourite colour of lingerie were. He didn't say anything though, and just ended the interview by mumbling about another review in a few weeks' time.

'Until then, we'll be keeping a close eye on you,' he had said as she walked out of his office.

Catherine walked into the kitchen, drying her hair with a bright green towel.

'Do you want a cup of tea, Catherine?' Emily asked her flat mate.

'Is it too early for a glass of wine?'

'Probably a bit early,' Emily laughed, looking at the clock on the kitchen wall. It was just before six. 'Have a cuppa first, then a glass of vino after.'

'Sounds good to me,' Catherine replied. 'Ooh, you've got flowers.'

'Yeah, right.' Emily watched Catherine examine the sad bouquet on the table. 'Emergency flowers from the corner shop. Reduced, as well. Even when they were full price, they were only a fiver.'

'Well, it's the thought that counts. Who are they from?'

'That bloke who I kneed in the testicles a few days ago. There's a card attached to them.'

'To Emily,' Catherine read from the card. 'Sorry for grabbing your tits. It was an accident. Andy.' Catherine started laughing and, despite her bad mood, Emily joined in. 'Who says romance isn't dead?' Catherine said. 'Even after you kicked him in the bollocks, he's left a phone number. Talk about treat them mean, keep them keen. Are you going to call him?'

'Am I heck,' Emily said, crossing to the kitchen table. She picked up the flowers and threw them in the bin. 'I'm waiting for that bloke from the lab to call. Gary.'

'Do you not think Gary would have phoned by now if he was interested?'

'Give him time,' Emily replied. 'He'll come round. I've got another sample in the fridge at work to take to the lab at some point.'

'Stalker.'

'Oh shut up, Catherine. You've not seen him.'

'Well, good luck to you girl.'

Emily made them both a cup of tea and they sat in the lounge for a while watching television. Catherine flicked through the channels, but didn't settle on one for more than a few minutes.

'We should go out tonight, Emily,' Catherine said after eventually settling on a re-run of *Friends*. 'What do you think?'

'I don't know,' Emily replied. 'I was thinking more along the lines of a long, hot bath, several glasses of wine, and a good book.' She needed to get her diary up to date as well, before she fell too far behind with it.

'A good book?' Catherine said. 'My God, how old are you exactly? You're in the prime of your life. You should be out there playing the field before you are actually old.' Emily laughed. This was a conversation they'd had many times before.

'Whatever, Catherine,' she said, getting to her feet. 'I'm going to have the first of those glasses of wine now. You want one?'

'Of course,' Catherine said. 'Listen, how about the Waterfront? Later on? There's a band playing tonight that are supposed to be brilliant. My mate Becky at work said the lead singer is to die for.'

'Maybe,' Emily said. 'Let me have a bath first and I'll see how I feel. But if we do go out, I'm only having a couple. I've got work tomorrow.'

'Yeah, yeah, yeah,' Catherine mumbled as Emily walked back into the kitchen, a wry smile on her face.

30

Andy laid his head down on top of his folded arms and groaned. He felt like shit and knew that he didn't look much better. There was a ding from the computer on his desk, but he didn't bother looking up. It would just be another instant message from Martin about last night. Andy held Martin personally responsible for what had happened by starting them both off on flaming sambucas before the band had even started. Martin's rationale for starting early was that as there was no sign of Karen from Accounts, they might as well get smashed.

'Andy, wake up,' Rob's sharp voice cut through Andy's headache. He raised his head and peered at the marketing manager.

'Sorry, Rob,' he said, almost in a whisper. 'I'm not feeling so good.'

'Andy, you look like shite and you stink of booze.' A packet of extra strong mints rolled their way onto his desk. 'Suck on some of those, and sort yourself out. We've got a brief in the conference room in thirty minutes.'

'Do I have to?'

'Yes, Andy. You do. Charles has said everyone has to be there. Even the bloody useless interns. So, zip up your man suit and suck it up.' Andy put his head back onto his forearms and groaned again.

Twenty-five minutes later, Andy was sitting in the conference room in one of the chairs nearest the door. He was feeling marginally better, courtesy of some strong coffee and aspirins that one of the marketing team had brought to him with a sympathetic smile. Andy had been drinking the coffee when another message popped up from Martin. Andy had opened the message to see that there was an attachment. With a sinking feeling in his stomach, Andy had opened the attachment to see a picture of himself from last night. It was right at the end of the evening, and in the photo he could be seen being ejected from the Waterfront by a couple of burly security guards. Apart from a smiley faced emoji that someone had thankfully photoshopped over his groin, he wasn't wearing a stitch of clothing. The looks of disgust on the bouncers' faces said it all.

'Mate, you're trending on Twitter,' the text under the picture said. 'And Pinterest.'

'Ladies, gentlemen,' Charles stormed into the room, making Andy jump. 'Good morning everyone.' Charles sniffed the air. 'My God, what's that smell?' Andy looked down, hoping that it wasn't him. 'Thank you all for coming.' The room was filled with everyone from the marketing team Rob sat at the front of the room like an expectant puppy looking for a treat. Charles strode over to join him. 'Right, before I start, could you give an update on tomorrow's events please, Rob?'

'Certainly, Charles,' Rob replied. 'Thank you. Now, I did want to say a few words while I've got the whole team here. The last couple of weeks have been extremely busy

for the whole marketing department, and while I've done
the bulk of the work, I wanted to thank you all for playing
your part. Being a leader's not easy at the best of times, so
your support and all the little bits and pieces you've done
under my supervision have really helped.'

'Rob, Rob,' Charles laughed, slapping him on the back.
Slightly too hard from the look on Rob's face. 'You're
doing yourself down. There's no 'I' in team, is there?'

No, Andy thought. *But there is a 'u' in cun—*

'Andy?' His thoughts were interrupted by Rob shouting
at him. 'Could you open the door at bit please? It's getting
a bit stuffy in here.'

Rob spent the next twenty minutes or so outlining the
plans for the competition at The Forum in the morning.
There was nothing in his speech that hadn't already been
covered several times in the numerous meetings that they'd
had. The only difference was that now it sounded as if Rob
had done absolutely everything. Andy recognised his
speech for what it was — an attempt to impress the Big
Cheese. From the look on Charles' face, it was working,
and the bored expressions on everyone else's faces told
Andy it wasn't the first time Rob had done this.

'Rob, thank you,' Charles said when Rob had wound
up his one-man band act. The Big Cheese extended his
hands out to the room. 'And a huge thank you to all of you
for everything you've done to help Rob out.' There were
one or two wry smiles in the room. 'Now, I do have one
thing to talk to you all about. There was a lot of produce
bought for the competition. I was amazed by just how
much Rob had managed to get hold of when I went
through the fridges in the Executive Suite last night. But
when I went to the fridges this morning, I noticed that
some of the produce was missing.'

Charles picked up his phone and the room watched as

he prodded at the screen with fat fingers. 'Yes,' Charles continued when he had finished messing with his phone. 'There was some missing.' He furrowed his eyebrows as he looked around the room before breaking into a wide smile, tilting his head back, and laughing. 'Some sausage meat, no less.'

Andy thought back to the butcher's shop he'd gone to the other day where he'd met Emily from the Food Standards Agency, who was increasingly replacing Karen in Accounts as his current favourite daydream. That was the only place he'd bought sausage meat from, so that must be the one. He wondered if Emily had got the flowers he'd dropped off at the front desk, and if she had, what she'd thought of them? It was a very long shot, thinking that she might text him or something, but as Martin always said, 'Nothing ventured, nothing gained.'

The door of the conference room opened, and a short, round woman with grey hair walked through. Mrs Lebbon, her name was, and she ran the staff canteen. With an iron fist, according to the other staff who worked there. She was carrying a large silver tray in her hands with a sheet of grease proof paper over the top of it. As she walked toward the front of the room, Charles beamed at her and at everyone else. When she put the tray on the table, Charles removed the paper with a flourish.

'It was me who stole the sausage meat,' he said with a broad grin. 'And it was Mrs Lebbon here who made it into sausage rolls.' He picked up the tray and started working his way round the room.

'My God, these smell amazing,' one of the marketing managers said. The woman sitting next to him picked up a sausage roll and bit into it with an exaggerated 'Mmmm' noise. Andy watched, disgusted, as a trickle of fat ran down her chin. She mopped it up with an obese finger which then disappeared into her mouth. The smell of the freshly cooked meat water round the room, and Andy started salivating. From the churning in his stomach, it wasn't from hunger. By the time Charles got to the back of the room, there were only a few sausage rolls left.

'You there, new boy,' Charles said, looking at Andy and waving the tray under his nose. 'Sausage roll?' Andy looked at the tray and the sausage rolls as he caught a really strong whiff of the meat. He jumped to his feet, almost knocking the tray from Charles' grasp.

'Sorry, gonnabesick,' Andy muttered as he pushed past the Big Cheese and out of the door. He made it to the toilet cubicle just in time, wrapping his arms around the white bowl and filling it full of half-digested coffee and extra-strong mints. Andy groaned before retching again. He was looking through teary eyes at the contents of his stomach when he heard a voice from behind him.

'Are you okay?' the voice asked. A woman's voice. He looked over his shoulder to see who it belonged to. 'You do know this is the Ladies' toilet, don't you?'

'Hi Karen,' Andy managed before his stomach contracted again.

31

Tom leaned his head back to enjoy the early morning sunshine. He would have closed his eyes, but that would have meant he wouldn't be able to see the road in front of him.

'It's a lovely day, Frank,' Tom shouted over the noise of the tractor. Frank replied with something that Tom couldn't hear, but the fact that he had replied was good enough for Tom.

The brothers were half way to Norwich, Tom at the wheel of the tractor and Frank sitting snugly behind him on a seat that was only designed for one. Tom chuckled to himself as he remembered how the two of them used to cycle round Norfolk on the single bicycle they owned between them in much the same way. Most of the time it had been Frank in front, which was his prerogative as the older brother, but every once in a while, Tom was allowed to take the handlebars. These days it was different. Frank hated driving the tractor, so Tom always got to sit in the front.

The tractor rumbled past a layby, one of several on this

stretch of single carriageway road, and Tom heard several angry car horns behind him. He couldn't work out why, when the weather was as nice as it was today, people were in such a hurry. A few miles ago, a silver Audi TT had powered past them on a blind bend and only just missed another tractor coming in the opposite direction. Both brothers had laughed at the way the silver car had fish-tailed as the driver fought to keep his car on the road and away from the solid trees at the side of the road. There'd been enough accidents around here for Tom to know that when a car went head to head with a tree, the tree usually won.

A mile further on toward Norwich, the road expanded out into a dual carriageway. Tom kept the tractor in the middle of the two lanes for a couple of hundred yards, as he normally did, before finally moving over to the left-hand side to let the cars behind him overtake. Of the twenty or so cars that passed them, only one driver didn't react in some way. Tom counted eleven middle fingers, two long blasts on car horns, and three hands held out of the window with the index finger and thumb curled in a circle doing a strange wave. He'd seen football fans do the same wave when they disagreed with the referee, but Tom wasn't quite sure what it meant. He made sure that he copied the gesture back at the drivers, which made Frank laugh at least.

The only driver who didn't react was a little old lady driving a clapped out little green car. She inched past the tractor, hands grasped on the steering wheel. Tom could hear the car engine screaming above the rattle of the tractor and wondered why she didn't change up a gear or two. A few hundred yards before the dual carriageway turned back into a single lane road, she managed to coax the car past the brothers.

Tom drove down Newmarket Road, one of the main approaches into Norwich from the countryside. It wasn't known as Millionaires' Row for nothing. As they drove past one mansion, Frank pointed at the huge house and leaned into Tom's ear.

'When we win the lottery, Tom,' he shouted, 'we'll have that one.' Tom nodded in reply.

A few minutes later, Tom approached the familiar glass-fronted facade of the Forum. There weren't many parking spaces in Norwich for tractors, so he decided to park in the open space just outside the front of the building. Several depressed looking teenagers, dressed almost entirely in black, scattered as he manoeuvred the tractor into position. Tom turned the ignition off and sighed as the engine died.

'We're here, Frank,' he said.

'Yep,' his brother replied as he climbed down from the back of the seat, using Tom's leg as a handle to get to the floor. 'We are indeed.'

The two brothers walked toward a coffee shop outside the Forum, leaving the tractor where it was. Tom was fairly sure that they wouldn't get a ticket parked where they were, and Frank had agreed. After all, he'd asked Tom, how was a traffic warden going to put a ticket on the windscreen when there wasn't a windscreen to stick it to? As they got to the door of the coffee shop, a young man approached them with an equally young woman in tow. Tom took in the stranger's pale white face, blonde dreadlocks, and emaciated frame under a baggy hoodie and what looked like bright red pyjama trousers. The man's companion was equally oddly dressed, and she stared at Tom through pale grey eyes. Her hair matched his trousers — it was dyed bright red.

'Take a leaflet, brother,' the man said, offering Tom a

dog-eared piece of paper. Tom caught the smell of his breath and was reminded of the time his father had tried to diversify into mushroom farming. The venture hadn't gone well, but the smell of compost and rotting mushrooms was still familiar.

'Er, yeah. Thanks,' Tom managed to say before Frank leaned over his shoulder and grabbed the leaflet from the stranger's hand.

'What's this about?' Frank asked. Tom sensed the anger in the question.

'Meat is murder, man. We're protesting against this competition on behalf of the Norfolk Vegan Alliance.'

'Really?'

'Yeah, man. Animals have feelings, you know? They're sentient.'

Tom looked at the leaflet in Frank's hand. There was a picture of a pig on the front of it, with some text that Tom couldn't make out properly apart from the words 'murder', 'cruelty', and 'vegetables'. He was just about to say something when Frank pushed past him and leaned toward the protester.

'Animals are meat, fella,' Frank snarled. 'Why do you think some of your teeth are really pointy?' Tom didn't understand what Frank meant, but from his tone of voice and the look on the other man's face, he didn't think Frank was trying to make friends with him.

'There's another way. It's your choice to be a carnivore.' Tom realised that Frank and the other man's foreheads were only inches away from each other. Tom was just about to try to step between them when the stranger's companion intervened.

'Rupert, leave it,' she said in a reedy voice as she placed a bony hand on his chest. 'He's too far gone for help. Look at his eyes.' Tom looked at Frank's eyes, but they looked pretty normal to him. The woman tugged at her companion's sleeve. 'Come on, he's not worth it. Just leave him.' Frank and Rupert stared at each other for a few seconds until finally, to Tom's relief, Frank broke off the confrontation. He pushed past the protestor and his companion, and strode toward the doors of the coffee shop. Tom followed him, flashing a quick smile at the man holding the leaflets.

Inside the coffee shop, Tom stood next to his brother while they waited in the queue to order.

'What was that about, Frank?' Tom asked.

'Just some nut job,' he replied. 'I wouldn't worry about it. He was protesting against people eating meat. I'll go and grab us a table while you get the coffees.' Frank walked through the coffee shop toward the front window where there were a couple of empty tables. Tom thought about Frank's reply as he watched his brother glare out of the window at the protestors who were talking to a couple of teenagers. If people didn't eat meat, Tom thought, then what did they eat? That didn't make any sense to him.

'What would you like?' a female voice interrupted his thoughts. He looked at the young woman behind the counter. According to her name badge, she was called Christine.

'Can I have two coffees, please?'

'Sure,' the woman said with a broad smile. 'What type can I get you? Cappuccino? Americano? Flat white perhaps?' Tom stared at her, not sure what to say. 'How about a mocha with a chocolate sprinkle?' Her smile was starting to falter.

'Can I have ones with milk in please?' Tom asked. Christine hiked her smile back up again.

'Sure, coming up.'

32

'Do you want a cup of tea, Catherine?' Emily called through her flat mate's bedroom door. She heard a grunt from the other side of the door. 'Is that a yes?'

'Yes.' The reply was half shout, half groan.

'One sugar or was it a two sugars kind of night?'

'Just the one, ta.'

Emily went back into the kitchen and bustled around to make them both a cuppa. She glanced at her watch. It was nearly eleven o'clock in the morning and Emily wanted to get into the city. She had no idea what time Catherine had got back last night, or whether she'd been on her own when she got back. A couple of months ago, Emily had walked into the kitchen to find a very good-looking man tiptoeing across the floor toward the front door. She had stared at him, open mouthed, as she pulled her dressing gown across her chest. The man just looked at her with bleary eyes and raised his index fingers to his lips.

'Shhh,' he'd said as he tiptoed past. 'Don't wake her up. She's bloody bonkers, she is.' When Catherine had got up later on that morning, Emily had asked her if she had a good night.

'It wasn't too bad,' Catherine had said, not even batting an eyelid. It had taken Emily three days and a full bottle of wine in Catherine's stomach before she'd spilled the beans. The bloke's name was James, he was proper posh and worked in a bank somewhere in Norwich. Catherine never wanted to see him again, much less sleep with him. Apparently at one point, during a particularly intimate moment, he'd called her 'Mummy'.

By the time the kettle had boiled, Catherine had surfaced. Emily heard the shower start up, so held off on the tea until Catherine made an appearance.

'Morning,' Catherine said when she came out of the shower, wet hair plastered over her shoulder.

'Morning,' Emily replied. 'Get up to much last night?' Catherine smiled wryly, which told Emily that something had happened at some point.

'Yeah, was okay. Ended up at the Waterfront again.' Emily handed Catherine her cup of tea. 'Cheers mate.' They both sat at the table. 'I don't know if it's me getting old, or if it's the crowd there getting younger, but I didn't half feel ancient.' Emily smiled at her flat mate.

'Sure, Catherine,' Emily said. 'You must have been at least three years older than most of them.'

'Seriously,' Catherine replied with a laugh. 'I was talking to one lad who said he had a thing about MILFs, so when he saw me he just had to buy me a drink.' Emily giggled at the thought of it.

'Let me guess,' she said. 'You let him buy you a drink and then told him to piss off?'

'Yep, you got it,' Catherine replied. 'I told him he wouldn't last two minutes with a cougar like me, and that he should go home to his mother. I ended up talking to a bunch of Spanish blokes.'

'What, tourists? This time of year?'

'No, football fans,' Catherine said. 'Norwich City are at home today.'

'Who are they playing?'

'Barcelona, I think.'

'Oh, okay. So, any gossip?' Emily asked.

'Possibly,' Catherine smirked. 'There may have been a small exchange of fluids with one of them.'

'Catherine, you are such a slapper,' Emily smiled as she got to her feet.

'I think the term you're looking for is 'cultural ambassador' as opposed to 'slapper',' Catherine replied. 'At least when Jose goes back home to Barcelona he's got a positive experience of our fine city to tell his amigos about.'

'Jose?' Emily laughed. 'Really? He was called Jose?' She looked at Catherine who just shrugged her shoulders and tried to look innocent. It didn't fool Emily for a minute. 'Do you actually know what his name was?'

'What are we doing today anyway, Emily?' Catherine ignored Emily's question. 'Are we going into the city?'

'Yeah, if that's okay,' Emily replied. 'There's a Pride of Anglia competition at the Forum.'

'I thought Pride was in the spring?'

'Not that sort of Pride,' Emily said. 'It's an agricultural competition. One of the local supermarkets is trying to find the best local produce.'

'An agricultural competition? You want me to go to an agricultural competition with you?'

'Catherine, come on,' Emily pleaded. 'There's loads of people from the Food Standards Agency going. I can introduce you to some of them.'

'Is there a certain young gentleman from the laboratory going, young lady?'

'There might be, I don't know. But if he is there…'

'Don't worry, I get it,' Catherine held her hands up in mock surrender. 'Hands off. What was his name again? Gareth, was it?'

'Gary,' Emily replied with a broad smile. 'His name's Gary, and he's all mine.'

An hour later, Emily and Catherine were sitting on a bus heading into the city centre. It had only taken Catherine twenty minutes to get ready, and by the time she came out of her bedroom, she looked as if she was dressed up for another night out. That was one thing that never ceased to amaze Emily. It took her ages to get ready, and even then she knew she was never going to look as good as Catherine. Emily hadn't been sure whether or not to wear one of her suits, but Catherine had talked her out of it on the ground that she wasn't at work. On top of that, Catherine had reasoned, if Gary was there it wouldn't do Emily any good if she was dressed in one of her lesbian outfits.

In the end, Emily had settled on a pair of brown slacks and a cream silk blouse. Nothing too slutty, but at the same time, she thought she looked okay. Just the right balance between a work-related outfit, and something that she thought Gary might like. If he was there, that was. Emily and Catherine spent most of the bus journey ignoring a bunch of pre-teenage lads at the back of the bus shouting increasingly vulgar obscenities at them. To be fair, most of the comments were aimed at Catherine, and Emily was surprised that Catherine just sat there and didn't respond. Looking at her flat mate's expression, Emily realised that she was enjoying the male attention, even if was from kids.

They got off the bus and walked through the city

centre toward the Forum, dodging groups of Barcelona fans who were spilling out of the pubs between the bus station and the city centre. Bored looking clusters of policemen and women stood close by, but the police presence was minimal. Emily had read the Evening Daily News website on her phone while they were on the bus, and everyone was predicting an easy win for Norwich City. She looked at the away fans as they walked past the pubs, and most of them looked resigned to losing but determined to have a good time regardless.

'Let me know if you see Jose,' Emily said to Catherine as they walked past a group of half-drunk Spaniards.

'Bugger off,' Catherine muttered with a smile. 'I wouldn't recognise him in daylight, anyway. The alleyway behind the Waterfront's pretty dark.'

The glass fronted facade of the Forum rose above them as they walked up toward the competition venue. A large banner was draped across the front of the building, welcoming visitors to the Pride of Anglia competition. The banner announced that the event was sponsored by Kett's of Norwich. In the open space in front of the building, a traffic warden was looking at an abandoned red tractor, scratching his head as he tried to work out where to put the parking ticket he was clutching in his hand. Emily and Catherine swerved their way past a couple of hippie types who were determined to press a leaflet on them.

'No thanks,' Emily said to the man in baggy trousers as they swept past him and into the main foyer of the Forum. She turned to Catherine as they stood just inside the doors. 'My God, Catherine. Did you see his eyes?'

'Oh yeah,' Catherine replied, looking over her shoulder at the man outside and his companion. 'I did indeed. They were something else, weren't they?'

33

F rank made his way through the crowded coffee shop to an empty table, picking up an abandoned copy of the Eastern Daily News from another table as he did so. He sat down, putting the paper on the glass top, and read the front page. Across the top of the paper was a banner advertisement for the competition they'd come to watch. Frank hadn't been convinced at all about coming, but Tom had been really keen on the idea. Neither of them had been in city for a while, and Frank hadn't been in during the day in ages, so they'd decided to make a day of it. They were going to do the competition in the morning, have lunch somewhere and maybe a pint or two, then head home.

He opened the paper to the double page spread advertising the competition and was reading it carefully when Tom reached the table with two cups of coffee.

'Here you go, Frank,' Tom said as he put them down, spilling a bit of coffee in each saucer.

'Why didn't you get take-out cups?' Frank asked, frowning.

'I didn't have enough money,' Tom replied. 'It would have been an extra two pounds a cup for take-out ones.'

'Two quid? Bloody hell.'

'That's that plastic tax, that is. The coffee on its own is expensive enough.'

'Yeah, well, that's because it's foreign,' Frank said. 'I read in the paper a while ago about some idiot farmer in Suffolk trying to grow coffee to get round the import tax, but it didn't work.' He returned to the paper, and the two of them sat in silence for a few moments.

'Hey, Frank?' Tom said. Frank looked up from the paper to see Tom pointing out of the window. 'There's that woman from the Food Standards Agency.' Frank followed Tom's finger to see the young blonde woman and her friend from the pub dodging the weird bloke with the dreadlocks and leaflets. The two women walked toward the revolving door at the front of the Forum and disappeared from sight.

'So it was,' Frank replied, his lips pressed together. He'd not told Tom about the night in the pub when the friend had been taken ill. Deciding against telling Tom about their disappearing act, he returned to the paper. At the very bottom of the second page of the advertisement was a list of contributors. To his surprise, about halfway down the sausage category were the words 'Frank Pinch, Butcher.'

'Tom?' he said. 'Did you know we've been entered into this thing?' It would be just like Tom to enter them and not say anything, and that would explain why he'd been so keen to come.

'No,' Tom replied, his eyes widening. Frank knew straight away that he was telling the truth. One thing that his brother definitely wasn't was a very good liar. 'No, I didn't know. Honest.'

Frank's frown deepened. He glanced around him and leaned forward, beckoning Tom with his hand to do the same thing.

'The meat that I've been selling in my shop the last week or so,' he whispered. 'Should not have been entered into a bloody competition.'

'I told you, Frank,' Tom hissed back. 'It wasn't me.'

'I know that, Tom. I'm just saying, that's all.'

'But it's still meat.'

'Yes, it is. But if anyone finds out where it comes from, we could get into trouble.'

Tom span the paper round and started reading the advertisement. Frank left him to it, thinking through the potential implications. The more he thought about it, the more he relaxed. Tom was right, it was still meat.

'Oh, Frank. I see what you mean.' Frank looked at his brother, who was pointing at a paragraph in the paper. 'We could get into trouble, you're right.' Frank sighed. My God, his brother could be thick as anything sometimes. 'It's only for local produce.'

'What?' Frank asked.

'It says here. It's only for local produce.'

'Tom, I'm not with you.'

'Well,' Tom said, leaning forward and dropping his voice back to a whisper. 'He was a foreign, wasn't he? I don't know where he was from, but it wasn't Norfolk.' Frank felt his mouth open of its own accord. 'We could get disqualified.'

'Disqualified? Are you fucking serious?' Frank said. 'Tom, we could get in a lot more trouble than that.' They stared at each other for a few seconds.

'I don't like it when you swear, Frank.'

'I know. I'm sorry.'

They spent the next few minutes sipping their coffee

which Frank thought that, despite the price and the fact it was scalding hot, was very good. The sound of a band drifted across the coffee shop, and Frank looked at his watch. It was almost eleven o'clock, time for the competition to begin.

'Come on, Tom,' Frank said. 'The competition's starting. We should head over there.'

'But we've not finished our drinks,' Tom replied, looking down at his half empty cup.

'We can take them with us.'

'What, steal them?'

'No, we can bring them back after.' Frank got to his feet and picked up his cup, angling his body so that he had his back to the counter. Tom did the same, and the two of them shuffled their way to the door. As they walked through the door and across the floor of the Forum, both Frank and Tom were giggling like schoolchildren.

The competition was in one of the conference rooms off the main foyer, and Frank managed to get through the door without spilling any of his coffee. The interior of the room was decorated with yellow and green balloons and banners announcing the 'Pride of Anglia Competition sponsored by Kett's of Norwich'. Along two walls of the room were trestle tables with plates of various types of food laid out on them, all labelled with what they were, and which firm they were from. People were milling about the room in small groups, some sitting on the chairs laid out facing the stage in the corner of the room. Frank was itching to go and find his and Tom's sausages, but the band was beginning to quieten down and a man holding a microphone was walking toward the stage.

'Come on, Tom,' Frank said. 'Let's get a seat before it kicks off.' They found two seats next to each other on the back row and sat down. A moment later, the band finished whatever song they'd been murdering, and shuffled off the stage to be replaced by the man with the microphone. He looked around the room at the expectant crowd. There were, Frank thought, maybe thirty people in the room.

'Hello Norwich,' the man on the stage shouted, and the entire room winced as his words were followed by a high pitched whine through the speakers. 'Hello Norwich,' he repeated, less loudly. There was a silence in the room that lasted for a few seconds before a muted 'Hello' echoed around the room. Another silence followed.

'Fantastic, thank you all for coming. My name is Charles, and I'm the Chief Executive Officer of Kett's of Norwich. Welcome to Pride of Anglia.'

34

A ndy stood to the left of the stage and watched Charles go through his welcome address. Like the rest of the whole marketing department, Andy had heard it three or four times already, and it didn't get any better the more he heard it. Andy's job at the competition was quite simple. He was the media manager for the event. Rob had spent ages telling him what a vital role it was, how he would be crucial to the success of the competition. Andy knew that if it was successful, it would be because of Rob, but if it went wrong, it would be because of everyone else.

Despite sending out press releases to all the local media outlets, magazines, and local television, the only person who'd applied for a press pass was a young lad from the Eastern Daily News. Not surprising really, considering how much they'd spent on advertising in the paper. Andy had met the lad, Josh, in the foyer earlier this morning. It turned out that they'd been at college at the same time. The Eastern Daily News had been so pumped about the competition that they'd sent one of their interns.

The turnout for the presentation wasn't quite as many people as they'd hoped. Rob had even made Andy write an annex to the schedule that dealt with 'crowd management'. The elaborate plans they'd made to deal with hordes of agricultural enthusiasts filing through the room weren't going to be needed. He looked around the room as Charles launched into what Andy knew was the last part of his welcome speech. The front row was full of staff from Kett's of Norwich, with Rob front and centre lapping up every one of Charles' words. Again. A few rows behind them was a small group of elderly ladies, and sitting next to them a couple of confused looking men in Barcelona football shirts were deep in conversation. Andy squinted as he saw the two people sitting at the end of the row. Was that the woman from the Food Standards Agency? Emily? He muttered her name under his breath when he realised it was her. He'd wasted a fiver on a bunch of flowers if the discount to three pounds fifty was ignored and not heard a dicky bird in response. Not even a thank you.

On the stage, Charles was just building up to his final joke. Josh, from the Eastern Daily News, was lurking at the back of the room with a camera, no doubt waiting to capture the standing ovation that Charles so badly wanted. In the end, it was a lukewarm round of applause, but the newspaper intern snapped away anyway. Andy thought Charles hid his disappointment well as the CEO went on to introduce the guest of honour, Tina Lovett. The night time weather presenter from ITV Eastern. Andy saw Emily mouth the word 'who?' to her friend who just shrugged her shoulders in return.

Over the next thirty minutes, Charles and Tina announced the winners of the competition. Apart from a burst of excitement when an ostrich egg was announced as winning the 'Egg-cellent' category, Andy could tell the crowd was getting restless. He was pretty sure that if one person got up and left, most of the rest of them would follow.

'So, we're now building up to the grand winner,' Charles said, trying to keep the momentum going, but in reality coming across to Andy as sounding desperate. The CEO was holding a large golden envelope in his hand which he handed to the weather presenter. 'Tina, would you be so kind as to open the envelope and announce which local producer has won an exclusive contract with Kett's of Norwich?' Tina Lovett fumbled the envelope and had to lean forward to catch it. Andy chuckled to himself as he saw Charles' eyes glance down at her chest as her dress fell away from her not insignificant breasts. She was stick thin, but had tits that must have cost a fortune.

'Ladies and Gentlemen, the winner of the Pride of Anglia competition is...' Tina Lovett pulled out a small piece of paper from the envelope. '...Mr Frank Pinch, butcher, for his artisan sausages.'

At the sound of a china cup smashing, several heads in the crowd swivelled round to look at the back of the room. Andy followed their stares and saw the two men sitting on the rear seats. When he recognised the man who'd dropped his cup, Andy tugged at Charles' sleeve.

'Charles? Charles?'

'Who are you?'

'Andy, one of your interns. That's him, at the back.'

'That's who?'

'The butcher. That's Frank Pinch, the butcher. The winner.'

Charles grabbed the microphone back off the surprised weather presenter.

'Ladies, Gentlemen,' Charles said. 'I've just been told by Mandy, one of my staff, that the winner is actually here this morning. Mr Pinch? Would you like to come up to the stage?' Andy watched as the butcher and the man with him, who were by this time half-way to the door, stopped in their tracks. Frank looked toward the stage, his eyes wide. 'Please, Mr Pinch. Come on up.'

Rob, from his position in the front row, started a round of applause which was picked up by the rest of the marketing department. Andy laughed as the butcher made his way to the front of the room and past the Barcelona fans who obviously hadn't got a clue what was going on. As Charles tried to do an impromptu interview with the terrified winner, Rob pulled Andy to one side of the stage.

'Listen, Andy,' he said, his excitement obvious. 'This is fantastic. Make sure you get the butcher's details. Get the lad from the paper, see if you can get to the shop where the sausages came from for some photos. This could make the front page of the Eastern Daily News.' Rob pointed at the butcher. 'Him, in his butchering outfit, standing outside the front of his shop with a string of award-winning sausages round his neck. My God, this is magic.' Andy wasn't sure if Rob was still talking to him or just thinking out loud. 'Pride of Pinch. Pinch's Pride. Yes, Pinch's Pride. That's the headline right there. Now go, grasshopper. Go and make the news.'

Andy shrugged his shoulders and walked over to the door of the room, leaving Rob muttering to himself. There was only one way out of the room, so Andy could catch the butcher as he tried to leave. As he walked past the rows of chairs, he looked to see if Emily from the Food Standards Agency was still there, but there was an empty seat where she'd been sitting.

'Bugger,' Andy muttered as he reached the door of the room.

35

Tom watched from the back of the room with a broad grin on his face as Frank made his way onto the stage. His brother hadn't wanted to go up there at all and had sworn quite a lot when he realised that the fat man with the microphone was talking to him. Even from this distance, Tom could see that his brother was sweating.

When Frank had dropped his cup on the floor as he realised he'd won the competition, Tom had almost dropped his as well from the fright it had given him.

'Come on, Tom,' Frank had said in a fierce whisper. 'Let's get out of here.' But that didn't happen, and that was why Frank was perspiring up there now, a microphone inches from his face, stuttering answers to the fat bloke's questions. Tom decided that he should leave, just in case Frank decided that he wanted him to go up there as well. Besides, he needed to take the cup back to the coffee shop. That's what Frank had told him when they left earlier, and there was no way that Tom was going to steal anything. He'd get in trouble for that.

Tom sidled to the door and after checking that no-one

was watching him, he slipped through it and back into the main foyer. With a sigh of relief, he started walking toward the tables outside the coffee shop. He could just leave the cup on a table and then someone would come and collect it, he figured. But what about Frank's cup? It was in pieces on the floor back in the room he'd just left. Tom slowed down, thinking hard. He didn't want to go back and get the pieces. Perhaps he should tell Christine from behind the counter about the broken cup so that she could get the bits and glue them back together? But then she would know that the cup was broken, and Frank could get into trouble. Tom carried on thinking about what would be the best thing to do when a woman's voice broke his concentration.

'Excuse me?' the voice said from behind him. 'Excuse me?'

'Oh no,' Tom muttered under his breath. It must be the woman from the coffee shop, and he was in the middle of the foyer. Nowhere near the tables. Not only that, but he still hadn't decided what to do about Frank's broken cup. Turning round to see who had spoken to him, he breathed a big sigh of relief when he saw the woman from the Food Standards Agency, and another woman Tom didn't recognise. Not Christine from behind the counter.

'It's Tom, isn't it?' the young woman said. Frank had mentioned her name earlier, and Tom frowned as he tried to remember it. He started going through the alphabet in his head to see if it jogged his memory. As soon as he got to the letter 'E', he broke into a wide smile.

'Emily. You're Emily.'

'Oh wow,' the woman said, mirroring his smile. 'I can't believe you remembered my name.'

'You remembered mine.'

'Yeah, but I had do a load of paperwork about your

farm for the inspection on Tuesday. I had to write your name about a hundred times.' The woman was still beaming at him, and Tom took the opportunity to look at her more closely than he'd been able to when he met her briefly before. One thing he did remember was that she'd nearly looked in the pot on the stove. She was quite pretty, Tom thought, but her nose was a bit small. As he looked at her, her smile faded and her mouth formed a small 'oh' shape. Now her mouth was a bit too small as well. 'Oops. You're not supposed to know when the inspection's going to happen.'

'Er, okay,' Tom replied. 'When is the inspection going to happen?' Emily crossed her arms across her chest and gave him a weird look. That was why Tom didn't talk to women much. He just couldn't understand them.

'Are you going to introduce us then, Emily?' the other woman said. Tom turned to look at her, and decided that the new woman was far nicer looking than Emily.

'Sorry,' Emily said. 'Tom, this is Catherine, my flat mate. Catherine, this is Tom. He's a pig farmer.'

'A pig farmer?' Catherine said. 'Wow, really? How cool is that?'

'Hello Catherine,' Tom said. 'You're much prettier than your friend is.'

Catherine started laughing, even though Tom didn't think he'd made a joke. He was just saying what he thought, like he always did.

'Oh, I like you, Tom,' Catherine said. 'You've got very good taste.' As she said this, Emily punched her on the arm, but Tom could see from their smiles that they were messing around. He smiled as well, thinking for a few seconds that this was unexpected, and great fun. Maybe he should ask Frank to buy him some lucky pants for his next birthday, and they could come into the city together and both talk to women?

Tom's phone buzzed in his pocket, so he pulled it out and thumbed at the screen.

'Text message,' he said out loud. 'From Frank. He's my brother.'

'Now he's an award-winning butcher as well,' Emily said, winking at Catherine. Tom read the message and put the phone back into his pocket. He glanced toward the front of the Forum and noticed it had just started raining. 'Everything okay, Tom?' Emily asked.

'Yeah, it's fine. Frank's going back to his shop to have some photographs taken, and the man from the supermarket is going to give him a lift home.' They stood in an awkward silence for a few seconds. 'Right, I need to put this cup on the table so Christine doesn't think I've stolen it, and then I think I'll drive home and wait for Frank.' He walked over to the table, put the cup down, and returned to the women.

'Are you parked close by?' Emily asked with a look at the rain. It was coming down quite hard and Tom knew from the look of the sky that it was going to rain for a while.

'Yep, just out the front,' Tom replied.

'You're not going past Riverside on your way, are you?' Catherine asked, curling a lock of hair around her finger and smiling. 'Only we don't have coats.'

'Why didn't either of you bring coats? Didn't you know it was going to rain?'

'They never said anything on the weather forecast,' Emily said, 'but if you could give us a lift down there, that would be magic. We're going to go to the cinema.'

'Oh, that'll be nice,' Tom said. 'I've only got room for one of you, though.'

'I'll see you down there, Emily,' Catherine said, taking a step toward Tom. He managed not to take a step away from her, but he still flinched when she slipped her hand through the crook of his elbow, grabbing his arm. 'I'll be in the Wetherspoons by the cinema. Don't worry, I'll get a drink in for you.' Tom looked at Catherine and saw her wink at Emily.

'Bye Emily,' he said. 'See you soon.'

'Yeah,' Emily said. 'See you soon.' She had a funny expression on her face that Tom couldn't work out. He was just about to say something else when Catherine tugged at his arm, pulling him toward the doors at the entrance to the Forum. He turned away from Emily and walked with Catherine to the entrance, enjoying the way people were looking at them. This was going to be a great story to tell Frank this evening. The rain was teeming down, and outside the Forum people were rushing back and forth, trying to avoid the rain. Very few of them seemed to know it was going to rain, as they didn't have coats or umbrellas. Tom was just about to mention this to Catherine when she spoke.

'Right then, Tom.' She looked at him and smiled. She was definitely prettier than Emily, or at least Tom thought she was. 'Where's your car?'

36

F rank felt ridiculous. Not only did he feel ridiculous, but he knew he looked it as well. This was his shop, his bread and butter, and he was standing outside it with his apron and hat on. A couple of elderly ladies, customers almost certainly, were standing on the other side of the road watching as Frank draped sausages around his neck.

'Eyes to me, eyes to me,' the young man with the camera shouted at him. Frank looked at the youngster, crouched in the middle of the road. 'Yeah, that's perfect. Now just push the sausages slightly to the left.' Frank did as instructed and was rewarded with a flurry of clicks from the camera. 'Now, hands on hips. Yeah, that's it. You've done this before. Now just lift up the end of the string of them. Perfect. Hold the end one like it's your, er, like it's a sausage. Excellent.'

When the photographer had finally finished taking what seemed to Frank like an inordinate number of photos, he spent a few minutes talking to Andy, the lad from the supermarket. Just before he raced off in his souped-up Ford Ka, the photographer called over to Frank.

'Thanks very much, Mr Pinch,' he shouted with a wave. 'Keep an eye out in the papers tomorrow, yeah?' Frank didn't reply, but just raised his hand.

'Is he a real photographer?' Frank asked Andy who was leaning against the wall. 'He seems a bit, I don't know, young.'

'As far as I know he is,' Andy replied. 'He's the best one the Eastern Daily News has got, I heard.' Frank took his butcher's hat off and mopped his brow with the sleeve of his white jacket.

'Are we done then?' he asked Andy.

'Sure, I think so. I'll give you a lift back to your place.'

'Thanks. I've got car trouble at the moment.'

'Yeah, you said. No problem,' Andy said. Frank went back into his shop and put his jacket and hat on the coat rack in the back. He glanced around the shop to make sure everything was as it should be. The shop was fine, but most of the cabinets were empty. He locked the door and walked round to the car park.

On the drive back to the farm, Andy did most of the talking, which was fine by Frank. He learned that Andy was an intern, got paid an absolute pittance by Kett's of Norwich, and that Andy thought both his direct boss and the main man in the company were absolute arseholes. Frank had never worked for anyone else, so he couldn't really sympathise with the lad.

'Are you going to work there for long, then?' Frank asked when Andy had run out of bad things to say about the place he worked at.

'Not sure,' Andy replied. 'I need a bit more than just experience to go to one of their competitors with.'

'What, like a trade secret or something?'

'I guess so, yeah,' Andy laughed.

'I saw a programme on telly the other night about a

bloke who tried to nick the secret recipe for Louisiana Fried Chicken,' Frank said. 'He got caught, though. Not sure what happened to him.'

'How come?'

'I turned over. It was shit and I got bored. Next left here, Andy. Just after that tree that looks like a swastika.'

'Oh my God it does, doesn't it? How come it looks like that?'

'Lightning. A few years ago. Frightened the living shit out of me and Tom it did,' Frank said. 'Heard a crack, and we looked out of the window to see a burning swastika at the end of the lane.' Andy turned the car into the track and the car ground to a halt. 'What's up?' Frank asked.

'Am I going to get up there in this?'

'Should do.'

'It's just that the car's a bit low to the ground.'

'Well, if you get stuck we've got a tractor.'

Frank saw Andy give him a nervous glance before putting the car back into gear and inching his way forward. Apart from a few scraping noises from underneath the car which were accompanied by sharp inhalations from Andy, they made it to the farmhouse without any problems.

'Do you want to come in for a cup of tea?' Frank asked. 'You said you wanted to go over this contract thing with me and Tom.'

'Sure, but all I was told to do was give you the paperwork. It's not like I'm a lawyer or anything like that.'

'Well I'm a butcher and my brother's a pig farmer, so I reckon you've got more of an idea about it than we have.' The two men walked into the farmhouse, and Frank pointed Andy toward the kitchen table. 'Have a seat, I'll put the kettle on. Looks like Tom isn't back yet, although it might take him a while to get here.'

'I thought he left before we did?'

'He did, but he's in a tractor and he drives it like a golf buggy to piss people off. Milk and sugar?'

'Both please, thanks.'

Frank and Andy spent the next thirty minutes going through the contract between them, and Frank was pretty sure he'd got the gist of it. He certainly wasn't going to pay some twat from a posh school who'd grown up to become a lawyer look over it and charge him a thousand pounds for the pleasure. Andy was getting ready to leave when the front door opened, and Tom walked in. The first thing Frank noticed was a stupid grin plastered across his brother's face.

'Tom, this is Andy,' Frank said, frowning at his brother. 'He works for Kett's of Norwich, the lot who sponsored the competition we won.'

'I saw him earlier,' Tom replied, still grinning.

'Nice to meet you Tom, but I've got to head away,' Andy said.

'Cool. Nice to meet you too.'

Frank shut the door behind Andy after saying goodbye to him. He turned to Tom who still looked like a Cheshire cat.

'Tom, what's with the shit-eating grin?' he asked. Despite his curiosity, Frank felt himself starting to smile.

'Nothing.'

'Bollocks.' Normally, Frank swearing would wipe any smile off Tom's face, but it didn't even falter. 'What you been up to, little brother?' Frank didn't think it was possible, but Tom hitched his smile even higher.

'Can you keep a secret?' he asked.

'Er, Tom. I'm your brother, and we've got a fair few secrets already. Of course I can.'

'I've met a girl,' Tom said. It was all Frank could do to not laugh out loud.

'Really? A real one?'

'Yep.'

'Wow, that's fantastic. What's her name?'

'Catherine. I gave her a lift from the Forum to Riverside,' Tom said. 'It was raining.'

'You gave her a lift?'

'Yep.'

'In the tractor?'

'Yep. She sat where you sat earlier.'

'What's she like?' Frank asked.

'Lumpy.'

'Er, lumpy?'

'Yeah,' Tom replied. 'Not like you. She's got lumpy bits. I could feel them pressing into my back.'

Frank walked over to the cupboard to stop himself from roaring with laughter. He opened the cupboard and took out two glasses and a bottle of whisky, waiting a few seconds to control his laughter before he turned to return to the table.

'Well that, little brother, calls for a celebration. I suggest we drink to Catherine,' he said. 'We've got some other stuff to discuss, but first, you need to tell me all about this young woman you lured onto your tractor.'

A while later, Frank wasn't sure how long, the two brothers had made a fair old dent in the bottle. Frank hadn't found out much about Catherine. Yes, Tom thought she was from Norwich. No, Tom didn't get her phone number. Yes, as well as being lumpy she was also very pretty. No, Tom hadn't arranged to meet her again. No, Tom didn't know anything about her other than the fact her name was Catherine. Frank was starting to feel really sorry for his poor lovestruck brother and the fact that he would probably never be able to find Catherine again when Tom mentioned that she'd been with the woman from the Food Standards Agency. In that case, Frank had reassured Tom, they would be able to get in touch with her.

'So,' Tom said, his face brightening at the news that all was not lost. 'What was the other stuff you wanted to talk about.'

Frank scraped his chair back from the table and crossed the kitchen with a slight wobble. He returned to the table with the paperwork that Andy had left behind.

'Tom,' Frank said, staring at his brother's glazed over eyes.

'What?' Tom replied. Frank tapped his finger on the paperwork and took a deep breath before replying.

'We need more meat.'

'Oh.'

'A lot more meat.'

37

Emily yawned and stretched her arms as the final credits started to roll up the screen. The lights in the cinema flicked on, and she looked around at the other people in the cinema blinking in the bright light. From the number of people who were also yawning, it didn't look as if Emily was the only one who'd not enjoyed the film.

'What did you think?' Catherine said as Emily fished around behind her to retrieve her bag. 'That was great, wasn't it?'

'Er, yeah,' Emily replied. 'It was okay.'

'Okay?' Catherine got to her feet. 'It was more than okay. Benedict Cumberbatch was awesome. Oh my God, he's so handsome as well.' Emily tuned Catherine out as they made their way toward the exit. By the time they left the cinema, Emily had had enough of Catherine going on about how good the film was.

'Catherine,' Emily said. 'It was rubbish. He's acting his little heart out, desperate for a bloody Oscar.'

'Oh, he was not,' Catherine slapped Emily's arm playfully. 'You're just grumpy because you slept through most of it.'

'I did not,' Emily said. 'I might have nodded off once or twice, but that was only because it was so bloody boring. Who was that Harvey Weinstein bloke anyway?'

'Well, if you'd been watching the film, you'd know that he was a misunderstood genius,' Catherine replied. 'I thought Benedict did the inherent tragedy of the man perfectly. Did you know he had to put on over three stone to play the part?'

'Inherent tragedy? Where'd you get that from?' Emily knew Catherine wouldn't have thought that one up on her own.

'Heard it on the radio.'

'Well, I'm glad you enjoyed it.'

'I did,' Catherine replied. 'Sour puss. Right then, let's go for a drink or three. Where do you fancy going?'

'How about the Queen of Iceni?' Emily said. 'Just the one, though. I'm tired, and not really dressed for being out.'

'I don't know why you're still tired after your power nap, but you're right about not being dressed for a night on the tiles,' Catherine said, and Emily laughed as they walked toward the doors of the pub.

The Queen of Iceni was a huge pub right on the riverfront of Norwich. It used to be even bigger, but since Brexit, the chain that ran it discovered that well over half of their workforce had disappeared, so they'd had to scale down. It still did what it did best though, which was sell cheap booze and even cheaper food. Emily grabbed them a table and looked around while Catherine went to the bar to order. The pub was maybe half-full, with a mixture of families eating and young people getting fuelled-up before heading round the corner to the more expensive bars and clubs on the Prince of Wales' Road.

Emily smiled to herself as she watched a man eating a soggy pizza with his wife and young kids. He was trying to get a good look at the young women, who were definitely on their way out, on the table next to them without anyone noticing.

'There you go, mate,' Catherine said as she put a large glass of wine on the table in front of Emily.

'Oh Jesus, Catherine,' Emily replied. 'I said a small glass.'

'That is a small glass. It just looks big to you because, er, because you're small.'

'Ha ha, very funny,' Emily laughed as she picked up the glass. 'Let's drink to Benedict's chances at the Oscars.'

'I'll drink to that.' Catherine said. They clinked their glasses off each other's. 'So, Emily,' she continued. 'It's Saturday night, we're both young, free, and single. The entire male population of Norwich is at our disposal, and you're heading back to the flat for a night in your pyjamas in front of the telly.' Emily looked at Catherine, not wanting to tell her that her plan was to have a bath and curl up in bed with the latest Peter James novel.

'I just don't feel like it, that's all.'

'Are you okay?' Catherine said. The look on her face was deadly serious.

'I'm fine.'

'Are you sure? You seem really down at the moment.'

'Honestly,' Emily said. 'I'm fine. It's just work's getting on top of me what with the warning and everything. The last thing I need at the moment is a relationship.'

'Who said anything about a relationship?' Catherine replied with a theatrical wink. Emily looked at her friend and started giggling.

'I'm not you, Catherine,' Emily said, laughing.

'Bloody right you're not.'

'So how was the ride down from the Forum, then?' Emily asked. 'With Tom the pig farmer?' It was Catherine's turn to start giggling.

'Oh my God, he was hysterical. The only way I could get on the bloody tractor was to jam myself right up behind the poor man and every time I touched him, he flinched.'

'Let me guess, you touched him quite a lot?'

'I might have done. He's hiding his light under a bushel, that one is. Very well put together from what I could feel, but I guess that's from working on a farm.'

'Do you not think he's a bit odd?'

'In what way?'

'I don't know,' Emily said. 'I mean, I've only spoken to him a couple of times, but he seemed a bit weird.'

'I think he's quite sweet.' Emily raised her eyebrows. 'Oh, don't give me that look,' Catherine said. 'I don't mean in that way. I just don't think he gets out much, that's all.' She took a sip of her drink. 'Bit like you at the moment.'

'Ha bloody ha,' Emily said.

They spent the next twenty minutes in quiet conversation, interrupted only by a loud but brief argument at a table behind them. Emily turned to see an angry woman dragging two crying children toward the door while her husband sat looking down at his lap. From the giggling of the women at the table next to him, Emily guessed he'd been busted.

'So, are you sure you're not going to join me and the girls, then?' Catherine said, draining the last of her glass of wine. 'Last chance?'

'Nope, honestly. I'm fine,' Emily replied. 'I'm going to walk up to Castle Meadow and get a bus home.'

'Up to you, mate,' Catherine said. 'But don't wait up for me.' She winked again at Emily, who just smiled.

Emily shivered as she walked along Rose Lane toward the bus stop. It was colder than she thought it would be, and getting soaked walking through the rain earlier hadn't helped. She noticed a plaque she'd not seen before on the wall of a multi-story car park advertising the fact that it had won the 'Britain's Best Car Park' award five years in a row. Emily was just considering how much fun that award ceremony must have been when she heard a male voice calling her name.

'Emily?' She looked around to see who was calling her. 'Emily, over here.' On the other side of the road was a group of four young men queuing up outside a bar with a nightclub attached to it. One of them was Gary. The lovely Gary from the laboratory. Emily crossed over the road to talk to him.

'Hey, Gary,' she smiled as she walked up to him. 'You never write, you never call.' One of the lads with Gary laughed.

'I'm sorry,' Gary replied with a broad grin that showed off his straight teeth and square jaw. He really was very good looking, dressed in jeans and a white shirt with just the right amount of chest hair poking through the top. 'Where you off to, then?'

'I've just been to the cinema to see that God-awful film about Harvey Weinstein,' Emily said. Gary leaned back and laughed, a deep throated chuckle that suited him perfectly.

'I saw that last week,' he said. 'Benedict's last chance for an Oscar, I reckon.'

'Yep, couldn't agree more,' Emily smiled. They stood looking at each other for a few seconds, when the bouncer at the door of the bar called out to get Gary's attention. There was room inside when they were ready, the bouncer told them.

'Hey, come for a drink,' Gary said. Emily looked at him, a wry smile on her face.

'Thanks, but I'm heading home,' she replied.

'Come on,' one of Gary's friends said. 'We don't bite.'

'It's really kind of you, but I'm fine,' Emily said. 'It's been a really long day.'

'Are you sure?' Gary said as one of his friends tugged at his shirt, pulling him toward the door.

'Yeah, I'm sure. Have a great evening, though.'

As Gary and his friends disappeared into the bar, Emily rubbed her hands up and down her arms to warm up a bit. She continued up the road for a few yards before turning to look at the bar. The Loft, it was called. Above the entrance was a large rainbow flag and a banner declaring that it was Norwich's one and only premier gay nightclub.

'Oh well,' Emily muttered under her breath as she carried on toward the bus stop.

38

Tom burped and rubbed his sternum with the palm of his hand as the whisky put in a second, unwelcome, appearance. He glanced at the bottle on the kitchen table. It was almost empty. Frank got to his feet and went to the cupboard to fetch another one. Tom blew his breath out of his cheeks. At least tomorrow was Sunday.

'So, Tom,' Frank said as he returned to the table with the bottle. 'What do you think?'

'About what?' Tom fought another burp. 'About the plan?'

'Yes, Tom,' Frank said. From the tone of his voice, Tom knew that Frank was getting tetchy. 'About the plan.'

The brothers had spent the previous couple of hours going over how they could get hold of more meat. Tom had been confused at first. He'd thought after Kyle had his accident with the shovel that Frank was dead against any more meat like that. But, as he'd explained to Tom, winning the competition had changed everything. With the sows still a couple of months away from producing anything, if they didn't get hold of more meat now, they would miss the opportunity. As well as that, they'd already done two immigrants, so they were in for a penny, in for a pound. That had been one of their father's favourite sayings, but he usually said it as he cracked open another bottle of something.

'If we do this right, Tom,' Frank had said, 'this could set us up properly. The money that this supermarket lot are offering would see us debt-free, with enough left over to completely restock the farm.'

'Debt-free?'

'Yes Tom. Debt-free, and with cash to spare. We could buy a new tractor.'

The chance of a new tractor got Tom's attention straight away. When Frank had said that, Tom allowed himself a few minutes to day dream, imagining the look on Catherine's face when he pulled up outside her place sitting on a brand-new Massey, or maybe even a John Deere. Bright green livery with huge canary yellow wheels, like one of the 6R series he'd seen in the showroom window the last time he'd gone past the dealership. Tom could see Catherine's face drop when she saw him pull up outside. She would gasp, and put her hands over her mouth to stop herself exploding with delight...

'Tom?'

'What?' Tom replied, irritated at having his concentration broken.

'I said, what do you think of the plan?'

'I don't know,' Tom replied, trying to remember exactly what the plan was. 'I mean, we need more meat, but you told me that it wasn't right, what I done with Kyle.'

'That was then, Tom,' Frank fixed him with a hard stare. 'This is now. Now zip up your man suit.'

Tom leaned across the table, grabbed his glass, and emptied it. While Frank poured Tom a very generous measure and topped his own glass up, Tom thought of something to ask his brother.

'How much more meat do we need, then?' he asked. Frank looked at him, almost surprised, before picking up a pencil and paper from the table. Tom watched him for a few moments, doing sums on the paper and looking at the paperwork from the supermarket. Tom had never been any good at sums, but Frank knew all about them, so that didn't matter. A few minutes later, Frank nibbled at the end of the pencil before writing a single number on the paper and drawing a circle around it.

'Five,' Frank said. 'We need five more of them.'

'That's a lot.'

'Well, yeah, but that would fill the freezers until the sows do their thing.'

'Right.'

'Based on how much meat we got off Kyle, who wasn't the biggest bloke who's ever worked on the farm, five of them would give us enough to deliver what the contract says.'

'Okay,' Tom replied, not one hundred percent sure what Frank meant, but happy to go along with it.

'So, we're agreed then. Five?' Frank said. Tom just nodded in response. If Frank thought it was five, then that was what they would need.

'How're we going to get five, though?' Tom said. 'Marko might not be that fussed about the odd immigrant here and there buggering off, but five of them?'

'Fair one, Tom,' Frank replied. 'That's a fair point.' Tom nodded. He was pleased that Frank was listening to him, so decided to carry on.

'What if we didn't use Marko, though?' Tom asked. 'What if we got our own workers?'

'How are we going to do that?' Frank said. 'Take out

an advert in the Eastern Daily News? 'Farm workers wanted. Legal workers and skinny people need not apply'. Can't see that working, little brother.'

Tom remembered the ad for the canoe. He'd not discussed that with Frank yet, but thought that maybe now wasn't the time. He started to wonder if Catherine had ever been in a canoe when he stopped himself.

'Well Marko must get them from somewhere,' Tom said. 'If we find out where from, and then just get some for ourselves. Marko doesn't need to know, does he?' Frank looked at him with his thinking face on.

'I think you might be onto something, Tom.' He poured another couple of fingers into Tom's glass even though he'd not finished the last lot.

'We could follow him,' Tom said, picking up the glass.

'He's going to notice that, though.'

'Yeah, he is. Especially as it would have to be in the tractor until you get your car fixed.' Frank started laughing.

'Can you imagine that?'

'No, it wouldn't work. Well, it would be okay as long as Marko didn't go any of the big roads. I wouldn't be able to keep up,' Tom said. He watched Frank's face as his smile slipped for a few seconds before he started laughing again.

'You're right, Tom,' Frank said, patting his trouser pockets. Tom took another sip of his whisky. He was going to have to go to bed soon, or he'd have a really sore head tomorrow. Sunday or no Sunday, he'd still have to get up early to feed the sows. 'Oh bugger,' Frank said. 'Lost my bloody phone.'

The brothers chatted for a while until finally Frank put the top back on the whisky bottle and placed it back in the cupboard. Tom was quite relieved, but he didn't say anything. He didn't want Frank to call him any names for not wanting more whisky. Tom got to his feet, unsteady for a second.

'Need a pee,' he said.

'Thanks for sharing,' Frank replied. 'Don't forget to lift up the lid.'

In the toilet, Tom relieved himself with one hand and thumbed at his phone with the other. He almost dropped the phone into the toilet, but managed to hang on to it. By the time he got back to the kitchen, Tom was smiling from ear to ear. Frank was going to love this.

'What're you grinning at, Tom?'

'Shop.'

'What?'

'Shop. In the shop.'

'What's in the shop?' Frank asked. Tom held his phone up for his brother to see the screen and the blue dot on the map.

'Your phone's in the shop.'

Frank stared at Tom, and for a few seconds Tom was worried that he'd done something wrong. Did Frank know that he'd nearly dropped the phone in the toilet? That would make him very angry, but Tom couldn't work out how Frank would know. Frank got to his feet and stood in front of Tom, his eyes going between the phone and Tom's face.

'Little brother, that is it. That's how we do it.' Frank pulled Tom into a bearhug and Tom nearly dropped the phone again. 'That is a fantastic idea.'

Tom wasn't sure what was a fantastic idea, but he hugged his brother back anyway.

39

The worse thing about Monday mornings, at least as far as Andy was concerned, was that the whole week stretched ahead like a prison sentence. Not only that, but the weekend was over and the next one was as far away as it ever would be at any point in the week. Andy had been forced last night by Martin to choose between putting some petrol in his car or going out last night. The faint hangover he was nursing, and the fact he was currently sitting on the top deck of the Number 24 bus from Thorpe St Andrew into Norwich city centre, was the result of his decision. At least he got paid on Friday, for what that was worth.

Andy put his headphones in as the bus pulled up to a stop with a whole bunch of schoolchildren waiting. He knew they would all come upstairs, sit as far toward the back as they could, and just be generally irritating until they got into the city. A moment later, he sighed and selected something loud from his music collection as they filed past him, already shouting at each other. He leaned back and closed his eyes, resigned to the next twenty minutes or so.

By the time he got to Partridge Towers, Andy's headache was building. It hadn't been helped by the bus journey, but at least the pain wasn't too bad. Probably two paracetamol and some strong coffee would sort it out. The only thing Andy had on that morning was the marketing department wash up from the competition. He got to his desk and checked his e-mails for anything urgent. There was a couple of emails about the marketing wash up, and one from the event's organiser at the Forum, Jessica. Andy read the e-mail, which started off thanking him for the good publicity. He was just about to print the e-mail off to show Rob when he read the last line. Jessica was wondering if Andy might be free for a drink and something to eat one evening perhaps? Andy swallowed and deleted the e-mail. From what he remembered of Jessica, it would be quite a lot to eat.

'The Thought Factory' on the top floor was almost full when Andy got there. Seven, maybe eight people from the marketing department were chatting between themselves. There were a couple of empty beanbags, so Andy slipped himself into one. A few minutes later Rob arrived, a flip chart tucked under his arm.

'Morning, team,' Rob said in a bright voice. There were a few mumbled replies from the beanbags, but Andy thought that Rob was by far the most enthusiastic person in the room. 'Right, we need to wash up the competition, and identify our yellow brick road.' He fixed the flip chart on the wall. 'So, who's here?'

They went round the room, a voice coming from each beanbag. When the introductions got to Andy, Rob pointed a marker pen in his direction.

'Andy, what are you doing down there? You should be up here, wielding this weapon of words.' Grumbling to himself, Andy got to his feet and walked to the front of the room. Why was it always him who had to do the bloody writing on the flip chart? 'So,' Rob continued. 'We need to come up with a strap line for the next stage. We've got 'Pride of Anglia', but we need more to pull in the punters. 'Thoughts, people?' There was silence in the room. 'Oh come on, this was in the e-mail I sent round. You should all have at least thought about it.'

A thin hand emerged from one of the beanbags in the corner.

'Who's that?' Rob asked, peering at the beanbag.

'It's Tony,' the man's voice said.

'Cool, Tony. You're the man. Can you sit up a bit so we can see you?' There was a rustling from the beanbag and Tony emerged. He was one of the older members of the team, and it looked to Andy like he'd just woken up. Maybe he had? 'So, Tony. What've you got, big man?'

'Well, Rob,' Tony started in a voice so quiet Andy struggled to hear him. 'I was thinking about how we can —'

'Tony, speak up. Own the idea.'

'Right,' Tony said, clearing his throat and starting again. He was marginally louder, but not much. 'I was thinking about how we can increase the diversity of our marketing strategy.'

'Like it, like it,' Rob said, clapping his hands together. 'Increase the diversity of our marketing strategy. Great stuff, carry on.' Andy looked at his boss and knew he would be using that particular phrase again at some point. Probably at the next board meeting.

'So I did some research, scoped it out a bit more. Do we know how the meat is killed?'

'What?' Rob said. There was some rustling in beanbags as the other people in the room started to get interested.

'Do we know how the meat is killed?' Tony continued.

'I heard you, but what are you talking about?'

'I mean, is it shot with a bolt thing? Is it a knife to the jugular?'

'Tony, I'm not sure where you going with this. I'm not seeing how this can be used for marketing.'

'Because, Rob,' Tony said, a look of triumph on his face. 'If it's been killed with a knife, then that opens up a whole new marketing channel.'

'You're going to have to explain that one, Tony.'

'Well that makes it Halal meat,' Tony said, a broad smile on his face. 'Which means we can go with the diversity angle.'

There was a silence in the room, which went from being awkward to uncomfortable within seconds. Andy, trying to suppress a grin, looked at Rob who quite obviously hadn't got a clue what to say.

'Tony,' Rob said after a few more seconds of deafening silence. 'It's pork.'

'So?'

'Muslims don't eat pork. You can't have a Halal bloody pork sausage.'

'Oh,' the look of disappointment on Tony's face was replaced a second later by another smile as he thought of something else.

'What about if it's Kosher, then? We could go with that angle instead.'

'Oh sweet Jesus,' Andy heard Rob mutter under his breath, followed by what Andy was pretty sure was the word 'fuckwit.'

Almost an hour later, the flip chart was full with ideas for marketing that didn't involve insulting any of the world's major religions, or at least as far as Andy knew. The attendees at the meeting were getting to their feet when Rob turned to Andy.

'Andy, could you hang back for a few minutes?' Rob said. 'Got a task for you.' They stood in silence as the room emptied. The last man to leave was Tony, who hadn't said another word in the meeting. He looked as if he was going to say something to Rob, but he just glanced at Andy and shuffled out of the room.

'My God, can you believe that?' Rob said. Andy didn't say anything, but just smiled. 'I know this part of the country isn't the most ethnically diverse as some areas, but even so.'

'So what's the task, Rob?' Andy asked, sure he was just about to be stitched up with something crappy.

'Patience, young grasshopper,' Rob replied. Andy just stared at him until Rob looked as if he'd decided that Andy had been patient enough. 'We need a non-disclosure agreement signed by the butcher. Legal are concerned that he could sell his sausage recipe to a competitor. It would be worth a fortune, so we need to nail it down. So, get round there this week and get it signed.'

'Okay,' Andy sighed. It could have been worse. 'Anything else?'

'Yeah, one more thing. Charles the Big Cheese has decided we need to make some cutbacks, so one of the intern posts is going to be axed at the end of the month.'

'Which one?' Andy asked, a sinking feeling in the pit of his stomach. If he lost this job, he'd have nothing. He didn't have anywhere near enough experience to start looking for another one.

'He's not decided yet. I thought I'd tip you the wink though, give you a chance to make a real impression.'

'Yeah, thanks Rob,' Andy said. 'That's magic. Thanks.'

40

F rank drummed his fingers on the kitchen table and glanced at the clock on the wall. Marko had said that he would be here by eight o'clock, and it was now ten past eight. One thing that Frank disliked was people who weren't punctual, but there was nothing he could do about the fact that Marko was late. Frank picked up his phone, but there was nothing from Marko, so he guessed he would have to be patient.

Tom and Frank had spent the previous day working out the best way to approach the next few days. They'd not got much done in the morning, but by the time their hangovers had worn off, they'd been able to put together what Frank thought was a pretty damn good plan. Mike had come round for a while, so they'd had to pause what they were putting together, but as the main reason he'd come round was to fix Frank's Land Rover, they'd had no choice. Frank had paid Mike with a free session of man love with Boris. By the time Mike left, everyone was happy. Frank was happy as his car was up and running again, and Mike was happy with a jar full of pig semen in his pocket. Even Boris looked as if he had a smile on his face.

Just before the big Tesco on the outskirts of Norwich had closed, Frank had been able to nip in and buy the cheapest smartphone they sold. It would be able to run the 'Find My Phone' app, and had a battery life of three days, so would do nicely. Tom, currently hiding in one of the sheds out of the front of the farmhouse, had the phone in his pocket with a roll of gaffer tape, waiting for Marko to put in an appearance.

Frank picked up his phone again, and as he did so he heard a noisy engine outside followed by the gravel crunching outside the front door. He got to his feet and made his way to the door, opening it to see Marko's van outside. The gangmaster got out of the van and made his way to where Frank was standing.

'Marko,' Frank said, extending a hand toward the visitor. Marko just looked at Frank's hand, making no attempt to shake it. 'How are you doing, mate?'

'Good,' Marko replied after a few seconds silence. Out of the corner of his eye, Frank could see Tom's face peer out of the barn door.

'Do you want to come in? Have a cup of tea?' Frank asked.

'No, is good. How many you need?'

'Er, two?' Frank replied, ignoring Tom who was now inching his way toward the back of Marko's van.

'When?'

'Oh, well. Now, from what Tom told me, he's got to sort out the pens at the far end of the farm. The ones nearest the woods?' Frank raised his voice a bit to cover the sound of Tom's footsteps. Tom was nearly at the back of Marko's van, and as Frank watched out of the corner of his eye, his brother disappeared behind the van. Just as

Tom vanished from sight, Marko followed Frank's eyes and turned around. 'So, could we just get two when they're available?' Frank continued.

'Yeah, okay. Couple of hours' time. Extra for short notice, though.'

'How much extra?'

'Fifty quid.'

Frank bristled at the thought of paying an extra premium just to get some workers at short notice, but he knew that Marko had him over a barrel. If they waited until tomorrow, there was a risk that the battery on the phone Tom was hiding in the wheel arch of Marko's van wouldn't last.

'Right, fifty quid it is,' Frank said. Marko turned and took a step toward his van. 'Hey, Marko?' Frank called after him. The gangmaster stopped and turned back round.

'What?'

'Er,' Frank said, trying to think of something to say that wouldn't sound too odd. Over Marko's shoulder, Frank could see Tom scurrying back to the barn. 'What do you think of Norwich City's chances in the Champion's league this year?' Marko didn't reply, but stared at Frank for a few seconds before grunting. Behind him, Tom slipped through the barn door just seconds before the gangmaster turned back round.

Frank watched Marko's battered Transit van wobble its way back down the track, the occasional puff of black exhaust smoke coughing into the air. Tom made his way back to the front door, his phone in his hand. As the van turned onto the main road, the brothers looked at the screen on Tom's phone. A small blue flashing dot told them both that their plan was, so far, working well.

'Did you put enough tape on?' Frank asked his brother.

'I put loads on, like you said.'

'But you didn't cover up the top of the phone, did you?' Frank had done some rudimentary research on the internet that had suggested the signal for the phone came out of the top of it. Not covering that part with layers of gaffer tape made sense to him, but he wasn't one hundred percent sure it would make any difference at all. Tom nodded toward the screen where the blue dot could be seen making its way onto the A11 dual carriageway and heading away from Norwich and toward Thetford.

'It's working okay, isn't it?' Tom said.

'Yeah, I just hope it doesn't fall off,' Frank replied. 'Come on, let's go and get a cup of tea and boot up the laptop.'

They sat in the kitchen, sipping tea and watching the blue dot on the screen for almost thirty minutes. Marko certainly wasn't to get pulled over for speeding by the police, Frank noticed with a wry smile.

'Look,' Tom prodded a finger at the screen. 'Looks like he's stopped. Where is that?'

'Thetford Forest, I think. Hang on a second.' Frank fiddled with the mouse attached to the laptop. 'There's a way of bringing up a view that's like from a satellite or something.' The screen changed to show an aerial view instead of a map. Frank studied the screen for a few moments.

'A satellite as in one of them things up in space?' Tom said. Frank nodded.

'Yeah, that's right. I know where the van is. There's a layby not far off the A11 with a small car park. That's where he is.' They watched the screen for a few moments. The van had definitely stopped. Either that, or the phone had fallen off.

Frank had been to that exact layby once a couple of

years ago. He was driving back from Cambridge after going to the Cambridgeshire County Show. It was quite late at night, and because he'd spent a bit too long in the beer tent before leaving the show, he was busting for the toilet so had pulled into the layby. To his surprise, there were quite a few cars there already. He was relieving himself up against a tree when one of the cars flashed its headlights, lighting him up like a torch.

'Idiots,' he had mumbled as he got back into his car. As he drove past the car that had flashed its headlights, he slowed down to give the driver a look, but he'd not been able to see anything as the windows were all misted up.

'So is that where we're going to go then, Frank?' Tom asked, interrupting Frank's thoughts.

'I reckon so, little brother,' Frank said. 'First thing in the morning, though. I'm not going there at night.'

41

Tom woke up with a start and thrashed around his bed looking for the alarm clock. It was still pitch-black outside and he couldn't see a thing. He eventually found the clock, considered throwing it against the wall for a second, and turned the alarm off. Knowing that if he lay back down on the bed he'd fall asleep, he threw his legs over the side of the bed and got to his feet. As he walked past Frank's room, Tom tapped on the door to make sure he was awake as well. When he didn't hear anything he tapped again, harder this time. A muffled shout came from inside the room. Tom was pretty sure it was a swear, but as he'd not heard it properly, it wasn't worth getting upset about it.

By the time Frank came into the kitchen, Tom had two mugs of tea ready. He was also fully dressed, right down to a beanie on his head and black puffy jacket.

'My God, Tom,' Frank said. 'You look like a bloody burglar.'

'At least I'm dressed,' Tom shot back. 'You said four in the morning. It's now almost twenty past.'

'Alright Tom,' Frank said. 'Keep your beanie on. It'll take me two minutes to get ready. We'll be out of the door by half past.'

Frank was true to his word, and ten minutes later they were climbing into the front of Mike's white transit van. Frank had collected it the night before, explaining to Tom that they shouldn't use one of their own vehicles just in case they were spotted. Tom settled himself into the passenger seat when Frank turned to him.

'Hang on a second, we need to do something.'

'What?' Tom asked as Frank got back out of the van.

'Number plates.' Tom watched as Frank kicked mud and pig shit from the floor up against the front of the van. 'You do the back one.'

'What am I doing to it?' Tom asked as he undid his seatbelt.

'Covering up the number plate. Just cover it in mud in case someone sees us.'

Tom did as he was told, and after Frank had inspected his handiwork, the two of them climbed back into the van.

Twenty minutes later, they pulled into the layby that Marko had stopped at the day before. Tom and Frank had watched the laptop like hawks. According to the app on the phone hidden in the wheel arch of Marko's van, he'd left the farm, travelled to this layby, and then come straight back to the farm. When he got back to Frank and Tom's, there were two young lads in the back of it. They were maybe mid-twenties, both looked terrified and didn't speak a word of English between them, but they turned out to be hard workers. The pig sheds had never been so clean as they were by the time they'd finished. Tom had even got them to clean the abattoir on the basis that it was about to be used a fair bit. Frank had cooked them some sausage sandwiches for lunch. Normal sausages, from Lidl. Or at least that was what Frank had said. Seeing as Tom had eaten one of the sandwiches as well, he hoped his big brother was telling the truth.

'Is Marko still at his house?' Frank asked. Tom looked at the screen. The blue dot was static, showing Marko's van to be at what the two them presumed was his home just off Newmarket Road.

'Yep, according to this at least,' Tom replied. 'How can a bloke who runs illegal immigrants for a living afford a place there, anyway?'

'No idea,' Frank mumbled as he opened the door. 'Come on, let's get going.' Frank got out of the van, and Tom joined him. They stood in the car park for a moment, looking around. As far as Tom could see, they were the only ones there.

'What do we do now?' Tom asked. He wasn't sure what to expect when they got here, and neither did Frank. They'd talked about it a bit in the van on the way over, but Frank had said they would find out what happened when they got there. The best that they'd been able to come up with was that maybe all the illegal immigrants were living in the forest, and that they'd come when they heard a car. Tom had seen a film a while ago with Mexican immigrants queuing up for work, so maybe it was a similar setup.

'Not sure,' Frank said. 'Maybe there's a signal or something?'

'I could do an owl noise?'

'An owl noise?'

'Yeah,' Tom said, 'to let them know there's someone here.' Frank turned and stared at his brother.

'We're in the middle of a bloody forest, Tom,' he said. 'If there is anyone here, they'll think it's an owl.'

'Oh,' Tom replied. 'I hadn't thought of that.' Tom knew that he could not just do an owl noise, but also a dog, cat, or even a pig, but from the look on Frank's face none of them would be any good either.

A few minutes later, Frank had said that he would whistle to see if there was anyone about. Tom watched him put his fingers in his mouth and take a deep breath when there was a voice behind them.

'Help you?' the voice said in heavily accented English. Tom jumped at the noise, and Frank did exactly the same thing.

'Sweet Jesus,' Tom said, putting a hand on his chest and turning to see a man standing behind them. He was dressed almost completely in black and had crept up on them in total silence.

'You frightened the crap out of us,' Frank said, his face dark with anger.

The man laughed in response before repeating his question. 'Help you?'

'We're looking for workers,' Frank said. 'You know, people to help out on a farm.'

'No-one here,' the man said, shaking his head from side to side. Tom watched Frank pull a ten pound note out of his pocket. 'Okay, maybe someone here.'

'How many someone?' Frank asked. 'We need five. For one day.'

'I need five,' the man said, nodding at the ten pound note. 'Finding fee.'

Frank pulled a couple of twenties out of his pocket and put them with the tenner. He handed the money over to the man who folded it carefully and put it in his back pocket.

'Okay,' he said. 'Wait.' He walked toward the trees and was lost from sight within seconds.

Tom blew a breath out of his cheeks.

'Blimey, I nearly shit myself when he appeared,' he

said, looking at Frank. 'So what, do we just wait here then?'

'I guess so.'

'Do you think he'll come back?'

'He'd bloody well better,' Frank replied. 'He's just had fifty quid off me.'

Tom and Frank got back in the van a few minutes later, both feeling the chill. They sat in silence, waiting for the strange man to come back. Tom wondered what Frank would do if he didn't. There wasn't much that he could do, as far as Tom could see. Thetford Forest was huge, and if he was living in there like some sort of modern day Robin Hood, Frank would have no chance of finding him. Tom was just about to ask Frank what he would do when he heard rustling and saw branches moving in some bushes at the edge of the car park. Tom tapped Frank on the leg and pointed toward the bushes.

'Yep, got it,' Frank replied, opening the door and getting out. Tom watched as five scruffy men emerged from the bushes and stood huddled in a small group. They were followed by the man who Tom had given the money to. Frank walked over and was talking to him for a few seconds before he turned to Tom and motioned for him to open the van doors. Tom hopped from the van and ran round to the back to open them. It was all he could do not to giggle. This was just like being in a film or something.

The five men walked to the rear of the van and started getting in. Frank followed them and stood by the doors.

'Okay?' Tom jumped again and turned to see the same man dressed in black next to him.

'How the hell do you do that?' Tom asked. The man just smiled and extended his hand. Tom looked at it for a second, and decided that it would be okay to shake it. As they shook hands, the man introduced himself.

'I'm Alfonso,' he said. 'You need more, you come back?' Tom thought hard before replying. He couldn't give this strange man his real name. Frank had told him on the way over that they mustn't give anything away about themselves. Tom needed a name, or the man would think he was rude. The problem was that Tom wasn't very good at thinking things up on the spot. He had a sudden flash of inspiration.

'Hi Alfonso,' Tom said. 'My name's Mike. Pleased to meet you.'

42

E mily hummed along with the song on the radio as she drove along the dual carriageway. She was so engrossed in the music that she almost missed the turn off to the farm. Realising at the last minute, she braked hard and flicked her indicator on, causing the motorist in the BMW behind her to lean on his horn as he almost rear-ended her Mini. Emily turned to look at him as she slowed down on the slip road, and he gave her a one finger salute as he accelerated away. She could see his lips moving as he shouted at her. From the brief glance she got of the man, he looked like an overweight businessman.

'One step closer to that heart attack, my friend,' Emily muttered as she reached the end of the slip road. Ten minutes later, just after the sign for Hill Top Farm, she pulled into a track that led to her next inspection. The Pinch farm, co-owned by Tom and Frank Pinch, and home to the now famous Pride of Anglia winning sausages.

As she approached the farmhouse, she realised that it looked as if no-one was at home. She swore to herself under her breath and got out of the car to knock on the farmhouse door. Several sharp raps later, she realised that she was right. Massaging her bruised knuckles, she returned to her car and dug her mobile phone out. She could call Mr Clayton at the office, explain that the farm was empty, and ask him what to do. At least if she did that, she couldn't get into any trouble. The phone screen lit up as she touched it, and Emily realised that there was no signal.

'Oh, for God's sake,' she said aloud. Her mobile phone provider had the worst coverage of all of them, especially out in the sticks. In fact, getting a signal anywhere outside the inner ring road of Norwich was patchy at best, non-existent at worst. She slid her phone back into her trouser suit pocket and thought for a few moments. Emily decided to give it twenty minutes and then head back to Norwich. It was only Tuesday, so she could come back later in the week and still have the report done by the weekend. That would have to do.

Just over ten minutes later, Emily was sitting in her car listening to the radio when her patience was rewarded. In the rear view mirror, she saw a white Transit van turn into the track and head up toward the farmhouse. Emily got out of the car and stood next to it to wait for the van. When it got to about fifty feet away, it stopped. She could see the two men in the front of the van — the Pinch brothers — having an animated discussion about something. Emily crossed her arms over her chest and waited.

Both doors to the van swung open, and Emily saw the two of them get out and change places. The one who had been driving, the butcher, ran around to the back of the van while his brother, Tom, got behind the wheel. Emily heard the rear doors open and shut again a few seconds later. A few minutes later, with the butcher now in the passenger seat, the van pulled up to where Emily was standing.

'Morning,' the butcher called out through the open window before getting out of the van. Tom, now driving, gave Emily a broad smile and waved through the windscreen.

'Morning,' Emily said. 'It's Frank, isn't it?'

'Yep, that's me. And you're Emily. We should stop meeting like this. People will talk.' Emily looked at the butcher and tried not to shiver. There was definitely something odd about the man. Even just the way he was looking at her now made her uncomfortable. He had a kind of half-smile on his face, not quite a leer but not far from it.

'Yes, well,' Emily tried to put an authoritarian note into her voice. 'I'm here for the farm's annual inspection.'

'Of course you are. Does it have to be today, though? Tom's not feeling very well.'

Emily looked at Tom sitting in the driver's seat. He waved at her again, still smiling.

'He looks okay to me,' she said.

'He just hides it well. Proper Norfolk boy, he is. He could chop his arm off and it'd only be a scratch.'

'Well, it does need to be today, really. I'm on quite a tight schedule, you see,' Emily replied. Frank's smile dropped for a second.

'If you insist. Tom just needs to drop the van off at the sheds, so how about a cup of tea while we wait for him to come back?' Frank walked toward the door of the farmhouse, a key extended in his hand. When he reached the door, he turned and stared at his brother before jabbing the key in the direction of the pig sheds Emily could see in the distance. Tom put the van in gear, and as it lumbered down the track toward the sheds, it hit a large pothole. Emily wasn't sure, but she thought she heard a thud come from inside the van followed by laughter. That Tom bloke definitely wasn't right if he laughed at potholes, she thought as she walked toward the farmhouse.

The inside of the kitchen was just as Emily remembered it from her previous visit. Minimalist. She glanced toward the stove, recalling the bubbling stock pot, but there was nothing there today.

'How do you take it?' Frank asked. 'Tea, I mean?'

'Oh, white with no sugar, please.'

'Coming right up. Have a seat.' Frank gestured toward a lumpy looking armchair in the corner of the room. Emily walked across to it and sat down, sinking so far into it she had to grab the arms with her hands before it swallowed her up. Springs in the armchair were either optional or long gone. She shuffled her way back to the front of the armchair and perched on the edge of it, trying her best to look businesslike.

'So, how did you get on with the pre-inspection assessment?' she asked. 'Tom said you were going to help him out with it.

'Yeah, I think we're there,' Frank replied. 'So which bits do you need to inspect, anyway?'

'Same as last time,' Emily said, reaching for her bag. She pulled a sheaf of paperwork out of it. 'Pig pens, general husbandry areas, outside livestock spaces.' She ran her finger down the sheet of paper. 'That's pretty much it.'

'Not the abattoir then?'

'Don't think so. I don't think it's even on the list,' Emily said. She looked again at her paperwork. 'It's not in use, is it?'

'Oh no, it's not been used in years,' Frank replied. 'Would you excuse me for a moment? I just need to make a quick phone call.' He held his mobile up for her to see. 'Won't be long.'

'Sure, no problem,' Emily said. 'At least you can get a bloody signal,' she added as Frank disappeared into another room.

43

A ndy walked into the foyer of Partridge Towers and was just about to leave through the glass double doors when a security guard stopped him. The term security guard was a bit of a stretch, as the man in the white shirt and tie must have been in his seventies, but he was one of the few people at Kett's who'd always been friendly to Andy.

'Door's closed, son,' the security guard said. 'You'll have to go out the back way to get to the garage, if that's where you're going.'

'Why is it closed?' Andy peered through the glass doors and noticed a small group of people standing outside.

'There's a demonstration.'

'Really? Cool. What about?'

'Meat,' the security guard said with a tired sigh. 'It's murder, apparently.'

As he stepped toward the glass door, Andy got a better look at what was happening on the steps to Partridge Towers. Although Norwich wasn't a hotbed of political activism, it wasn't the largest demonstration Andy had ever seen in the city. There were less than twenty protestors outside, several of them carrying posters on bits of wood. One of the posters read 'End Carnism'. Another had the words 'If you wouldn't eat a cat, why eat a pig?' in angry red letters. 'There is another way' was daubed on another poster, carried by an emaciated, pale woman who looked like she needed a good meal or two.

'Bloody liberals, look at them.' Andy turned to see the security guard standing next to him. 'Bunch of wasters. Need to get a job, they do.'

'What's Carnism?' Andy asked. 'Never heard of it.'

'Meat eating, I guess,' the guard replied. 'I'd eat a cat, though. Wouldn't think twice about it. Especially if it was next door's. That'd teach him to shit on my broccoli patch, that would.' Andy glanced at the security guard, realised that he wasn't joking, so kept silent.

The two of them spent the next ten minutes or so watching the demonstration. On the other side of the road, a bored looking policeman also watched. At one point, the demonstrators turned their attention to the policeman, who was a bit on the large side in Andy's opinion. Watching him chase after someone would be quite amusing, if short-lived.

'Burn, piggy, burn,' the protestors chanted for a minute or so, pointing at the policeman who looked utterly disinterested.

'It's not a very good demonstration, is it?' Andy asked the security guard. 'They all look a bit, I don't know, apathetic?' The guard just nodded in response. As they watched, one of the protestors who was carrying a poster sank to his knees, breathing heavily. He was relieved of the placard by a man with dreadlocks and red trousers, and helped to a nearby bench by one of the other protestors.

Andy watched the protest for another few minutes

before deciding that a major riot by militant vegetarians was unlikely to occur any time soon. He said 'good luck' to the security guard, and made his way out of the back door and into the garage. Retuning his radio to Canary FM just in case there was any breaking news such as Partridge Towers being stormed, he drove onto the A11 and plugged the postcode for Frank Pinch's butcher's shop into his sat-nav.

By the time he reached the shop, Andy had sat through a full thirty minutes of country and western music on the radio. He'd almost changed the radio channel several times, but the thought of Partridge Towers being razed to the ground was an entertaining enough daydream, so he kept listening until the top of the hour. The headline news on Canary FM was an article about an accident between a cyclist and a large goose in Wroxham, so Andy flipped the radio off just as the announcer was getting riled up about careless cyclists with no regard for Norfolk's wildlife.

Andy got out of the car and walked through the car park to the front of the shop. To his dismay, it was closed. He checked his watch. It wasn't even ten o'clock, so it wasn't shut for lunch. He put his hands up against the glass to look inside for any signs of life when an elderly lady sidled up to him. At her feet was what Andy thought was a Chihuahua, attached to a lead strong enough for an Alsatian.

'Ooh, that's a shame,' the woman said in a high-pitched warble. 'Is he closed then?' Andy looked at the sign on the door, with the word 'CLOSED' in large capital letters.

'I think he might be,' Andy replied.

'Bollocks,' the woman said. 'I'll have to go all the way to bloody Lidl now.' She shuffled off, leaving Andy with a smile on his face from her unexpected language.

When he was back at his car, Andy pulled his phone out from his pocket and called Martin. He needed a Plan B.

'Yo, big man,' Martin said as he answered. 'What's occurring?'

'Hi, mate,' Andy replied. 'I need a favour.'

'Of course. Your wish is my command. Just wait for a second while I drop everything I'm doing so that I can assist you.'

'Yeah, right. Minesweeper or Solitaire?'

'Solitaire. Not doing so well, though. What are you after?'

'Can you look up the address of that butcher bloke?' Andy asked. 'The competition winner. I need to get him to sign something, but his shop's closed.'

'Why is it closed? It's not lunchtime.'

'I don't bloody know, do I Martin?'

'Alright, keep your knickers on. Where is the address?'

'Er, it's on my desktop. In a Word file. You'll have to log on as me.'

'Hang on,' Martin said, and Andy heard him tapping the keyboard. 'Right, I'm logged off. What's your password?'

'Password,' Andy replied.

'Yeah, what is it?'

'Password. With a capital P.' He heard Martin chuckling down the line.

'Very original, mate,' Martin said. 'Wait one, Word's just creaking its way open. Here we go.' He recited the postcode down the line, and Andy scribbled it on an old receipt.

'Nice one, cheers buddy.'

'No problem, have fun at the farm.'

Andy tapped the postcode into his sat-nav and set off

in the direction it told him to. Twenty minutes later, he was stationary in a lane swearing at the sat-nav, which was pleading with him to turn left. Into a field. Just as he was about to turn the sat-nav off, his phone buzzed with a text message. It was from Martin.

Who do I message first as you, mate? Karen or the Big Cheese? Swearing under his breath, Andy tapped out a reply threatening Martin with a painful death if he messaged anyone, knowing that it wouldn't make a blind bit of difference. He put the car back into gear and kept going down the lane.

'Yes,' he said as he saw a crude handpainted sign for Hill Top Farm. 'Turn left my arse.'

44

F rank handed Emily her cup of tea.

'There you go, pet,' he said. If she was offended by being called 'pet', she didn't show it. 'Sorry about that. I just had to give Tom a quick bell to let him know that we'll be down there in a few minutes.' He watched as Emily sipped her tea.

'Okay, no worries,' she said. There was an awkward silence for a few moments.

'So, have you been working for the Food Standards lot for long, then?' Frank asked, figuring that he might as well try to make some conversation.

'A few months,' she replied.

'Going well, is it?'

'It's okay.'

'I bet you've got a few funny stories.'

'Er, not really.' Frank saw Emily frown for a second before shrugging her shoulders. She put the mug of tea, half finished, down on the floor and got to her feet. 'Shall we get cracking?'

They left the farmhouse and Emily walked over to her

Mini, pulling a pair of wellies out of the boot and putting them on. She also grabbed a clipboard from the car and returned to where Frank was standing.

'Mind if I ask you a few questions while we're walking to the sheds?' she asked.

'As long as you're happy with me answering them. I'm only a butcher,' Frank replied. Emily looked at him with a curious expression.

'But it's your farm as well as your brother's, isn't it?'

'It is, but all I do is chop meat up. Tom does everything else.'

'Well, I'm happy if you're happy,' Emily said, flashing a smile at Frank. 'It'll make the whole inspection quicker.'

'Sure, fire away.'

The two of them walked toward the sheds, Frank answering as many of Emily's questions as he could. There were a few that Tom would have to answer, like how often the pens were cleaned out, but Frank thought he did okay. At one point, Emily stepped in a puddle that was a lot deeper than it looked. Frank thought she was going to lose her balance and reached out his hand to grab her arm.

'Getoffme,' she barked, jerking her arm away from his hand and lifting her boot out of the hole in the track. Emily stood on one foot to pull her wellie off and poured water out of it. 'Sorry, that was a bit sharp.' Another brief smile. 'It's been a long day, and now I've got a soaking wet leg.'

'No problem,' Frank said, grinning and nodding toward the pothole. 'That's why we've got a tractor.'

When they reached the sheds, Frank walked with Emily toward the largest shed in the complex. As they approached the door, Frank saw Tom appear from the abattoir. Before he walked across to join them, Tom pulled a thick chain through the handles of the doors and padlocked them shut. At least Tom followed instructions sometimes, Frank thought.

'This one's the main shed,' Frank said to Emily as they stepped through the doors. 'We've not got much in here at the moment, just Boris the boar and a few pregnant sows.'

'Should be a lot fuller in a few months' time,' Tom added. 'Once they've popped.' Emily walked over to the pen with the sows in. Behind him, Frank heard Boris stir and get to his feet. The boar made a strange noise that Frank hadn't heard him make before.

'Did he just growl?' Frank whispered to Tom.

'Think so,' Tom replied. Frank looked across at Emily, who was leaning over the gate and petting one of the sows on the head. There was a deafening crash behind them, and Frank jumped as Boris threw himself at the gate of his pen.

'Jesus, Tom. Make sure the gate's secure, would you?' Frank looked at the boar and the stringy white saliva that was dripping from his mouth onto the floor of the shed. As Tom checked the latches on the gate, Frank followed Boris's eyes. The boar was staring at Emily's backside. She was still bent over the gate, scratching one of the sows behind the ear. Emily stood up and walked back to join them.

'Blimey, he looks a bit angry,' she said, nodding in Boris' direction.

'I don't think he is,' Tom said. 'I think he likes you.'

They spent the next thirty minutes going round the complex, Emily asking questions about the way it was run. Frank answered most of them, deferring to Tom when needed. When they got to the abattoir, Emily pointed her pen toward it.

'What's in there?' she asked, looking at Tom.

'Nothing,' Frank replied. 'That's the old abattoir. Not been used in years.'

'Didn't you just come from there though, Tom?'

'No,' Tom replied.

'Yes you did. I saw you chaining it shut.'

'What Tom means,' Frank said, 'is that it's not used for any sort of agricultural preparation. Tom's got an office in there. It's where he comes up with his secret recipes, like the one that won the competition. Isn't that right, Tom?'

'No,' Tom replied. Frank smiled at Emily and kicked Tom's leg, hoping that she wouldn't notice. 'I mean yes,' Tom said. 'Yes, I've got an office in there.' Emily paused, looking at Frank and Tom for a few seconds.

'Right,' she said, slowly. 'Okay. No problem. It's not on the schedule anyway. The only thing left is, hang on a second…' she looked down at her clipboard, 'the feeding stations in the fields.'

'Tom,' Frank said. 'Can I leave you to take Emily to the feeding pens? I need to nip back to the farmhouse, get some stuff sorted.' That wasn't strictly true. All Frank had to do was sharpen his knives, but the sooner he did that the sooner he and Tom could get cracking once Emily had gone.

'Yep, no problem,' Tom said.

'Take her to the pens, and then come back to the farmhouse,' Frank said, staring at his brother. 'Nowhere else, yeah?'

'Yep, got it.'

Frank made his way back to the farmhouse, dodging the potholes as he did so. He was thinking about what was actually in the abattoir, and how they could separate them out one by one. It wasn't going to be easy when none of them spoke any English, but he was sure that he could work something out. As long as they dealt with them one at a time, and without any of the others realising what was going on, it would be fine. He was just putting the finishing touches to the plan in his head when he heard tyres crunching on gravel. Looking up, he saw a bright yellow MG sports car pull into the yard in front of the farmhouse and park up next to Emily's Mini. A young man got out and stood next to the Mini, looking in through the windows. As Frank got closer to the yard, he recognised the visitor as the man from Kett's who'd collared him after the competition.

'Hi,' Frank said. 'You're from Kett's, aren't you? Alex, isn't it?' The man looked up at him.

'Andy. My name's Andy.'

'Oh, sorry.'

'It's okay, I'm used to it.' They looked at each other for a few seconds.

'So, can I help you?' Frank asked. Andy glanced at the Mini before looking back at Frank.

'I've got some paperwork for you to sign,' he replied. Frank sighed. They didn't get many visitors to the farm, and now they had two at the same time. Just when they had other work to be getting on with.

'Will it take long?' Frank asked.

'Nope, ten minutes tops.'

'Okay, cool. Come on in.' As they walked toward the farmhouse door, Frank noticed Andy looking back at the Mini again. He might only be a butcher, but he couldn't work out why a young man who drove an MG sports car would be so interested in a Mini.

45

T om whistled to himself as he walked back toward the farmhouse door. Emily, who had told him on the way back to the farmhouse that Catherine had really enjoyed the ride on the tractor, had just left. Tom had asked Emily to say 'hello' to Catherine for him, and to offer her a guided tour of the pig farm any time she wanted. Emily had smiled, taken his mobile number, and said that she was sure Catherine would love to have a proper look round the farm. Tom was just about to open the farmhouse door when it swung open and the young man from Kett's came out. That must be his yellow sports car in front of the farmhouse, then.

'Hi,' Tom said. 'Sorry, can't remember your name.'

'Andy,' the man said, looking at the yard in front of the farmhouse. He looked distracted. 'Has she gone?'

'Who?'

'Emily.'

'Who?'

'Jesus wept, Emily. From the Food Standards Agency.'

'Oh yeah, she left.'

'Bollocks.'

'That's a swear.'

When the man from Kett's, Andy, had left, Tom walked into the kitchen. Frank was wrapping his butcher's knives up in their oilskin on the kitchen table.

'Are we good?' Tom asked. Frank looked at him through dark eyes.

'I think so,' he said. 'Come on, let's get it done.'

As the brothers walked back down the track toward the shed complex, Tom listened carefully as Frank outlined the plan. He — Frank — would get the immigrants one at a time into the abattoir, where Tom would dispatch them. Frank was quite clear on that bit. He wasn't going to do the actual killing, that was all up to Tom. The plan was fine with Tom. After all, they were just meat. That was what Frank had told him, so it must be okay.

The first one was easy. Frank had brought him into the abattoir while Tom had hidden behind the door. The immigrant had started sweeping the floor when Tom stepped behind him and put the electrodes on either side of his head. Thirty seconds later, the man was upside down and hanging by the ankles from the pulley system on the roof of the abattoir. A quick jab to the neck from one of Frank's favourite knives, but delivered by Tom, and that was it. Tom hauled the now pale body on the pulley into the back room while Frank hosed the floor down, and that was it. Once the doors to the back room were closed, there was no sign of anything untoward. Job done, as far as Tom was concerned. One down, four to go.

They left thirty minutes or so before they did the next one. Frank had said that it would be a good way of stopping the others from getting suspicious. If it had been up to Tom, they would have done them all straight away, one after the other like they used to do when they slaughtered pigs on the farm. The second one went without a hitch. If anything, it was smoother than the first one. It was the same with the third one.

'We're getting this down to a fine art, Frank,' Tom said as his brother hosed the floor down again. Frank didn't reply, but just grunted. 'Are you sure you don't want to change over? I feel a bit bad using your favourite knife. Do you want a go?'

'No,' Frank said. 'I'll be using them enough preparing the meat.' Tom laughed. Frank had always been a bit squeamish with live animals, though. Tom thought back to when they were younger, and their father was trying to teach them how to kill a pig. The first time Frank had watched one being slaughtered, he'd run from the abattoir, screaming and in floods of tears. Tom hadn't been bothered in the slightest when his father had offered him the knife instead.

'Just here, son,' his father had said, pointing with the tip of the knife at the best part of the pig's neck. Tom had been surprised how easily the knife had slipped into the flesh, and he couldn't work out why Frank had been so upset. Mind you, Tom thought, he had only been seven at the time.

By the time the fourth immigrant was hanging upside down in the back room, Tom could see that Frank was starting to get tetchy. At least they only had one to go, and then they could go to the pub. Tom took up his position behind the door as Frank went to get the last of the workers. When Frank walked him into the abattoir, Tom could see that he was by far the biggest of all of them. He wasn't that tall, but he was pretty wide. Tom stepped forward, his button on the trigger of the stun gun, and put the electrodes on either side of the man's forehead. Just as Tom pulled the trigger, the man jerked and one of the electrodes slid away from his skin. Tom jabbed at the button, but nothing happened.

The immigrant whipped round and looked at Tom holding the electrodes in his hands. The next thing he knew, Tom was sitting on the floor, his back against the wall, blood streaming out of his nose. He'd been punched in the face for the first time in his life, and it bloody well hurt. The immigrant was standing over him, fists clenched. He leaned forward and pulled one fist back.

'Frank, do something,' Tom shouted through his blocked nose. 'Quick, do something.' Tom couldn't see where Frank was as the immigrant was blocking his view, but he hoped that he was doing something. Tom didn't want to get punched again, and the man looked really angry.

Tom flinched at the deafening bang which echoed off the stone walls of the abattoir. His ears whined, the high-pitched noise blocking everything else out. His attacker jerked upward, and threw his arms back as if he was trying to get to something on his back. A few seconds later, he started sliding to the floor to reveal Frank standing behind him, the captive bolt gun in his hand. Tom's brother's jaw had dropped, and he looked at the man on the floor with a look of utter surprise while a wisp of grey smoke made its way from the barrel of the bolt gun.

'Get his legs,' Tom shouted, the high-pitched whining still ringing around his head. Frank shook his head from side to side and dropped the gun. Between them, they got the immigrant strung up so that Tom could jab him in the neck, just in case. The blood didn't pump out of the wound like it had done with the others, so he was probably already dead, but it didn't hurt to be careful. At least, that was what Tom thought.

'Blimey, Frank,' Tom said once they had moved the last

body into the back room. 'That was a bit close.' He picked up the gun from the floor and re-set the bolt before putting it carefully back on the table.

'Er, yeah,' Frank replied, almost in a whisper.

'He was going to punch me again, cheeky sod.'

'In fairness, Tom, you were trying to kill him,' Frank said. 'Your nose okay?'

'Yeah, it's fine. Just a bit sore.'

'Fuck me, I need a drink.'

'Frank,' Tom replied, 'you know I don't like it when you swear.'

46

E mily flipped through the channels on the car radio until she found one that didn't fade out every few seconds. That was the good news. The bad news was that it was Canary FM, which wouldn't have been her first choice of channel. When she got onto the A11, she could retune to something else. Preferably something that wasn't playing country and western music.

As she drove, the thought about the inspection back at the Pinchs' farm. It had gone okay, she thought. Emily still couldn't see what Catherine saw in the farmer, Tom. He was a strange chap. To be fair, they were both a bit odd, but they must be doing something right to have won the competition. Hopefully, they'd leave her some good feedback on the inspection. God knows, she'd dropped enough hints to the butcher about overlooking some of the minor infractions in return for a decent writeup.

What had surprised her was the bright yellow MG parked next to her Mini in front of the farmhouse. She knew it belonged to the young lad from Kett's of Norwich, as she remembered seeing him at the competition. He must have popped round to talk to them about the contract or something like that. What was his name again? She tutted while she tried to remember. The best she could come up with was that it began with 'A'. Or was it 'O'? Oscar?

Emily was just about to turn the channel over to see if she was in range of something other than Dolly Parton, when an announcer interrupted the wailing.

'We're interrupting this program with some breaking news,' a woman's voice said. There was a pause, and Emily could hear papers rustling in the background. 'Exclusive to Canary FM, stay tuned for a newsflash.' Emily turned the radio up as she joined the slip road to the dual carriageway.

'Canary FM has received reports confirming that Norfolk Police are investigating the discovery of what appears to be human DNA in sausages being sold by a popular local supermarket, Kett's of Norwich,' the woman on the radio said, breathless with excitement. 'We're going to cut now, live, to a press conference with the Chief Superintendent of Norfolk Police.'

'Bloody hell,' Emily whispered as she inched the radio up another notch. She could hear people whispering on the radio before a woman's voice cut across them.

'Ladies and Gentlemen, good afternoon.' The voice was stern, authoritarian. 'My name is Chief Superintendent Jo Antonio, Norfolk Police. I can confirm that, this afternoon, following a report from the Food Standards Agency, we are investigating the discovery of human DNA within a sample of meat we believe to be from Kett's of Norwich.' Emily winced as the room erupted into a sea of voices, and she turned the radio down a notch.

'Jo Jo? Jo Jo?' a man's voice cut through the tumult.

'Yes,' the policewoman said.

'Bob Rutler, Canary FM,' the man continued. 'Have you confirmed the source of the meat?'

'We think it's probably from a human being, Bob.'

'Er, yeah, sure,' Bob said. 'Got that bit. But where did it come from? Who supplied it?'

'We're not sure,' the superintendent replied. 'There was a mix-up at the laboratory. The tray of samples was dropped, but we have been able to narrow it down to one of a few farms.'

'How many farms?' a woman's voice shrieked.

'I cannot comment on an active police investigation.' As the policewoman said this, the room erupted again. The noise from the press conference faded out, and the announcer's voice came back on the radio.

'Well, goodness. We'll bring you more updates as they come in. In the meantime, here's an old favourite from Tim McGraw.' An electric guitar began playing as the woman spoke over the intro. 'Do you want fries with that?' she breathed.

'Shit, shit, shit,' Emily muttered as she flicked the radio off. She needed to get back to the Food Standards Agency as soon as she could.

Half an hour later, after breaking most of the speed limits on the way, Emily pulled her mini onto the road outside the Food Standards Agency. As she drove past the head offices of Kett's of Norwich, she saw a crowd of people milling about outside the building, some of them waving banners. An overweight policeman was standing at the front door with his arms outstretched, and over his shoulder Emily could see a scared looking elderly man in a security guard's uniform looking out from the other side of the door. Emily pulled over to the side of the road at the sound of sirens behind her, and she watched as a couple of police vans screamed past before screeching to a halt outside the building.

'Oh my God,' Emily whispered as she crept her car past the demonstration. The police vans had discharged a whole bunch of coppers in riot gear, who were busy hitting anyone they could reach with rubber truncheons. When she was clear of the fighting, she accelerated toward the ramp that led to the garage under the Food Standards Agency.

Once she was in the building, Emily spoke to a couple of people to try to find out what was going on, but no-one seemed to know anything. She made her way toward Mr Clayton's office and walked in, forgetting to knock on the door. Inside the office was a tough looking policewoman, deep in conversation with Mr Clayton. In the corner of the room, Emily saw Gary from the lab. He was sitting on a chair, his head in his hands. Mr Clayton glanced across at Emily.

'Emily, have you given the lab any samples in the last week?'

'Er, yeah, I have.'

'Which farm?'

'It wasn't from a farm, it was from a butcher's,' Emily replied. 'But the meat was from Hill Top Farm.' The policewoman looked at the clipboard she was holding. 'I've just done their inspection,' Emily added.

'I've already done that sample from the butcher's,' a quiet voice said in the corner. Emily turned to Gary. 'It's not that one. I already said, all the samples were from the competition.'

'Well that's just great.' The policewoman scribbled on the clipboard. 'So how many different producers were in the competition?'

'About twenty,' Mr Clayton said. 'But of those, there

were only five different sausage meats. The samples Gary dropped were all from sausages, so it must be one of those five.'

'Right,' the policewoman said with a grim smile. 'That narrows it down a bit at, least. We're just going to have to go round them, one by one.' She pulled a mobile phone from her pocket, and prodded the screen. 'Not fucking ideal at all.'

Emily walked over to where Gary was sitting. She put a hand on his shoulder, and he looked at her with red-rimmed eyes.

'Are you okay?' she asked him.

'It wasn't my fault,' he replied, his voice faltering. 'I didn't mean to drop the bloody tray. I was in a hurry to get to the phone, that was all. I didn't do it on purpose.' Emily wasn't sure quite what to say, so she just squeezed his shoulder and tried to look sympathetic.

47

A ndy shivered and pulled his coat tighter around him. He was sitting in his car, parked in a layby not far from the turnoff to Hill Top Farm. It wasn't a bad spot in terms of keeping an eye on what was going on at the farm. He could see the farmhouse, and just about see the sheds further away. He'd been sitting there for well over an hour, thinking about what he was going to do next.

The conversation with the butcher had been interesting. When Andy had got him to sign the non-disclosure arrangement, he'd seemed friendly enough, so Andy had taken the opportunity to ask him about the recipe that they'd used to win the competition. The butcher had laughed, saying that his brother had the recipe in an office on the farm. Not in the farmhouse, the butcher had said, but in one of the outbuildings. From where he was sitting, Andy couldn't see any other buildings other than the farm-house and the barn next to it, so the office must be in the sheds in the distance. With the beginnings of an idea in the back of his mind, Andy had tried to get some more information, but the butcher wouldn't give anything else up. The only other piece of information that he'd managed to get was that the butcher and his brother were going to the pub that evening, once they had 'attended to some business'.

While he sat in the car, wondering how long it would be before they left the farm, Andy thought about the young woman from the Food Standards Agency. Emily. Even though she'd kneed him in the bollocks, there was something about her that was growing on him. When he'd seen her car outside the farm, Andy was chuffed to bits at the thought of speaking to her again. The fact that the butcher had commented on the look of disappointment on his face when he left the farmhouse and her car had gone pissed Andy off no end, but there was nothing he could do about it.

Andy had never broken the law in his life, at least not deliberately. The fact that he was sitting in the car contemplating what he thought was breaking and entering just showed how desperate things had become. He hoped that the shed with the farmer's office would be open, and that he could just walk in and look for the recipe. Surely it wouldn't be breaking and entering if he didn't break anything? Andy thought about what Charles the Big Cheese would say when he walked in with a copy of the secret recipe. Or maybe he could approach one of Kett's competitors and sell it to them to teach Kett's a lesson? It wasn't as if they had treated him that well, after all. He was chewing over the options of what to do with a copy of the recipe when he heard an engine starting up. Andy looked over at the farm and could see a pair of headlights in front of the farmhouse. They moved forward, and onto the track leading to the road Andy was sitting at the side of.

As the headlights got to the end of the track and

turned onto the road, Andy shrugged himself as far down in the driver's seat as he could. Hiding in a bright yellow sports car wasn't ideal, but Andy had pulled his MG as far over to the bushes at the edge of the layby as he could without damaging the paintwork. It was almost dark as well, which would help. The headlights illuminated the car for a brief second, and Andy slid over and lay down on the passenger seat as a Land Rover pulled past him.

He stayed where he was for a few minutes until he was sure that the car had gone and not stopped to turn around. Andy sat back up in the car and watched the farm for any signs of life. Shivering, he gave it a good five minutes before deciding that they had both left. He started the car, turned the heater up to full, and crept along to the track leading up to the farm.

Andy parked the car in front of the farmhouse, just like any other visitor, and got out. He walked up to the front door and rapped hard on the solid wood. If anyone answered, he had a cover story prepared about wanting to check a couple of things in the non-disclosure agreement, but in the end that wasn't needed. There was no-one home. He took a deep breath and looked past his car to the pig sheds a couple of hundred yards from where he was standing, and although the light was fading, he could see that the condition of the track leading to the sheds was far worse than the track he'd just driven down. The clearance under his MG was limited at best, and the last thing he wanted to do was to drive up the track and risk snapping an axle, so he set off on foot toward the silhouetted complex.

By the time he was half-way to the pig sheds, both his feet were sopping wet up to the ankles. More than once, he'd almost stumbled after stepping into what he had thought was a shallow puddle. The problem was that a lot of them weren't puddles, nor were they shallow.

'For fuck's sake,' he muttered as his foot disappeared up to mid-shin in yet another pot hole. At least he could see his destination a bit more clearly now. The sheds were in darkness, with only the faintest glimpse of light coming from one of them. On any other night, the sun setting behind them would have been quite spectacular, but tonight Andy wasn't in the slightest bit bothered about the sunset. He focused in on the shed on the far right of the complex, where a thin strip of light was shining from underneath the door. Was that the office?

He reached the group of sheds a few moments later, all thoughts of his wet feet forgotten. This was it. Andy stopped for a few minutes. He crouched down, listening hard for any signs of life, but there was nothing. Creeping his way toward the shed with the light on inside, he circled the building to see if there was another way in apart from the main door. There wasn't. It was a squat, brick-built building, with no entrance apart from the front door. There weren't even any windows. One way in, one way out.

Andy took a deep breath and nudged at the door with his foot. To his relief, it swung open.

'Hello?' he called through the open door, just in case. Andy didn't know what he would say if there was someone there, but there wasn't, so he didn't need to worry. He stepped into the shed and looked around. There wasn't much in the shed apart from a large table, a free-standing cupboard with some equipment on top of it, and a drain in the middle of the floor. The air inside was stuffy and smelled of something that Andy couldn't place. A hosepipe lay coiled near the drain, attached to a tap on the wall. There certainly wasn't an office in the shed. Muttering to himself, Andy tip-toed over to a door at the back of the shed. The office must be in there. It took him a moment to work out how to open the door, but when he pressed down on the latch, it opened with a satisfying 'clunk'.

'Hello?' Andy called out again as he swung the door open.

48

F rank swung the Land Rover into the pub car park
and squeezed it in between a brand-new Audi TT
and a red BMW that wasn't much older. He opened the
door of his vehicle and smiled as it bounced off the front
wing of the Audi.

'Oops,' he said with a grin. Bloody people from the
city, coming to the countryside to remind anyone living in
the countryside how little money they had. Frank didn't
bother to check to see if his door had left a mark on the
Audi or not. He couldn't care less if it had.

Inside the pub, Mike was already sitting at their usual
table near the fireplace. He had three pints of lager in
front of him, one of them half empty. Frank walked across
to join him, nodding at the landlady as he did so. She
didn't nod back, but just stared at him with her arms
folded tightly across her ample chest. Frank had got a bit
too drunk in the pub a while ago, and might have said a
few things to her that he wouldn't have said if he had been
sober. He risked another glance at her. Thank God she'd
chosen to be offended at what he'd said and not actually

taken him up on his offer, Frank thought, and not for the first time. One thing the landlady of the Dog and Duck wasn't employed for by the brewery was her looks.

'How do, mate,' Mike said as Frank arrived at the table. 'You alright, then?'

'Mustn't grumble,' Frank said, sitting in the chair. It complained loudly as he made himself comfortable. 'You?'

'All good,' Mike replied, taking a sip of his lager. Frank picked up a glass from the table and took a large slug.

'Cheers,' he said before wiping foam off his top lip.

'He in the toilet, then?' Mike asked, nodding at the third glass.

'Who, Tom?'

'Yep.'

'No, he's back at the farm,' Frank said. 'Changed his mind about coming out to play. When I left he was up on the far field, trying to fix a hole in the fence.'

Mike started laughing. 'I didn't think you'd got any stock to escape from that field.' Frank looked at his friend before deciding that although he was taking the piss, there was no point being upset about it.

'We will have, soon,' he said with a brief smile. 'Got three sows getting ready to do their thing.'

'Tom did mention that. Old Boris was a good buy after all, then.'

The two men sipped their pints in companionable silence for a few moments before Mike changed the subject.

'Saw your ugly mug on the front page of the Eastern Daily News the other day,' he said.

'Really?' Frank replied. 'I've not seen that.'

'Hang on there for a second. I'll ask Randy Rachel if she's still got a copy behind the bar.' Frank grimaced as Mike got to his feet, returning a moment later with a dog-eared copy of the local paper. 'Here you go, mate.' He put the paper on the table.

Frank looked at the front page. Sure enough, there he was, gurning at the camera. Not his best look, all things being considered, but he'd never been on the front page of the paper before. It was unlikely, Frank considered, that he ever would be again.

'Cool,' he said. 'Not the most flattering photograph, though.'

'Better than the one on the next page,' Mike said. Frank opened the paper. On the inside page was a picture of the bloke who'd been running the competition, standing next to Tina off the telly. The cameraman had caught him staring down the inside of Tina's dress as she tried to catch a falling piece of paper.

'Oh dear,' Frank laughed. 'Talk about being rumbled.'

'I bet his wife wasn't impressed,' Mike said. 'So, what's she like, then?'

'Who? His wife? No bloody idea.'

'Not her, you prat. The weather woman. You had a bit of thing for her a while ago, didn't you?'

'You know they say that being on television puts ten pounds on you?' Frank said. From the look on Mike's face, he'd not heard that, but Frank carried on anyway. 'Well, in her case it's more like twenty. It's not just that though, but when you see her up close...' Frank bared his teeth into a rictus grin, '...you can see she's had quite a bit of work done.'

'Oh, right,' Mike laughed. 'Got you.' He paused before continuing. 'She still worth a squirt, though?' Frank laughed, spluttering into his lager.

'That's what I like about you, Mike,' Frank said, still laughing. 'Your uncanny ability to cut right to the heart of the matter.'

A few minutes later, they were sitting with full glasses in front of them. Frank had been to the bar and managed to buy two more pints and a couple of packets of crisps without any conversation whatsoever with the landlady.

'I think she likes you, mate,' Mike said, sipping his lager and nodding at Randy Rachel. 'She's not made of wood, after all.'

'Yeah, yeah,' Frank replied. 'I know. Her eyes aren't painted on.'

'So, this competition thing,' Mike said, 'what does it actually mean then, apart from you looking like Jimmy Saville on the front page of the paper?'

'Got a contract now with Kett's of Norwich, so we have,' Frank replied. 'Exclusive providers of their Pride of Anglia range.'

'Sounds impressive.'

'I had to sign a non-disclosure thing earlier today. Some work experience lad came round, can't remember his name. We're not allowed to sell the recipe to anyone else or we get sued to death.'

'You've actually got a recipe?' Mike asked.

'Well, Tom's got something up there in his head. I think he makes it up as he goes along, but we won the competition, so I'm not complaining.'

Mike leaned back in his chair and frowned.

'When are those sows due?' he asked. Frank looked at his friend and knew exactly where he was going.

'Few months.'

'In which case,' Mike said, leaning across the table and continuing in a conspiratorial whisper that half the pub could probably hear. 'Where's the meat coming from?' Frank took a second to compose himself before replying.

'I've got a source.'

'I'll bet you have, sunshine.' Mike lowered his voice to a proper whisper. 'Is it Aldi?'

Frank raised his glass and took a long drink of his lager. He arched one eyebrow in Mike's direction.

'Don't ask, don't tell, fella. But it's amazing what a handful of herbs and spices can do to shit quality meat.'

'Ah,' Mike replied, winking. 'Gotcha.'

49

E mily made her way to her desk, ignoring the raised voices in the open plan office. She threw her bag onto the back of the chair, sat down, and sighed. Bloody hell, she thought. What on earth was going on? The look on Gary's face back in Mr Clayton's office was awful, and her heart had gone out to the man. She logged on to her computer and waited as it whirred into life. Knowing how long it would take her e-mail programme to start up, she considered going to the machine for a cup of coffee, but decided against it. When her in-box finally creaked into life, she saw that she only had a handful of emails, and that the majority of them were from Catherine. Emily clicked open the latest one.

Where are you? the message read. *What's going on.?? Call me or at least reply to your texts.* Emily reached into her pocket for her phone. She'd not felt it vibrate with any text messages. A few seconds later, she realised why. It wasn't in her pocket. She reached around for her bag, even though she hardly ever put her in there for fear of scratching the screen. It wasn't in there either.

'Bugger,' Emily muttered. The phone must be in the car, which was all the way down in the garage. She typed out a quick reply to Catherine to say that she was back at work, and they were trying to work out which farm the meat was from. Within seconds, there was a ping as an e-mail came in.

OMG!!! I can't believe it's true. I had a kebab on the way home last night from that dodgy shop on the Prince of Wales Road. Do you think it was human?? Emily thought for a moment before smirking and typing out a one-word reply.

Probably. She would apologise to Catherine later, but the opportunity was too good to miss.

Ten minutes later, Emily sat in the driver's seat of her car. She'd turned the car upside down looking for her phone, figuring that it must have slipped down the side of the seat or something, but it was nowhere to be found. She retraced her steps in her head, trying to remember the last time she had used it. Emily remembered trying to call Mr Clayton from Hill Top Farm, and not being able to get a signal. Then she'd put the phone in her pocket. Then she'd sat in that dilapidated chair.

'Oh, for fuck's sake,' she muttered, pulling the driver's door closed. Her phone must have fallen out of her pocket when she had slid back into the chair. There was no way she could survive without her phone until tomorrow. Emily didn't have a choice — she would have to go back and get it.

Emily decided to take a different way through Norwich to get onto the dual carriageway to avoid any demonstrators. She pulled out of the underground garage and flicked the radio on. There was a man singing about losing his wife, his house, and his dog on the station. As she listened, Emily realised that of the three, he was least fussed about losing his wife. The song finished, and the same announcer as before came back on.

'That was Hank Nelson, with his classic song, "I Miss My Dog the Most." Now, we're going back to the ongoing situation in the centre of Norwich.' The announcer took a deep breath. 'There're reports of widespread disturbances from the Station all the way up to the Castle. Norfolk Police are advising residents not to come into the city at all.'

'Blimey,' Emily muttered to herself.

'There was a report about a large crowd gathering at Carrow Road football stadium, but it turned out to be a peaceful demonstration against the cost of next season's home kit. There has been a lot of trouble elsewhere though, concentrated around Partridge Towers which is of course where the human meat is from.' In her excitement, the announcer's Norfolk accent got stronger, and she pronounced the word human as 'hooman'. 'We're going to go now to an outside broadcast with Canary FM's very own Bob Rutler, who is coming live to us from St Stephen's Street. Bob, can you hear me?'

The radio changed to static for a few seconds before a male voice cut in.

'Emilia, thank you. Yes, I can hear you. I'm in the middle of St Stephen's, right next to the dodgy computer shop that sells nicked stuff. It's madness here. There's groups of people running up and down the road, being chased by police. The police aren't messing about, either. There's a lot of people being hit with batons. I even saw an elderly lady with a shopping trolley get on the wrong side of the long arm of the law. There was blood piss... I mean pouring from her head, there was. '

'Bob, I hope you're safe where you are?' Just as the

female presenter said this, there was the sound of breaking glass in the background.

'Oh my Lord, Emilia,' Bob said, gasping. 'The front window of Poundland has just been smashed in. There's people streaming into the shop. They must be those looters they have down in that London sometimes.'

'Goodness me,' Emilia breathed. 'What are they stealing, Bob?' There was a long burst of static on the radio. 'Bob? Are you still there?'

'Yes, I'm fine, sorry.'

'What are they stealing, Bob?'

'Well Emilia, one woman has just run past me with a family size pack of value toilet roll. I'd say they're stealing whatever they can get their hands on. I've never seen anything like this in Norwich. The thing is though - ' Bob was cut off by a loud thud that made Emily wince. His voice came back on the radio. 'No, no, I'm press,' he screamed. 'Look, I've got ID.' There was another thud, followed by Bob swearing. Emily leaned in to the radio as another male voice came over the air.

'You're nicked, you beardy fuck,' the voice said. There was another wet thwack that was followed by a loud hiss. Emily could just hear Bob screaming something about his eyes when his voice was faded out.

'Oh my goodness,' the woman's voice said. 'That was Canary FM's very own Bob Rutler, being attacked by rioters during a live broadcast. I do hope he's okay, and on behalf of Canary FM, I would like to apologise for any bad language that listeners may have heard during that broadcast.' The woman took a deep breath. 'And now, another classic from Hank Nelson.'

As the country singer started telling the world about the day his dog went blind, Emily turned the radio down so that she could just hear the music. She could turn it back up again if there were any updates.

50

When Andy opened his eyes, he noticed several things in very quick succession. The first was that it was pitch-black. The second was that, apart from his underpants, he was naked. The final thing he realised, and this was the most disconcerting of the three, was that he was hanging upside down by his ankles with his hands tied behind his back.

'What the fuck?' he said, wriggling to see if he could free either his arms or his legs. He had the mother of all headaches, which wasn't helping, and his wrists felt as if they were tied together so tightly there was no way he was going to get them free. If he couldn't free his hands, there was no way he was going to be able to do anything about being upside down. Andy felt his heart racing in his chest, and he took a couple of deep breaths to try to calm down and work out what the fuck was going on.

The last thing he remembered was pushing the door to the back room open and trying to find the light switch. Everything after that was a complete blank. One thing he did know now though was that he hadn't been alone at the farm after all. Wincing with the effort, he bent at the waist to see if he could swing back and forth. Maybe he could dislodge something or work his ankles loose? He managed to get a bit of momentum going, but then knocked into something else that was also hanging from the ceiling. Stifling a scream, Andy realised that it must be a pig. A dead pig.

'Jesus wept,' he whispered.

Andy's heart started thudding in his chest as the seriousness of his situation became obvious. He thought back to the table in the other room. The drain in the middle of the room with the hosepipe. The fact that he was hanging upside down. Andy had never before had a panic attack, but he knew that he was about to have one if he couldn't get himself free. He was in a slaughterhouse.

He flexed his wrists and thought that perhaps there was a tiny bit of give in whatever they were tied together with. Over the next few minutes, he twisted his wrists, turned them, flexed and relaxed them. There was definitely some more movement around the ties, so he redoubled his efforts. By the time he eventually managed to squeeze one of his hands free, Andy was covered in a thin sheet of perspiration despite the fact he was almost naked. He shook the rope off his other hand and massaged his wrists to try to get the circulation back into them.

Andy stretched his arms down to find he could now touch the cold stone floor. He tried pushing them downward to relieve the tension on his ankles. Maybe he could work them free if there wasn't so much weight on them? After a couple of tries he realised that wasn't going to work. He didn't have the strength in his arms to support his entire body weight for more than a second or two at a time. The next thing he tried was pulling himself up in a bizarre parody of a sit-up to try to get his hands up to his ankles, but he had nowhere near the strength to do that, either.

'Think, for God's sake. Think,' he said. 'Come on, there must be something.'

He put his hands back on the floor and felt around to see if there was anything he could use. There was nothing in the immediate area, so he tried swinging himself again to extend the area he could search. On the third or fourth swing, his fingers brushed against something on the floor. Andy renewed his efforts to swing in that direction and was rewarded when his fingers closed around some material. Pulling it toward him, he worked his hands over it to work out what it was. When he got to a leather belt, he realised that it was his jeans.

'Oh, thank God,' he said. His phone was in the pocket of his jeans. He could phone the police, get them to come and rescue him. 'Thank God,' he repeated as he pulled the phone from his jeans pocket. Dropping the trousers back on the floor, he put his thumb on the home button to turn the screen on.

No signal.

'Oh, for fuck's sake,' he shouted, throwing the phone onto the floor. As soon as he heard it skittering across the stone tiles, he realised that was a stupid thing to do. The phone had a torch that he could have used to have a proper look round. Maybe find something that he could use to free himself?

Andy hung there for a few moments, blinking to try to shift his headache. The phone screen was still illuminated, and he could see the vague outlines of pigs hanging up around him. There were at least four, maybe more. A few seconds later, the screen turned itself off and he was plunged back into the pitch-dark. To his surprise, he felt tears at the corner of his eyes well up and drip down his forehead. He shook his head from side to side.

He didn't know if it was the butcher or the farmer that had strung him up. Either way, it didn't matter. Whoever it was wouldn't have stripped him and hung him upside down in a slaughterhouse unless they were going to kill him. He'd been so focused on trying to get free that he hadn't really considered that. Andy let the tears flow as he realised that this was it. It was going to be game over at some point in the not too distant future.

51

Tom was furious. He didn't get angry that often, but as he looked at himself in the mirror in his kitchen, he realised he was properly furious.

He'd been working on the fence line over at the far end of the farm near the woods when he'd heard an engine followed by car tyres crunching on the gravel outside the farmhouse. The noise had carried well over the field, and the car wasn't exactly subtle. He could see the low slung yellow sports car from where he was. Tom had watched as a young man had got out of the car and walked up to the farmhouse door, knocking on it. It was the young lad from the supermarket. What was he doing at the farmhouse? That was trespassing, that was. He'd not been invited. People turning up without being invited made Tom angry, unless they were official people who could visit whenever they wanted.

Tom had ducked down as he saw the visitor look around the farm and across at the sheds. A few seconds later, Tom risked lifting his head back up to see what was going on, and to his dismay he saw the lad walking down the track toward the pig sheds. Not only had this lad turned up uninvited, but he'd then decided to have a wander round.

'I am furious,' Tom said to his reflection. 'I am...' he dropped his voice to a whisper even though he knew he was on his own in the farmhouse, '...fucking furious.' There, that was how angry he was. He'd actually sworn, even if it was only to himself. Maybe he should swear a bit more?

Tom left his position in front of the mirror and walked over to the table. He picked up his phone and looked at the screen. A flashing blue dot showed that Frank was still at the pub, but the fact it was flashing meant that the app couldn't contact the phone. Which meant that Frank had no signal, so wouldn't have picked up any of the texts that Tom had sent in the last twenty minutes or so. He had no idea what to do about the man hanging upside down in the abattoir. The others had been easy. They weren't British, they weren't from Norfolk. They were just meat. But this one was different. He was almost one of their own.

Stunning him had been easy. Tom had got to the shed just after the man had slipped inside the outside door. Tom inched his wellies off so that he could tip-toe into the shed after him. One thing that Tom was looking forward to telling Frank about was how he'd thought of that, taking off his boots so he couldn't be heard. The man was just about to turn the light on to the back room, where the others were, when Tom had slipped the electrodes onto either side of his head and a split second later, the man had dropped to the floor. Tom had stripped him, resisted the urge to look inside his pants to see how big his pee pee was and if it was bigger than his own, before he'd strung him upside down with the others.

Tom had crouched next to the man for a few moments,

the knife in his hand, trying to decide whether to stick him without talking to Frank. The problem was, he didn't know what his brother's reaction would be. He could be really, really angry. Or he might not mind at all. Tom couldn't decide which, so in the end he tied the man's wrists behind his back and turned the lights off on his way out of the room.

'Come on, Frank,' Tom said with another glance at his phone. He crossed to the cupboard with the whisky in it and poured himself a large glass. Their father had always said that whisky was the best cure for anger, but seeing as the more their father drank it, the angrier he got, Tom wasn't convinced that was true. He took a large sip, enjoying the burning sensation as it worked its way down his throat.

Tom knew he had two choices. He could go back to the shed and stick the young man. Or he could wait until Frank got in touch with him to tell him what to do. The sensible thing to do would be to wait, so that's what Tom decided to do. It didn't stop him being angry, though. One thing he had done, which again he was again quite proud of thinking about, was to hide the stupid yellow car in the barn. The man had his car keys in his pocket, so Tom had used them to move the car from the front of the farmhouse. There was no way he would buy one of them, though. It was way too low down to be comfortable. Tom couldn't see what the point of a sports car was if you risked putting your back out getting in and out of them, no matter how quick they were.

He was on his third large glass of whisky when he heard the gravel in front of the farmhouse crunching.

'About bloody time, big brother,' he said, getting to his feet. Tom picked up the phone and looked again at the screen. The flashing blue dot was still over the pub. Tom frowned, not understanding why that would be. If Frank wasn't in the pub, why did the app say that he was? Maybe his phone was broken, or he'd left it in the pub or something? Tom walked over to the window to look out over the courtyard. When he saw the car that had pulled up, he ducked down again much like he had done earlier when he'd seen the little yellow car. What had parked in front of the farmhouse wasn't Frank's Range Rover. It was a bright red Mini, with the blonde woman from the Food Standards Agency getting out of the driver's seat.

52

E mily closed the car door behind her and stood looking at the farmhouse for a few seconds. She couldn't be sure, but she thought she caught a glimpse of movement at one of the windows. She walked over to the door and rapped on it several times before taking a step back. There was no reply, so she crossed to the window that she thought she'd seen something at and put her hands up against the glass to look inside. The kitchen looked exactly how it had earlier in the day, and there was no sign of anyone.

'Bugger,' she muttered as she walked back over to the car. A few feet away from it, she noticed something on the ground glinting in the light of her headlamps. Reaching down, she saw what she thought at first was a coin in the mud, but when she got closer, she could see that it was a silver disc. When she got her fingers under the disc, she realised that it was attached to something else, hidden in the mud. Emily pulled at the disc and a car key attached to it plopped out. She turned the disc over to see what was on the other side. It read 'MG Owners Club', with the distinctive MG logo in the middle of the key ring in large black letters. Emily had seen it before, but it took her a couple of minutes to work out where. When that lad had blocked her in at the butcher's shop, he had been twiddling the key ring between his fingers before he'd raced off.

Emily was intrigued. If he'd lost his car key, then where was his car? She looked around the ground to see if anything else had been dropped, but all she could see was gravel. Wincing as one of her knees clicked when she stood back up, Emily looked around to see if there were signs of life anywhere on the farm. The only thing she could see that indicated any sort of activity were some dim lights coming from the pig sheds.

She walked back towards her car, almost stepping in a puddle but managing to stop just short of it. Emily looked down and saw some wide, flat tyre tracks leading from the puddle toward the barn next to the farmhouse. They weren't from her car, as she hadn't driven this far into the yard. As far as she knew, the butcher drove a Land Rover and the farmer only drove a tractor. Emily smiled briefly as she remembered Catherine and her lift to the cinema, but her smile disappeared as she thought about the tyres on Land Rovers and tractors. Neither had wide, flat tyres.

Frowning, Emily walked over to the barn door. It was almost shut, but not quite, so she nudged it with her foot to open it. The inside of the barn was pitch-black, but when she swung the door open the headlights of her Mini lit up the interior. The inside of the barn was unremarkable. All she could see was agricultural machinery, sacks of God knows what piled up in one corner, and a dust cover over something in the middle of the barn. Something, Emily realised, that was not that far off the same shape as a car. She walked into the barn and pulled up one corner of the dust cover. In the light from her Mini's headlights, Emily saw the low-slung bonnet of a bright yellow sports car, complete with a badge on the front. A badge with large black letters that spelt out 'MG'. Well, that explained where the car had gone.

Emily left the barn and wandered back to her car, thinking about the best course of action. If she had her phone, and a signal, then she could phone the police? But what would she tell them? That she'd found a car? That wasn't going to get a response, what with everything that was going on in the city and the meat investigation. At the back of her mind was the thought that the farm she was on was one of the ones that the meat might have come from, but she'd been over the farm with a fine-tooth comb during her inspection. She'd seen nothing amiss whatsoever, and although the two brothers were weird, she couldn't see them being that weird.

She reached her car, turned her lights off, and locked it. The only sign of any activity was the light in the pig sheds on the horizon. Maybe the farmer was in there, doing whatever farmers did with pigs in the evenings. With a shudder, she realised that she'd rather not know what farmers did with their pigs in the evenings. She would be sure to knock loudly before going into any of the sheds whether the lights were on or not.

Avoiding all the puddles that she could, Emily made her way down the tracks towards the sheds. The fading light wasn't helping, but she managed to get to the complex without falling into any of the potholes. By the time she got to them, she was out of breath. They were farther away from the farm than she'd remembered. Ignoring the sheds in darkness, she crossed the yard to the one with a light on inside. If she remembered the layout correctly, this was the abattoir. Emily hadn't been inside it during the inspection as she'd had no need to.

She opened the door, forgetting to knock, and peered inside. It was the abattoir, she'd been right on that score. But, it was empty. Emily had hoped that she'd walk in and one or both of the brothers would be sitting there playing cards or something, her phone waiting for her in one of their pockets. She walked into the building and sniffed. Then she sniffed again. For an out of use abattoir, the musty odour inside smelled a lot like fresh blood.

There was nothing that she wouldn't expect to see inside an abattoir, used or unused. Cutting slab, drain, pulley system. All fairly predictable, except for the fact that the floor looked as if it had been freshly washed and rinsed down. On the other side of the room, a pair of double doors were closed. Emily glanced up at the ceiling. The rail for the pulleys ran across the ceiling and disappeared behind the doors.

'Drying out room,' she muttered as she made her way over to the doors. Emily swung one of them open, but couldn't see a thing inside, so she patted the wall just inside the doors. Her fingers closed over an industrial light switch, so she grabbed it and flicked it downwards.

53

'Please please please,' Andy scrunched his eyes tightly as the lights burst into life. 'Don't kill me, please don't kill me.' There was silence for a second, perhaps two, before he heard a scream. A very loud, very female, scream.

He opened his eyes, barely registering the figure at the door to the room before he saw what was hanging from the ceiling next to him. It wasn't a pig. It was a man. Andy couldn't help himself. He started screaming as well, and when he saw that the man's throat had been cut, he took a deep breath and screamed even louder.

'For fuck's sake, would you shut up,' a woman's voice shouted a few seconds later. Andy stopped mid-scream and looked at the person who had walked in and turned the lights on. She was upside down, obviously, but she looked very like the woman from the Food Standards Agency. Emily Underwood.

'Emily?' Andy gasped. 'Is that you?' The upside-down woman stared at him.

'Er, yep. That's me.' They looked at each other for a

couple of seconds, Andy suddenly acutely aware that he was hanging upside down in his underpants. 'Hi,' Emily said.

'Hi,' Andy replied. 'Er, can you help me get down please?'

Emily glanced around the room a couple of times before walking across to him. Andy saw her look her up and down before settling on his ankles.

'Bloody hell,' she said. 'What the fuck is going on?'

'No idea,' Andy shot back. 'But maybe we could discuss it when I'm the right way up?' He watched her eyes follow the pulley system from his ankles, across the ceiling, and over to a large wheel on the wall. She ran across to the wheel and tried to turn it.

'Jesus, that's not budging,' she said as she tried to turn it. Andy saw her try to turn it again, only giving up when she was red in the face.

'Can you lift me up, maybe?' he said. 'So I can get my hands to my ankles? I might be able to loosen the rope.'

Emily walked back over to where Andy was hanging and put her hands out.

'Give me your hands,' she said. 'I'll try to lift you up.' She pulled at his hands until he was bent at the waist and then shifted her grip to behind his shoulders. As the pressure on Andy's ankles started to ease up with Emily taking his weight, he could feel the waistband of his underpants start to slip down. He would rather be naked and free than dead in his underpants, so he reached up to the ties around his ankles.

Andy had just managed to loosen the rope holding him by the tiniest amount when he heard Emily groan.

'Christ, you're heavy,' she gasped.

'There's a bit of give. Can you hold on for a second? I

think we're nearly there.' The next voice he heard wasn't Emily's.

'This little piggy went to market,' a man's voice echoed round the room. Andy felt Emily squeal and move from under him. He swung back down to his original position with a thud, and the air whooshed out of his lungs as the rope holding his ankles tightened up. He could see a figure at the door of the room, and realised with horror who it was.

'This little piggy stayed at home. Which is where you should have both stayed,' the farmer said. Andy saw that he was holding something in his hands, but he couldn't tell what it was. He glanced across at Emily, who was standing in the corner of the room, fixated on whatever the farmer was holding. Around them, disturbed by Andy's weight yanking on the pulley, the bodies that were strung up next to him swung gently from side to side. He tried to ignore them and concentrate on what was going on in the room, but every once in a while, a dead set of eyes would appear to look at him as they spun round. 'This little piggy had roast beef,' the farmer continued, adjusting his hands until he had what looked to Andy like sticks in either one.

Emily and the farmer circled round each other, inch by inch. Even though he was upside down, Andy could see that Emily was terrified, but at the same time, her lips were pressed together in a determined way. She had her hands out to her sides as if she was balancing on a log.

'This little piggy had none,' the farmer said in a low, menacing voice as he moved toward Emily. She took a step back toward the corner of the room. Andy decided that he had to try to do something at least. He took a deep breath and shouted the first thing that he could think of at such short notice.

'Wanker!' Andy screamed. It had the desired effect as

the farmer's head snapped round and stared at him. At the same time, Emily stepped forward and delivered what Andy knew from bitter experience was her signature move when she was threatened.

The farmer crumpled to the floor a split second after Emily drove her knee into his groin. Despite his situation, Andy couldn't help but wince in sympathy. It had looked a lot harder that the knee that had put him on the floor, and that had bloody well hurt both at the time and for about a week afterward. Emily took a few steps back until she butted up against a low cupboard.

'Emily, just run,' Andy shouted. 'Get the police, but just run for fuck's sake.' She didn't respond, but stared at the farmer who was getting to his feet. His face was beetroot red, and he had tears at the corner of his eyes. Andy watched him getting up, knowing from experience that the farmer was made of sterner stuff than he was. Out of the corner of his eye, Andy could see Emily's hands scrabbling round on the top of the cupboard and pick something up, but he couldn't see what it was. 'Emily, run for fuck's sake!' he shouted, craning his neck to try to keep her in his line of vision as he spun around. Andy saw the farmer stumble, wincing as he did so. He tried to spin himself back round, wondering how the hell the farmer was on his feet after a blow like that?

'And this little piggy,' the farmer said, adjusting the prongs he was holding and lurching toward Emily, 'went wee wee wee all the way home.'

Just as he got to the word 'home', there was a deafening explosion.

54

E mily's ears rang, a high-pitched whine resonating
through her head. She opened her eyes, which had
been screwed shut, to see a man dressed all in black in
front of her. The first thing she noticed was the machine
gun in his hands, pointing directly at her. The second thing
was the word *POLICE* in white letters across his black base-
ball hat. His mouth was moving, but she couldn't hear
what he was saying. As the whining faded, his words
started to filter through.

'ARMED POLICE. DROP YOUR WEAPON.' Emily
looked at her hands. She was holding what looked like, and
what had felt like when she picked it up, a gun. 'Drop your
weapon. Turn around. Kneel down!' the policeman
shouted. Emily threw the gun on the floor, realising when it
was too late that it might go off, and turned around. She
could see the upside-down young lad from the supermarket
swinging gently from side to side, and just to his left, Tom
the farmer was sitting up against the wall. He had a black
hole in his upper chest, surrounded by a spreading circle of

red. He coughed, speckles of blood spraying out onto his clothes.

'Blimey,' he gasped. 'That smarts.'

'Kneel down, kneel down,' the policeman shouted again, waving his gun in Emily's direction. She sunk to her knees, looking up at the bodies. 'Shots fired, ambulance requested,' the policeman spoke into his radio before he looked around the room. 'Ambulances plural. Multiple casualties.' He let go of his radio mike. 'Bloody hell, what the hell's gone on in here?' His face whitened, and Emily could see his eyes widen as he took in the scene inside the abattoir. A few seconds later, there was a reply over his radio.

'You what, Dave?' a male voice asked.

'Just send everything,' the policeman said with a sigh.

Twenty minutes later, Emily and Andy were sitting in the back of a St John's Ambulance welfare wagon, fending off endless cups of tea from the well-meaning volunteer. The farm was surrounded by police vehicles and ambulances. Emily wrapped an itchy blanket around her, leaned back into her seat, and watched through the window as people in white smurf suits milled about. Flashes of blue light were bouncing off the walls of the pig sheds. She closed her eyes, sighed, and leaned back in her seat.

'Bloody hell,' she said. 'Wasn't expecting all that.'

'Me neither,' Andy replied. 'I suppose I should say thanks.' Emily looked at him through half-closed eyes.

'What, say thanks for saving you from a homicidal farmer by shooting him with a captive bolt gun?'

'Yeah, thanks.'

'You're welcome,' Emily said. 'I don't think you'd have made very good sausages, anyway.'

'That's nice.'

'I mean, I just wouldn't fancy eating a sausage and picking a bit of yellowed underpants from between my teeth.'

'They're not yellow.'

'They are a bit.' Emily smiled as Andy wrapped his blanket a bit tighter around himself, obviously uncomfortable. 'Just at the front, though.'

'Thanks,' Andy muttered, and Emily's smile broadened. 'Your turn.'

'What do you mean?' she asked.

'Your turn to say thanks.'

'What for?'

'Flowers.'

'Oh, right,' Emily laughed. 'Yeah, they were lovely, thanks.'

There was a knock on the door and the policewoman Emily had seen on the television looked in.

'You two free for a chat?' The policewoman asked. Emily looked at Andy and they both laughed.

'Sure,' Andy said. 'Come on in.'

The policewoman got into the van and sat opposite them.

'I'm Chief Superintendent Antonio,' she said. 'Jo.' She looked a lot more relaxed than when Emily had seen her at the Food Standards Agency earlier. 'So, bit of a long day for you both then?'

'You could say that,' Emily replied. 'So, what happens next?' The policewoman looked out of the window just as a dark van with blacked-out windows pulled up outside the abattoir.

'Well, we're going to be busy here for a while. As soon as we can we'll get you down to the station, take your statements.'

'Will he be okay?' Emily asked. 'The farmer, I mean?'

'I think so,' Jo replied with a kind smile. 'The paramedics seemed to think so, anyway. It'll be up to the Crown Prosecution Service, but I can't see them pressing charges. We certainly wouldn't support that under the circumstances.' Above their heads, a helicopter could be heard scuttling round the sky. 'We picked up the other brother as well. He had a brief argument with a tree after a very short chase.'

There was a knock at the door of the van, and a policeman's head appeared.

'Ma'am,' he said. 'They're ready to move the bodies now.'

'I'll be right there,' Jo said. 'Right then, I'll leave you two lovebirds to it.' Once the policewoman had left the van, Emily turned to Andy.

'Did you hear that?' she said. 'Lovebirds?'

'I did,' Andy replied with a smile. 'Do you think she knows something we don't?' Emily didn't reply, but just closed her eyes and sat back in her seat. 'Do you think that, er, maybe when this is all over...' Emily opened one eye and squinted at Andy.

'What?'

'Well, I don't know. Maybe we could go out for a drink or something?'

'Or something?'

'Er, we could go for a meal if you'd like?' Emily smiled as Andy said this.

'I think that sounds like a great idea. You've got a bloody cheek asking me now, though.'

'Don't ask, don't get.'

55

On the television in front of Andy and Emily, a press conference was about to start. They were snuggled up on the sofa in Emily's lounge, on their own for once. Catherine was visiting Tom in the hospital wing at Norwich Prison, so they had the place to themselves. On the television, the news anchor was describing the forthcoming trial of the Pinch brothers, Norfolk's first ever serial killers. Her excited description was cut with aerial footage of the night at the farm two months ago. Andy put his arm around Emily and pulled her closer to him.

'I can't believe your flat mate,' Andy said. 'Going to visit the serial killer that you shot.'

'Alleged serial killer,' Emily replied, and they both laughed. 'I've given up trying to work the woman out, though. She's quite smitten with him for some reason.'

On the screen in front of them, the Environment Minster was posing in front of the cameras. A few weeks ago, he'd been voted the most boring man in Parliament. Next to him was a small girl, maybe aged ten or eleven, who he had introduced as his daughter.

'Good Lord,' Andy said. 'She's a chunky little thing.'

'Big-boned, I think you mean,' Emily replied.

'Ladies and Gentlemen,' the Minister said, 'thank you all for coming.' As he looked toward the cameras, there was a flurry of flashes.

'What a knob,' Emily said, laughing.

'I can confirm that following the Norwich incident, the British meat supply chain is now one hundred percent free from any human DNA.' The Minister's voice was monotone, almost no inflection in it at all. At his side, his daughter grinned, showing a missing front tooth. The cameras whirred again as she smiled. 'Norwich was an isolated incident, quickly contained and dealt with. The disorder, while unfortunate, was entirely understandable under the circumstances. But, thanks to the swift action taken by us, the whole situation was diffused quickly and sympathetically.'

'He really is a cock,' Andy said, reaching for the remote control.

'As a display of confidence, I've asked one of the House of Parliament chefs to prepare some food for us,' the Minister droned on. Emily and Andy watched as a large woman in chef's whites brought a tray out full of sausage rolls.

'That child really doesn't need them now, does she?' Andy said.

'For Christ's sake,' Emily muttered as the woman put the tray on the table, and the cameras focused in on the look of anticipation on the Minster's daughter's face. Andy pressed the mute button on the remote control.

'I'm not listening to that. I'm sure we can think of something else to do,' he said, leaning into Emily. Their lips met, and within seconds they were both focused on something other than the television.

Had they been watching the television, instead of devouring each other in only the way that young people in the early flushes of a relationship can, they would have seen the Minister's daughter tucking into a sausage roll. They would have seen the young girl grimace, before pulling something out of her teeth. They would have seen her hold something up for the cameras to zoom in on. An earring.

Andy and Emily both missed the commotion following the discovery of the earring, and by the time they came up for air, the programme had cut to the weather forecast. Tina, who had been promoted to daytime weather forecasts, was talking about a moist warm front.

'Hmm,' Andy said, sliding his hand up the outside of Emily's thigh. 'A moist warm front?'

Emily slapped at his hand, laughing as she did so.

'Down boy,' she said. 'Plenty of time for that later. We've got an appointment to keep.'

'Really?' Andy groaned. 'Do we really have to go round to your Gran's?'

'Yes, we do,' Emily replied. 'You know how lonely she's been since Granddad died on the allotment. She's got a special joint of pork in.' She paused before continuing.

'And her crackling's to die for.'

A NOTE FROM THE AUTHOR...

Hi.

I hoped you enjoyed reading *The Butcher* as much as I enjoyed writing it! If you did enjoy it, perhaps you could do me a massive favour and consider leaving a review? Positive reviews make an enormous difference to independent authors, and it would be a real help to me.

The Butcher is the first in the *Rub-a-Dub-Dub Trilogy* which is available now on Amazon.

In the meantime, enjoy your sneak preview of the second book in the trilogy — *The Baker*.

Speak soon, *Nathan Burrows.*

IT'S FLOUR POWER...

THE
BAKER

NATHAN BURROWS

CHAPTER 1

Jennifer Jones — known as Jenny to her friends,
although she didn't have that many — stood on the
low wall at the edge of the very top of Partridge
Towers. In front of her and ten stories below her was the
fine city of Norwich, although her concentration was fixed
on the horizon. Jenny took a deep breath, and looked from
right to left, taking in the skyline of the city with the sun
setting behind it.

In the distance, the distinctive spire of Norwich Cathedral pierced the soon to be night sky. Between Jenny's
vantage point and the spire was the squat rectangular
outline of the castle, made spectacular only by the large
mound of earth it had sat on since the Middle Ages. There
was no other way to describe the sight — it was a fantastic
view. Jenny didn't look down. She didn't need to. What was
below her was only pavement and besides, she was fixated
on what was in front of her and where she was going.

Today had started off like any other day. Jenny had got
up, fed her elderly cat, and got ready for work. She was an
administration assistant in the city library, and had been

for the last ten years. Chances for promotion had come and gone. Jenny wasn't that interested anyway. She led a simple enough life, and her only regret was the fact that she was still single even though she was in her mid-forties. There had been one relationship in her past that she considered meaningful, and that had been a very long time ago. Nigel, his name had been, and despite promising her the world he'd delivered little of it. The last she had heard, Nigel was living in a caravan park in Great Yarmouth with a slapper called Betty who he'd met in 'Fallen Angels.' Great Yarmouth's Premier Lap Dancing and Gentlemen's Club, or at least it was according to their website. This was despite the fact that, in Nigel's opinion, the best thing to come out of Great Yarmouth was the A47 back to Norwich. Jenny had never bothered to find out how Betty had met Nigel, but if she was a dancer at Fallen Angels, Nigel was welcome to her.

Jenny's idea of a good night in these days was a few glasses of Pinot Grigio, a good book, and the company of her cat. She'd even listed 'reading' on her like of interests on the internet dating web site she'd signed up for. Jenny had only signed up on the site after meeting the young man that her friend Stacey had managed to find on it. He was young, fit, good looking, and way out of Stacey's league, at least in Jenny's opinion. After a few months of zero interest, even from the weirdos on the internet, she'd updated her interests to include 'Book Reviewing'. The truth was that Jenny wouldn't know a good book if the author themselves ran up and slapped her round the head with it, but that didn't matter to Jenny. She looked again at the horizon and at the large red disc of the sun about to disappear behind the now closed furniture shop on St Stephen's street. None of what had happened before today mattered to Jenny. Not anymore.

Since around four o'clock that afternoon, Jenny had grown wings. Not the sort of wings that drinking Red Bull gave you, but proper wings with feathers and everything that wings were supposed to have. She raised them from her sides, and looked at the light of the setting sun glinting off the multicoloured feathers. They were a fine set of wings indeed. She'd not had them this morning, she'd not had them at lunchtime. In fact, the first time she realised she had wings was about half an hour ago. Jenny had just been thinking about packing away her bag for the day when she was caught short by some vicious stomach cramps. She'd run to the toilet, thinking for a horrible moment that she was going to be sick but apart from a load of saliva, there was nothing untoward.

Earlier that day at lunchtime, Jenny had nipped out of the library to try something from the new sandwich van outside the Forum where the library was. Everyone, even her miserable sod of a manager, was raging about their artisan bread. Jenny had bought a halloumi and pickle sandwich, even though she wasn't sure what halloumi was, and had sat in the sun enjoying the sandwich. Halloumi, it turned out, was a type of foreign cheese. A few hours later, she was bent over the toilet, and a few minutes after that, she had emerged. With wings.

Jenny spread the wings now, allowing them to catch as much of the setting sun as possible, and marvelling at the multitude of colours reflecting from them. She looked again toward the cathedral spire. There was a pair of falcons breeding up on top of the spire, so she could swoop by and say hello to them. Then, she could bank to the right and buzz the castle. There were sure to be some Japanese tourists on the top who would jabber excitedly at the sight of a middle-aged, slightly frumpy librarian soaring past them.

She flapped her wings up and down, relishing the feel of the air filtering between her feathers. As she beat them faster, she felt her feet become lighter until she realised she was almost hovering above the low wall on top of the building. With a beatific smile, she stepped forward and prepared to escape the surly bonds of earth.

Whether Jenny was actually flying or not would depend on which definition of flying was being used. If it was moving through the air, flapping wings that didn't actually exist, then Jenny was in fact flying. If the definition included horizontal movement, as opposed to vertical, then she wasn't. She flapped her wings, a fixed smile on her face, as she waited for the air to get beneath them.

The wet thud as her head impacted the pavement ten stories below where she had started from confirmed the fact, at least to everyone that witnessed it, that Jenny couldn't actually fly. She was, however, quite good at falling.

CHAPTER 2

'Where the hell is this place, anyway?' Rupert strummed his fingers on the steering wheel of his mother's car. He turned to look at Hannah, his girlfriend. 'Any ideas?'

'Not a clue,' she replied, looking up from the map that was balanced on her knee. 'It can't be that far away. Not according to this map, at least.' Rupert peered through the grimy windscreen of the battered Citroen. If the washer worked, he would have put the wipers on to clear the screen, but his mother had forgotten to fill the washer bottle up and he wasn't going to do it for her.

'Must be round here somewhere,' he muttered through gritted teeth as he swatted at his blonde dreadlocks which were threatening to block his line of sight.

'Well, if we had a sat nav, that would help,' Hannah said. Rupert glanced across her with a frown.

'Well, we don't,' he said. 'I've told you, I don't like them. Why would you want something in the car that can track your every movement? You might as well put a chip

in your head so the government can keep tabs on you.'
Hannah folded her arms across her chest, creasing the
map. This wasn't the first time they'd had this argument,
but Rupert was insistent. According to him, sat navs were a
weapon of the establishment. She picked at a thread on
her tie-dyed skirt before looking out of the window.

'Oh wow, look at that tree,' Hannah said, pointing at
the side of the road. 'It looks just like a swastika.' Robert
looked in the direction she was pointing.

'It does, doesn't it?' He was just about to launch into a
potted history of the swastika and how it had been misap-
propriated by Nazis when he noticed a small cluster of
buildings a couple of hundred yards beyond the tree. 'Is
that the farm, do you think?'

'I don't know,' Hannah replied. 'It might be. There's
bugger all else out here, is there?'

Rupert slowed the car down and stopped by a turn off
on the left-hand side of the road. A rutted track led toward
the buildings. He got out of the car, careful to avoid the
puddles so he didn't muddy his new red trousers, and stood
on tiptoes to try to get a better view of the farm in the
distance. Parked by what looked like a farmhouse was a
silver car with a man in a suit standing next to it.

'I think that's the estate agent,' Rupert said, leaning
down and speaking to Hannah through the car window.
'He looks like one from here. What do you think?'

'Well, if nothing else we can ask him for directions,'
Hannah replied. 'Come on, let's get going.'

Rupert got back into the car and they drove up the
track, the Citroen bouncing from side to side as they did so.
More than once, Robert swore as the bottom of the car
scraped on the ground. It was a good job that Citroen made
cars that could at least get down a farm track. Or at least,

he thought as he looked at the tarnished blue bonnet of the 2CV, they used to make them. A few minutes later, Rupert pulled up next to the Mercedes in front of the farmhouse and he and Hannah got out. A young man in a nasty cheap suit walked over to them. Rupert's first thought when he saw the man up close was 'obsequious'. His second thought as the man extended a hand toward him was 'wanker'.

'Hey, you must be Rupert,' the man said, shaking Rupert's hand before turning to look at Hannah. 'And you must be the lovely Hannah. We spoke on the phone. I'm Marcus, from Nelson Estate Agents.' Rupert watched as Marcus shook Hannah's hand, holding on to it for far longer than Rupert thought was necessary. To Rupert's disgust, Hannah was smiling back at the smarmy estate agent, loving the attention from the looks of it.

'Yeah, right then Marcus,' Rupert snapped. 'Shall we get on with it?'

The first building that Marcus showed Rupert and Hannah round was the farmhouse. As he walked through the building, the estate agent kept muttering phrases like 'rustic charm' and 'so much potential'.

'It's a bit stark, isn't it Rupert?' Hannah whispered as they were shown into what was apparently a bedroom, but was only just larger than a cupboard. 'It doesn't look like anyone's ever lived here.'

'When do you think he's going to mention the history of the place?' Rupert whispered back. Hannah just shrugged.

'Now come through here, you must see this,' Marcus called to them from the kitchen. When Rupert and Hannah joined him, walking past the industrial sized oven, he threw open the back door with a flourish. 'Would you look at that view?'

Rupert looked out over the muddy field, the grey skies above it, and at the threadbare trees in the distance.

'Wow,' he said in a quiet voice. 'That's something else.'

Almost an hour later, Marcus had given them the grand tour of the whole farm. They'd looked around the pig sheds, and into a building that had at one point been an abattoir. The only positive thing that Marcus had said were some anaemic comments about how thick the stone walls of the buildings were. The three of them sat around the ancient kitchen table in the farmhouse, and Marcus had spread a pile of paperwork on the table. He pushed an A3 sized piece of paper over to Rupert and Hannah.

'This is an overhead aerial shot of the farm.' Marcus traced a red line that was drawn on the paper with a fat finger. 'This line here is the farm boundary. Just shy of twenty acres, so plenty of room for whatever you need it for?' It sounded as if the estate agent was fishing to try to find out what they were going to do with the property, but Rupert wasn't going to be fooled that easily. He looked across at Hannah, who to his irritation was staring at the estate agent. Rupert watched as Marcus glanced across at her and was rewarded with a smile. Rupert knew that smile well. It was the same one Hannah used when she saw something she wanted. It could be a cardigan, a new nose ring, or spontaneous middle of the afternoon sex. It didn't matter — the smile was the same.

'So, what can you tell us about the farm?' Rupert said, trying to stop Hannah's train of thought. The problem was that when she wanted something, she usually got it. Rupert was fine with that when it involved them both getting naked, but he didn't think that was the case here. 'Why is it so cheap?'

Rupert's last statement broke the moment for both

Hannah and the estate agent. Marcus's eyes widened, and he looked at Rupert.

'Well, er, now then,' Marcus stammered. 'It does have a bit of history, you see.'

'What do you mean, history?' Hannah said in a sweet voice, twirling a lock of hair around her finger. Rupert had to stifle a laugh.

'Oh, there was a couple of brothers living here until just recently.'

'So where are they now?' Rupert asked.

'In prison,' Marcus replied after a brief pause. 'They, er, they need some money for legal fees. That's why the farm's on the market for such a reasonable amount.' The estate agent glanced over his shoulder as if there was someone else in the room. Rupert was just thinking how much of a cock he was when Marcus continued in a stage whisper. 'I do know that they would be very amenable to sensible offers, given their circumstances.'

Rupert watched as Hannah leaned forward, placing her elbows on the table. He knew that Marcus would be able to see right down the front of her top, but to his credit, the estate agent never took his eyes off Hannah's. He went up in Rupert's estimation, but only slightly.

'So, Marcus,' Hannah breathed. 'What do you consider to be a sensible offer?' Rupert caught Marcus's eyes flicking down for a split second. The estate agent was human, after all.

'Well,' Marcus said, licking his lips. 'Perhaps an offer at about ten percent under the asking price would be reasonable?'

Rupert leaned back in his chair. Given the price that the farm was on the market for, ten percent under the asking price brought it well within his budget. He watched as Hannah arched her eyebrows in the estate agent's direction.

'And is there anything else that we can do to bring that price down a bit further?' she asked.

'Oh, gosh,' Marcus replied without even so much as a glance at Rupert. 'Possibly.'

CHAPTER 3

E mily Underwood rapped hard again on the door of 'Perfect Pizza'. She knew full well there were people inside. A few seconds earlier, she'd seen a head pop up from behind the counter before disappearing again. Even though the sign on the door said 'CLOSED', she could see a drunk bloke slumped in the chair of the waiting area. Emily knocked on the door again before taking a step back and looking at her reflection in the glass of the door.

She ran her hand over her blonde bob, swearing as the hair she'd spent ages earlier trying to tame just leapt back up again, making her look like a school science experiment. Emily ran a critical eye over her reflection. Her flat mate, Catherine, had been on at her for ages about the fact that Emily had lost weight over the last few weeks. The trouser suit Emily was wearing was definitely looser than it had been, so much so that she thought she might have to drop to a size six and buy some more outfits. She leaned forward and angled her head at her reflection, trying to see if there was anything stuck in her teeth, when she saw a tousled head pop up again from behind the counter. It disappeared a few seconds later.

'Oi, I can see you!' Emily shouted, banging her fist on the door. 'Let me in, or I'll close you down from out here.'

The Perfect Pizza wasn't the most hygienic facility in Norwich by a long stretch of the imagination, which was why the Food Standards Agency had sent Emily round to inspect them. In her bag were copies of the many complaints the council had received about the place. Everything from allegations of food poisoning to foreign objects in the pizzas. Non-edible foreign objects. There had even been a complaint about a condom hidden under several layers of pepperoni, but the Food Standards Agency had to stop the investigation when the complainant had admitted to eating it. He said he thought it was a piece of squid, according to the coffee room gossip.

Emily drew herself up to her full height of five foot three inches as a man appeared from behind the counter and walked across the waiting area to open the door.

'We is closed,' the swarthy looking man said with a heavy foreign accent as he opened the door a crack. Emily pulled the inspection notice from her bag.

'No you're not,' she said, waving the sheet of paper at him. 'This says you're open.' With a sigh, the man opened the door.

'Okay miss, welcome,' he said as Emily walked past him into the shop, wrinkling her nose at the sour smell. 'Come on in.'

'Right then,' Emily said, trying to sound business-like. 'Where shall we start?' She glanced at the drunk slumped in the waiting room. He took a deep breath before letting it out through his cheeks, a low rattle coming from his chest. The sour smell got worse. 'Is he okay?' she asked the restaurant owner.

'He fine. Too much beer.'

'Right,' Emily replied. 'Let's crack on.' She glanced down at her paperwork. 'Can we start with the food preparation area?'

An hour later, Emily was almost done. Most visits she did were much shorter, but this one wasn't one that she wanted to take short cuts on. There'd been too many complaints for one thing, and from what she'd seen in the last sixty minutes, Perfect Pizza was about to be closed down. Emily knew that she would have to phone for assistance if she decided to shut the restaurant straight away — an incident a few months back with a small Chinaman wielding a machete had taught her that the hard way — but she wasn't about to let the owner know that. She glanced down at her list of offences, the first page of them at least. Credit where it was due, the restaurant owner had almost got a full house. Dodgy storage of food, poor cleaning practices, abysmal food preparation areas. It was all there. The only thing that was missing was contaminated meat, and that was always a hard one for the Environmental Health Agency to prove anyway. If she'd found that, it would mean instant closure.

'Well?' the restaurant owner said as they stood behind the counter. 'What you think? We pass, yes?' He flashed a bright white smile at her.

'I need to check in with the office,' Emily replied. 'Let me speak to them, see what they say?' She returned his smile, but the way his face fell as she smiled at him told Emily that she'd not fooled him at all. She brushed past him into the waiting area. The drunk man was still there. Emily looked at him again, becoming concerned. Were unconscious drunks an Environmental Health offence?

Emily didn't think so, but she'd need to check the rule book to be certain. He was definitely pretty out of it — Emily couldn't see him moving at all. She walked over to him to take a closer look. Emily stood there for a few seconds before reaching out her hand and placing it on his shoulder, grateful she still had latex gloves on.

'Hello?' she said, shaking him back and forth. No response. 'Are you okay?' Again, no response.

A few moments later, Emily was standing in the car park on the phone.

'Hello, which emergency service do you require?' the male voice on the other end of the phone said.

'Er, not sure to be honest,' Emily replied.

'What's your emergency?'

'I think I need an ambulance. Or maybe the police.' Emily glanced back at the drunk man in the waiting area of the restaurant. 'Actually, how about an undertaker. Have you got any of them?' There was a silence at the other end of the line.

'An undertaker?'

'Yeah,' Emily said, taking a deep breath. 'I just found a dead bloke.'

$\sim$

The Baker is available now.

Printed in Great Britain
by Amazon

18392452R00181